OUR S[illegible]OR

(A LUK[illegible])

JACK MARS

ISBN: 978-1-64029-038-9

BOOKS BY JACK MARS

LUKE STONE THRILLER SERIES

ANY MEANS NECESSARY (Book #1)
OATH OF OFFICE (Book #2)
SITUATION ROOM (Book #3)
OPPOSE ANY FOE (Book #4)
PRESIDENT ELECT (Book #5)
OUR SACRED HONOR (Book #6)
HOUSE DIVIDED (Book #7)

"…we mutually pledge to each other our lives, our fortunes, and our sacred honor."

Thomas Jefferson
The Declaration of Independence

CHAPTER ONE

December 9th
11:45 p.m. Lebanon Time (4:45 p.m. Eastern Standard Time)
Southern Lebanon

"Praise God," the young man said. "Praise Him. Praise Him."

He took a long drag from his cigarette, his hand shaking as he reached to his mouth. He hadn't eaten in twelve hours. For the past four hours, the world around him had been entirely black. He was a truck driver, skilled at driving the biggest rigs, and he had driven this one across the border from Syria, then through the hilly Lebanese countryside, moving slow on winding roads, lights off the entire way.

It was a dangerous drive. The sky was filled with drones, with helicopters, with spy planes, and with bombers—Russian, American, and Israeli. Any one of these could become interested in this truck. Any one of these could decide to destroy the truck, and do so effortlessly. He drove the entire way expecting that at any moment, a missile would hit him without warning, rendering him a flaming skeleton sitting inside a burned out steel relic.

Now he had just pulled the truck up a long, narrow path and parked it under an awning. The awning, held up with wooden legs, was made to look from the sky like typical forest cover—in fact, the top of it was covered with dense brush. Its location was right where they had said it would be.

He turned the truck off, the engine farting and belching, black smoke pouring from a stack on the driver's side as the thing shut itself down. He opened the door to the cab and climbed down. As soon as he did so, a squad of heavily armed men materialized like ghosts, emerging from the surrounding woods.

"*As salaam alaikum,*" the young truck driver said as they approached.

"*Wa alaikum salaam,*" the militia leader said. He was tall and burly, with a thick black beard and dark eyes. His face was hard—there was no compassion in it. He gestured at the truck. "Is this it?"

The young man took another shaky drag from his cigarette. No, he almost said. Some other truck is it. This one is nothing.

"Yes," he said instead.

"You're late," the militia leader said.

The young man shrugged. "You should have driven in that case."

The leader stared at the truck. It looked like a typical tractor-trailer—perhaps something carrying lumber, or furniture, or foodstuffs. But it wasn't. The militiamen went right to work on it, two climbing the back ladder to the top, two kneeling near the bottom. Each man had a battery-powered screwdriver.

Moving quickly, they removed the screws one by one that held the tractor-trailer fiction together. Within moments, they pulled a large piece of aluminum sheet metal off the side. A moment later, they pulled a narrower sheet off the back. Then they were working on the other side, where the driver could no longer see them.

He turned and looked out at the nighttime hillsides and forest. Across the darkness, he could see the lights of a village twinkling several miles away. Beautiful country. He was very glad to be here. His job was done. He was not a militiaman. He was a truck driver. They had paid him to go across the border and pick up this truck.

He was also not from this region—he lived far to the north. He had no idea what arrangements these men had made for his return home, but he didn't care. Rid of the infernal machine he had just driven, he would gladly walk from here.

Headlights were coming up the narrow rutted road, a whole series of them. Seconds later, a line of three black Mercedes SUVs appeared. The doors opened in unison and gunmen poured from each car. Each man carried a heavy rifle or machine gun. The rear door of the middle car opened last.

A heavyset man with a salt-and-pepper beard and glasses pulled himself from the SUV. He leaned on a knobby wooden stick and walked with a pronounced limp—the residue of a car bomb attempt on the man's life two years ago.

The young driver recognized the man instantly—he was certainly the most famous man in Lebanon, and well known throughout the world. His name was Abba Qassem, and he was the absolute leader of Hezbollah. His authority—in matters of military operations, social programs, relations with foreign governments, crime and punishment, life and death—was unquestioned.

His presence made the driver nervous. It came on suddenly, like a stomach sickness. There were the nerves that came with meeting any celebrity, yes. But there was more to it than that. Qassem being here meant that this truck—whatever it might be—was important. Much more important than the driver had realized.

Qassem hobbled to the truck driver, surrounded by his bodyguards, and gave him an awkward hug.

"My brother," he said. "You are the driver?"

"Yes."

"Allah will reward you."

"Thank you, Sayyid," the driver said, calling him by a title of honor, suggesting that Qassem was a direct descendent of Mohammed himself. The driver was hardly a devout Muslim, but people like Qassem seemed to enjoy that sort of thing.

They turned together. The men had already finished removing the sheet metal covering from the truck. Now the real truck was revealed. The front of it was much as it had appeared to be—the cab of a trailer truck, painted a deep green color. The long rear of the truck was a flat, two-cylinder missile launch platform. Resting inside each of the launch cylinders was a large silver missile, shiny and metallic.

The two parts of the truck were separate and independent of each other, but were attached by a hydraulic system in the middle, and steel chains on either side. That explained why the truck had been difficult to control—the rear section was not secured to the front as tightly as the driver might have chosen.

"A transporter-erector-launcher, they call it," Qassem said, explaining to the driver what he had just driven here. "And just one of many the Perfect One has seen fit to bring us."

"Yes?" the driver said.

Qassem nodded. "Oh yes."

"And the missiles?"

Qassem smiled. It was beatific and calm, the smile of a saint. "Very advanced weaponry. Long distance. As accurate as anything in this world. More powerful than we have ever known before. God willing, we will use these weapons to bring our enemies to their knees."

"Israel?" the driver said. He nearly choked on the word. The urge came upon him to start walking north right this moment.

Qassem put a hand on the driver's shoulder. "God is great, my brother. God is great. Very soon, everyone will know exactly how great."

He stepped away, limping toward the missile launcher. The driver watched him go. He took one last drag on his cigarette, which he had smoked down to the nub. He was feeling a little better, calmer. This job was over. These maniacs could start another war if they wanted—it likely wouldn't reach the north.

Qassem turned around then and looked at him. "Brother," he said.

"Yes?"

"These missiles are a secret, you know. No one can hear of them."

The driver nodded. "Of course."

"You have friends, family?"

The driver smiled. "I do. A wife, three children. Little ones. I still have my mother. I am well known in my village and the nearby areas. I have played the violin since I was very young, and everyone demands a song from me."

He paused. "It's a full life."

The sayyid nodded, a little sadly.

"Allah will reward you."

The driver didn't like the sound of that. It was the second time Qassem had mentioned such a reward. "Yes. Thank you."

Near Qassem, two big men took rifles down from their shoulders. A second later, they held them ready, aimed at the driver.

The driver barely moved. This didn't seem right. It was happening so fast. His heart pounded in his ears. He could not feel his legs. Or his arms. Even his lips were numb. For a second, he tried to think of anything he might have done to offend them. Nothing. He had done nothing. All he had done was bring the truck here.

The truck… *was a secret.*

"Wait," he said. "Wait! I won't tell anyone."

Qassem shook his head now. "The All-Knowing has seen your good work. He will open the gates of Paradise to you this very evening. This is my promise to you. This is my prayer."

Much too late, the driver turned to run.

An instant later, he heard the loud CRACK as the first gun fired.

And he realized, as the ground came rushing up to meet him, that his entire life had been in vain.

CHAPTER TWO

December 11
9:01 a.m. Eastern Standard Time
The Oval Office
The White House, Washington, DC

Susan Hopkins almost couldn't believe what she was watching.

She stood on the carpet in the sitting area of the Oval Office—the comfortable high-backed chairs had been removed for this morning's festivities. Thirty people packed the room. Kurt Kimball and Kat Lopez stood near her, as well as Haley Lawrence, her Secretary of Defense.

The White House Residence staff were all here at her insistence, the chef, the servers, the domestic staff, mingling among other invited guests—the directors of the National Science Foundation, NASA, and the National Park Service, to name a few. A handful of news media personalities were here, as well as two or three carefully selected camera people. There were many Secret Service agents, lining the walls and peppered among the crowd.

On a large TV monitor mounted near the far wall, Stephen Lief, a man whom Susan could expect to never see in the flesh until her term as President was over, was about to take the Vice Presidential Oath of Office. Stephen was late middle-aged, owlish in round glasses, hair gray and thinning and receding across the top of his skull like an army in disordered retreat. He had a vaguely pear-shaped body, hidden inside a three-thousand-dollar blue pinstriped Armani suit.

Susan had known Stephen a long time. He would have been her main competition in the most recent election, if Jeff Monroe hadn't interceded. Before that, in her Senate days, he was the loyal opposition across the aisle from her, a moderate conservative, unremarkable—pig-headed but not deranged. And he was a nice man.

But he was also the wrong party, and she had taken a lot of heated criticism from liberal quarters for that. He was landed aristocracy, old money—a Mayflower person, the closest thing that America had to nobility. At one time, he had seemed to think that becoming President was his birthright. Not Susan's type—entitled aristocrats tended to lack the common touch that helped you connect with the people you were supposedly there to serve.

It was a measure of how deeply Luke Stone had gotten inside her skin that she considered Stephen Lief at all. He was Stone's idea. Stone had brought it up to her playfully, while the two were lying together in her big Presidential bed. She had been pondering out loud about possible Veep candidates, and then Stone said:

"Why not Stephen Lief?"

She had almost laughed. "Stone! Stephen Lief? Come on."

"No, I mean it," he said.

He was lying on his side. His nude body was thin but rock hard, chiseled, and covered with scars. Thick bandaging still covered his recent bullet wound—it was molded to his torso along the left side. The various wounds didn't bother her—they made him sexier, more dangerous. His dark blue eyes watched her from deep inside his weathered Marlboro Man face, half a mischievous smile on his lips.

"You're beautiful, Stone. Like an ancient Greek statue, uh, wearing a bandage. But maybe you better let me do the thinking. You can just recline there, looking pretty."

"I interviewed him at his farm down in Florida," Stone said. "I was asking him what he knew about Jefferson Monroe and election fraud. He came clean to me very quickly. And he's good with horses. Gentle. That has to count for something."

"I'll keep that in mind," Susan said. "The next time I'm looking for a ranch hand."

Stone shook his head, but kept smiling. "The country is fractured, Susan. Recent events have made the feelings worse than ever. You're still doing okay, but Congress has the lowest approval ratings in American history. If you can believe the polls, then politicians, the Taliban, and the Church of Satan all rate well with a similar percentage of Americans. Lawyers, the IRS, and the Italian Mafia have much higher approval numbers."

"And you say that because…"

"Because what the American people want now is for right and left, liberal and conservative, to come together a little bit and start to get some things done on behalf of this country. The roads and bridges need to be rebuilt, the train system belongs in a museum, the public schools are falling apart, and we haven't built a new major airport in almost thirty years. We're ranked thirty-second in healthcare, Susan. That's low. Can there really be thirty-one other countries ahead of us? Because I tell you, I've been around the world, and I run out of good countries at twenty-one or twenty-two. That puts us behind a bunch of bad ones."

She sighed. "If we had some buy-in from conservatives, we might be able to get my infrastructure package through…"

He tapped her forehead. "Now you're using your noodle. Lief did eighteen years in the Senate. He knows the game as well as anybody."

"I thought politics wasn't your thing," she said.

"It's not."

She shook her head. "That's what scares me."

He started moving toward her. "Don't be scared. I'll tell you what is my thing."

"Do tell."

"Getting physical," he said. "With someone like you."

Now she shook the memories away, a ghost of a smile on her face. She had drifted there for a bit. On the TV monitor, Stephen Lief was getting ready to take his oath. It was happening in her old study at the Naval Observatory. She remembered the room and the house well. It was the beautiful, turreted and gabled Queen Anne–style 1850s mansion on the grounds of the Naval Observatory in Washington, DC. For decades, it had been the official residence of the Vice President of the United States.

She used to stand at the big bay window that was visible on the monitor, staring out at the beautiful rolling lawns of the Naval Observatory campus. The afternoon sun would come through that window, playing incredible games with light and shadow. For five years, she had lived in that house as Vice President. She'd loved it there, and would move back in a heartbeat if she could.

In the old days, in the afternoons and evenings, she would go out jogging on the Observatory grounds with her Secret Service men. Those years were a time of optimism, of stirring speeches, of meeting and greeting thousands of hopeful Americans. It seemed like a lifetime ago now.

Susan sighed. Her mind wandered. She remembered the day of the Mount Weather attack, the atrocity that had catapulted her out of her happy life as Vice President and into the raging tumult of the past few years.

She shook her head. No thank you. She would not think about that day.

Through the looking glass, on a small dais, two men and a woman stood. Photographers milled around like gnats, snapping pictures of them.

One of the men on the dais was short and bald. He wore a long robe. He was Clarence Warren, Chief Justice of the United States. The woman's name was Judy Lief. She wore a bright blue suit. She was smiling ear to ear and holding a Bible open in her hands. Her husband, Stephen, placed his left hand on the Bible. His right hand was raised. Lief was often thought of dour, but even he was smiling a little.

"I, Stephen Douglas Lief," he said, "do solemnly swear that I will support and defend the Constitution of the United States against all enemies, foreign and domestic."

"That I will bear true faith…" Judge Warren prompted.

"That I will bear true faith and allegiance to the same," Lief said. "That I take this obligation freely, and that I will well and faithfully discharge the duties of the office which I am about to enter."

"So help me God," Judge Warren said.

"So help me God," Lief said.

An image appeared in Susan's mind—a ghost from the recent past. Marybeth Horning, the last person to take that oath. She had been a mentor to Susan in the Senate, and something of a mentor as Vice President. With her thin, small frame and her big glasses, she looked like a mouse, but she roared like a lion.

Then she was shot down and killed because of… what? Her liberal politics, you might say, but that wasn't true. The people who killed her hadn't cared about policy differences—all they cared about was power.

Susan hoped the country could move past that now. She watched Stephen on the TV monitor, embracing his family and other well-wishers.

Did she trust this man? She didn't know.

Would he try to have her killed?

No. She didn't think so. He had more integrity than that. She had never known him to be underhanded during her time in the Senate. She supposed that was a start—she had a Vice President who wouldn't try to kill her.

She pictured reporters from the *New York Times* and the *Washington Post* asking questions: "What do you like about Stephen Lief as your new Vice President?"

"Well, he's not going to kill me. I feel pretty good about that."

Then Kat Lopez was at her side.

"Uh, Susan? Let's get you over to the microphones so you can congratulate Vice President Lief and give him a few words of encouragement."

Susan snapped out of her reverie. "Of course. That's a good idea. He can probably use them."

CHAPTER THREE

11:16 p.m. Israel Time (4:16 p.m. Eastern Standard Time)
The Blue Line, Israel-Lebanon Border

"Listen not to the liars, to the unbelievers," the boy of seventeen whispered.

He took a deep breath.

"Strive against them with the utmost effort. Fight against them so that Allah will punish them by your hands and disgrace them and give you victory over them."

The boy was as battle-hardened as they came. At fifteen, he had left his home and family and joined the Army of God. He had crossed into Syria and spent the past two years fighting street-to-street, face-to-face, and sometimes hand-to-hand, against the apostates of Daesh, what the westerners called ISIS.

The Daesh were unafraid to die—indeed, they welcomed death. Many of them were older Chechens and Iraqis, very hard to kill. The early days of opposing them had been a nightmare, but the boy had survived. In two years, he had fought many battles and killed many men. And he had learned much about war.

Now he stood in the black dark on a hillside in northern Israel. He balanced an anti-tank rocket launcher on his right shoulder. In his younger days, a heavy rocket like this would drill into his shoulder and after a short time, his bones would begin to ache. But he was stronger now. The weight of it no longer made much impression on him.

There was a small stand of trees around him, and very nearby, a group of commandos were on the ground, watching the roadway below them.

"Let those who fight in the way of Allah sell the life of this world for the other," he said, very low, under his breath. "He who fights in the way of Allah, be he slain or be he victorious, he shall receive a vast reward."

"Abu!" someone whispered fiercely.

"Yes." His own voice was calm.

"Shut up!"

Abu took a deep breath and let the exhale slowly come out.

He was an expert with the anti-tank rocket. He had fired so many of these, and he had become so accurate with them, that he was now a very valuable man. That was something he had learned about war. The longer you lived, the more skills you amassed, and the better you became at fighting. The better you became, the more valuable you were, and ever more likely to remain alive. He had known many who didn't survive long in combat—a week, ten days. He had met one who died on the first day. If only they could last a month, things would start to become clearer to—

"Abu!" the voice hissed.

He nodded. "Yes."

"Ready? They're coming."

"Okay."

He went about his business, relaxed, almost as if he were just practicing. He hefted the rocket launcher and unfolded the stock. His placed his left hand along the length of the barrel, lightly, lightly, until the target came into view. You didn't want your grip too firm, too soon. The index finger of his right hand caressed the trigger mechanism. He put the gun sight near his face, but not to his eye. He liked to have his eyes free until the last moment, so he could acquire the entire picture before focusing on the details. His knees bent slightly, his back ever-so-slightly arched.

He could see light from the convoy now, behind the hillside to his right, approaching along the road. The lights reached upward, casting strange shadows. A few seconds later, he could hear the rumble of the engines.

He took another deep breath.

"Steady…" a stern voice said. "Steady."

"Lord Allah," Abu said, his words coming quickly now, and louder than before. "Guide my hands and my eyes. Let me bring death to your enemies, in your name and in the name of your most beloved prophet Mohammed, and all the great prophets in all times."

The first jeep came around the bend. The round headlights were clear now, cutting through the nighttime mist.

The boy Abu instantly became rigid under the weight of the heavy gun. He put his right eye to the sight. The vehicles in the line appeared, large, like he could reach out and touch them. His finger tightened on the trigger. The breath caught in his throat. He was no longer a boy with a rocket launcher—he and the launcher melded together, becoming one entity, a killing machine.

All around his feet, men moved like snakes, crawling toward the roadway.

"Steady," the voice said again. "The second car, you understand?"

"Yes."

In his gun sight, the second jeep was RIGHT THERE. He could see the silhouettes of the people inside it.

"It's easy," he whispered. "It's so easy… Steady…"

Two seconds passed, Abu slowly sweeping the rocket launcher from right to left, following the target, never wavering.

"FIRE!"

* * *

For Avraham Gold, this was the part he hated.

Hate was the wrong word. He feared it. Any second now, coming right up.

He always talked here. He talked too much. He felt that he would blurt anything, just to get past this place. He took a long drag from his cigarette—against the rules to smoke on patrol, but it was the only thing that relaxed him.

"Leave Israel?" he said. "Never! Israel is my home, now and forever. I will travel abroad, certainly, but leave? How could I? We are called by God to live here. This is the Holy Land. This is the land that was promised."

Avraham was twenty years old, a corporal in the Israeli Defense Forces. His grandparents were Germans who had survived the Holocaust. He believed every word that he said. But it still sounded hollow to his ears, like a corny pro-settler TV commercial.

He was at the wheel of the jeep, driving the third in a line of three. He glanced at the girl sitting next to him. Daria. *God, she's beautiful!*

Even with her close-cropped hair, even with her body covered primly in her uniform. It was her smile. It would light up the sky. And her long eyelashes—like a cat.

She had no business being up here, in this… no-man's-land. Especially with her views. She was a liberal. There shouldn't be any liberals in the IDF, Avraham had decided. They were useless. And Daria was worse than a liberal. She was…

"I don't believe in your God," she said simply. "You know that."

Now Avraham smiled. "I know, and when you get out of the army, you're going to—"

She finished the thought for him. "Move to Brooklyn, that's right. My cousin owns a moving company."

He almost laughed, despite his nerves. "You're a skinny girl to carry couches and pianos up and down flights of stairs."

"I'm stronger than you might—"

Just then, the radio screeched. "Abel Patrol. Come in, Abel Patrol."

He picked up the receiver. "Abel."

"Whereabouts?" came the tinny voice.

"Just entering Sector Nine as we speak."

"Right on time. Okay. Eyes sharp."

"Yes, sir," Avraham said. He clicked off the receiver and glanced at Daria.

She shook her head. "If it's so worrisome, why don't they do something about it?"

He shrugged. "It's the military. They'll fix it just as soon as something terrible happens."

The problem was right up ahead. The convoy was moving east to west along the narrow ribbon of roadway. To their right was a stand of dense, deep forest—it began fifty meters from the road. The IDF had cleared the land right to the border. Where those woods began was Lebanon.

To their left were three steep, green hills. Not mountains, really, but neither were they rolling hills. They were abrupt, and sheer. The roadway wrapped around and behind the hills, and for just a moment, radio communications were tenuous, and the convoys were vulnerable.

IDF command had been talking about those hills for over a year. It had to be the hills. They couldn't clear out the forest because it was Lebanese territory—it would cause an international incident. So for a while, they were going to dynamite the hills. Then they were going to build a guard tower atop one of them. Both plans were deemed unsuitable. Dynamiting the hills meant the road would have to be temporarily rerouted away from the border. And a guard tower would be under constant threat of attack.

No, the best thing to do was run patrols between the hills and the forest night and day and just hope for the best.

"Watch those woods," Avraham said. "Eyes sharp."

He realized he had just repeated the exact same words as the commander. What a fool! He glanced at Daria again. Her heavy rifle lay alongside her thin frame. She giggled and shook her head, her face turning red.

In the darkness ahead, a flash of light erupted from their left.

It slammed into the middle jeep, twenty meters in front of them. The car exploded, spun to its left, and rolled. The car burned, the occupants already incinerated.

Avraham stomped on the brakes, but too late. He skidded into the burning vehicle.

Beside him, Daria screamed.

They had attacked from the wrong side—the hill side. There was no cover over there. *It was inside Israel.*

There was no time to speak, no time to give Daria a command.

Gunfire came from both sides now. Machine gun fire raked his door. DUNK-DUNK-DUNK-DUNK-DUNK. His window shattered, spraying glass in on him. At least one of the bullets had pierced the armor. He was hit. He looked down at his side—there was a darkness, growing and spreading. He was bleeding. He could barely feel it—it seemed like a bee sting.

He grunted. Men were running in the darkness.

Instantly, before he knew it, his gun was in his hand. He aimed out the missing window.

BLAM!

The noise was deafening to his ears.

He had hit one. He had hit one. The man had gone down.

He sighted on another one.

Steady...

Something happened. His whole body bucked wildly in his seat. He had dropped his gun. A shot, something heavy, had gone right through him. It had come from behind him and punched through the dashboard. A gunshot, or a small rocket of some kind. Gingerly, numb with terror, he reached to his chest and touched the area below his throat.

It was… gone.

There was a massive hole in his chest. How was he even still alive?

The answer came instantly: he soon wouldn't be.

He didn't even feel it. A sense of warmth spread out through his body. He looked at Daria again. It was too bad. He was going to convince her… of something. Now that would never happen.

She stared at him. Her eyes were round, like saucers. Her mouth was open in a giant O of horror. He felt the urge to comfort her, even now.

"It's okay," he wanted to tell her. "It doesn't hurt."

But he could not speak.

Men appeared at the window behind her. With their rifle butts, they smashed away the remaining shards of glass. Hands reached in, trying to pull her out the window, but she fought them. She tore at them with her bare hands.

The door opened. Three men now, dragging her, pulling at her.

Then she was gone, and he was alone.

Avraham stared at the vehicle burning in the darkness in front of him. It occurred to him that he had no idea what had happened to the lead vehicle. He supposed it didn't matter now.

He thought briefly of his parents and his sister. He loved them all, simply and without regret.

He thought of his grandparents, perhaps standing ready to receive him.

He could no longer make out the burning vehicle. It was just bright red, yellow, and orange, flickering against a black background. He watched as the colors became smaller and dimmer, the darkness spreading and growing even darker. The inferno of the exploded car now seemed like the guttering of a spent candle.

He watched until the last of the color went out.

CHAPTER FOUR

4:35 p.m. Eastern Standard Time
Headquarters of the Special Response Team
McLean, Virginia

"Well, I guess the band is officially back together," Susan Hopkins said.

Luke smiled at the thought.

It was the Special Response Team's first day in their brand new digs. The new headquarters were their old headquarters from years before, but newly renovated. The squat, three-story, glass and concrete building was in the wealthy suburb of McLean, only a few miles from the CIA. It had a helipad with a brand new black Bell 430 hunched on the tarmac like a dragonfly, gleaming white SRT logo on its side.

There were four black agency SUVs parked in the lot. The building had offices on the first and second floor, and a state-of-the-art conference room that was nearly a match for the Situation Room at the White House. It had every technological bell and whistle that Mark Swann's fevered imagination could conjure. The workout center (complete with cardio equipment, weight machines, and a heavily padded sparring room) and the cafeteria were on the third floor. The soundproof gun range was in the basement.

The new agency had twenty employees, the perfect size to respond to unfolding events fast, light, and with total flexibility. Spun off from the FBI and now organized as a sub-agency of the Secret Service, the arrangement limited Luke's interactions with the federal bureaucracy. He reported directly to the President of the United States.

The small campus was surrounded by security fencing, topped with razor wire. But right now the gates were thrown wide open. They were having an Open House today. And Luke was happy to be here.

He strode the halls with Susan, eager to show the President of the United States all the things she already knew about. He felt like a five-year-old. He glanced at her from time to time, soaked in her beauty, but did not stare. He stifled the urge to hold hands, which she apparently felt as well, because her hand brushed his hand, his arm, his shoulder, almost constantly.

She needed to save all that touching for later.

Luke turned his attention to the building. The place had come together exactly as he had hoped, and so had the SRT. His people had agreed to join him. This was no small matter—with all the strife they had endured, and Luke's extended absence, it was a gift that everyone was willing to trust him again.

He and Susan entered the cafeteria and waded through the crowd, trailed by two Secret Service agents. About a dozen people snaked in a line around the food serving bar. Over by the window, Luke spotted the person he was looking for, standing between Ed Newsam and Mark Swann, dwarfed by the rippling muscle of Ed and the beanpole height of Swann. It was his son, Gunner.

"Come on, Susan, there's someone over here I want you to meet."

Suddenly, she looked stricken. "Wait, Luke! This isn't the right…"

He shook his head, and this time he did grab her—by the wrist. "It'll be fine. Just tell him you're my boss. Lie to him."

They emerged from the crowd and appeared next to Gunner, Ed, and Swann. Swann wore his hair in a ponytail, wraparound glasses on his face. His long body was draped in a black RAMONES T-shirt, faded blue jeans, with yellow-and-black checkerboard Chuck Taylor sneakers on his big feet.

Ed looked huge in a black turtleneck, beige dress pants, and black leather shoes. There was a gold Rolex watch around his wrist. His hair and beard were jet black, closely cropped, and meticulous, like hedges cared for by a master gardener.

Swann was information systems—one of the best hackers Luke had ever worked with. Ed was weapons and tactics—he had come through Delta Force after Luke. He was absolutely devastating in the use of force. Ed had a glass of wine—it looked tiny in his giant hand. Swann held a black can of beer with a pirate logo on it in one hand, a plate with several large sandwich slices in the other.

"Guys, you both know Susan Hopkins, don't you?" Luke said.

Ed and Swann shook her hand in turn.

"Madam President," Ed said. He looked her up and down and smiled. "Good to see you again."

Luke almost laughed at Ed giving the President the wolf's eye. He ruffled Gunner's hair. It was slightly awkward, because Gunner was just a little too tall to have his hair ruffled.

"Madam President, this is my son, Gunner."

She shook his hand and put on her friendly *I'm the President, and I'm meeting some random kid* face. "Gunner, very nice to meet you. How are you enjoying the party?"

"It's okay," he said. He blushed bright red and did not meet her eyes. He was still a shy kid, in some ways.

"Are your girls here?" Luke said to Ed, changing the subject.

Ed shrugged and smiled. "Oh, they're running around somewhere."

A woman appeared at the edge of their group. She was tall, blonde, and striking. She wore a red suit and high heels. Even more striking than her looks was the fact that she went straight to Luke, ignoring the President of the United States.

She held a smartphone out to Luke like a microphone.

"Agent Stone, I'm Tera Wright, with WFNK, DC's number one radio news."

Luke almost laughed at her self-introduction. "Hi, Tera," he said. He expected her to ask him about the reopening of the Special Response Team offices, and the mandate the SRT would have to fight terrorism at home and abroad. Nice. It was something he wouldn't mind talking about.

"How can I help you?"

"Well," Tera began, "I see the President is here at your agency's grand opening."

Luke nodded. "She sure is. I think the President knows how impor—"

The woman cut him off. "Can you answer one question for me, please?"

"Of course."

"Are the rumors true?"

"Uh, I'm not aware of any—"

"Rumors have been circulating for a couple of weeks," Tera Wright informed him.

"Rumors about what?" Luke said. He glanced around at the group, like a drowning man hoping for a rope.

Tera Wright raised a hand as if to say STOP. "Let's do this a different way," she said. "What would you say is the nature of your relationship with President Hopkins?"

Luke looked at Susan. Susan was an old hand at this. She didn't blush. She didn't look guilty. She merely raised an eyebrow and stared quizzically at the back of the reporter's head, like she had no idea what this person might be referring to.

Luke took a breath. "Well, I would say that President Hopkins is my boss."

"Nothing more?" the reporter said.

"Same as you," Luke said. "She's also my Commander-in-Chief."

He glanced at Susan again, thinking she would jump in now and steer the conversation in a new direction. But now Susan's chief-of-staff was there, pretty Kat Lopez, in a form-fitting blue pinstriped suit. Kat was still slim, though her face was not nearly as youthful as it had been when she took this job. Three years of constant stress and herding cats would do a number on anyone.

She was speaking low, practically whispering, directly into Susan's ear.

Susan's face darkened as she listened, then she nodded. Whatever it was, it was bad.

She looked up.

"Gentlemen," she said. "I hope you'll excuse me."

CHAPTER FIVE

6:15 p.m. Eastern Standard Time
The Situation Room
The White House, Washington, DC

"Amy," Kurt said, "please give us Lebanon and Israel. Focus on the Blue Line."

On the oversized screen behind him, a map appeared. A second later, it popped up on the smaller screens embedded in the walls. The map showed two territories, bisected by a thick, undulating blue line. To the left of the land area was a pale blue area, denoting the Mediterranean Sea.

Susan knew the area well enough that she could easily skip this geography lesson. Further, she was frustrated—she had already been back at the White House for an hour. It had taken this long to pull this meeting together.

"I'm going to race through the preliminaries, if no one minds," Kurt said. "I imagine everyone in this room is up on current events enough to know that there was a skirmish on the border between Lebanon and Israel nearly two hours ago.

"The Blue Line, which you see here, is the negotiated border, behind which Israel agreed to pull back her troops after the 1982 war and occupation. An unknown number of Hezbollah commandos made an incursion and attacked an Israeli patrol on the road that follows the Blue Line for much of its length. There were eight soldiers from the Israeli Defense Forces on the patrol, all of whom we know were killed, except one."

A formal photograph of a dark-haired young woman appeared on the screens. It looked like a photo taken for a high school yearbook, or before some kind of awards ceremony. The girl was smiling brightly. More than smiling—she was positively beaming.

"Daria Shalit," Kurt said. "Nineteen years old, and just beginning the second year of her compulsory two-year service in the IDF."

"Pretty," someone in the room said.

Kurt didn't respond. A long exhale escaped from him.

"Believe me, there is a lot of table-pounding and soul-searching in Israeli decision-making circles. Women have participated in the Israeli border patrols for the past several months. It seems clear now that this was a preplanned kidnapping with Shalit, or any young woman on the patrol, as the intended target. An assault force pursued the kidnappers across the border, but met with furious resistance within two kilometers. Another four Israelis were killed, along with an estimated twenty Hezbollah militants."

"Helen of Troy," a man in military dress greens said.

Kurt nodded. "Exactly. The effect on Israeli society has been visceral. It has been a punch to the gut, and this was probably the intent. Our intelligence suggests that Hezbollah is deliberately trying to spark a war, similar to the one that took place in 2006. Unfortunately, we suspect they are leading Israel into a trap."

"Hezbollah is tough," the military man said. "They are hard to root out."

"Amy," Kurt said. "Give me Hezbollah, please."

On the screen, an image appeared of a group of men marching with banners, fists in the air. Kurt gestured at the men with a laser pointer.

"Hezbollah—the Party of God, or Army of God, depending on which translation you prefer—is probably the world's largest and most militarily capable terror organization. They were created, and are trained, funded, and deployed, as a proxy of the Iranian government, with operations spanning Europe, Africa, Asia, and the Americas.

"As terrorists go, Hezbollah is vastly formidable. They enjoy worldwide legitimacy among Shiite Muslims, sophistication of operations, and an organizational ability that ISIS can only dream of having among Sunnis. In the areas of Lebanon where Hezbollah are based, they often act as the de facto local government, with the full cooperation of the population. They run schools, food, recreation and job programs, and they send a handful of elected representatives to the Lebanese parliament. Their military wing is far more effective and powerful than the Lebanese military. Because of the religious differences between Shiite and Sunni Muslims, Hezbollah and ISIS are enemies, sworn to destroy each other."

"What's so bad about that?" Susan said, only half-joking. "The enemy of my enemy is my friend, isn't she?"

Kurt almost smiled. "Careful. Hezbollah's policy toward our close ally Israel is one of open-ended holy war. According to Hezbollah, Israel is an existential threat, oppresses Lebanese society, oppresses the Palestinians, and must be destroyed at all costs."

"Do they have a chance of doing that?" Susan said.

Kurt shrugged.

"They could do some damage, the extent of which we don't know. Current assessments suggest that Hezbollah has between twenty-five thousand and thirty thousand fighters. Perhaps ten thousand to fifteen thousand of those fighters have combat experience, either during the 2006 war, or more recently fighting directly against ISIS in the Syrian Civil War. We believe as many as twenty thousand troops have received training from the Iranian Revolutionary Guards—five thousand or more have gone to Iran and received extensive training.

"Hezbollah has a network of deep tunnels and fortifications in the hilly region just north of the Blue Line, which during the 2006 war with Israel proved impossible to completely take out from the air. Israeli intelligence assessments suggest that these forts have only become deeper, more hardened, and more sophisticated since 2006. Our own intelligence suggests that Hezbollah has more than sixty-five thousand rockets and missiles, plus millions of rounds of small arms ammunition. Their arsenal is probably five times as large as it was in 2006. Throughout Hezbollah's history, Iran has been reluctant to provide them with anything more than slow-moving, short-range missiles and rockets, and we suspect that this is still the case."

"What is Israel doing?" the man in dress greens said.

Kurt nodded. Behind him on the screen, the Blue Line reappeared. All along the south side of it, small icons of soldiers appeared.

"Now we get to the meat of it. The Israelis have amassed a large incursion force at the border, with more units joining all the time. The Secretary of State has been on the phone with Yonatan Stern, the Israeli Prime Minister. Yonatan is a hardliner, popular with the right wing of Israeli society. To maintain his popularity with his base, he's going to have to deliver here. He needs a decisive victory, a return of the missing soldier—something. We understand he plans to send the Israeli incursion force across the border within the next few hours, essentially invading Lebanon."

"In a sense, you could say that Israel was already invaded by Lebanon," the military man said.

Kurt nodded. "You could say that. Combined with the invasion, Stern plans to conduct a bombing campaign. We have requested that the bombing campaign be limited to twelve hours in duration, be designed to avoid civilian casualties, and only target known Hezbollah military assets."

"What did Yonatan say to that?" Susan said. Yonatan Stern was not her favorite person in the world. You might even say that they did not get along.

"He said he would take it under advisement."

Susan shook her head. "Yonatan's another one of you men. He never met a war, or a weapon system, he didn't like."

She paused. This seemed like another low-grade Israel-Hezbollah skirmish, just like all the Israel-Hamas skirmishes, and the Israel-PLO skirmishes before those. Ugly, bloody, brutish, and in the end, inconclusive. Just another practice round for the next practice round.

"So what is our end game here, Kurt? What are the dangers, and what do you suggest that we do?"

Kurt sighed. His perfectly bald head reflected the lights recessed in the ceiling. "As always, the danger is that the fighting spills out of control and becomes linked to, or causes, other regional fighting. Hezbollah and the Palestinians are allies. Often, Hamas uses these wars with Hezbollah as cover to launch their own guerrilla attacks inside Israel. Syria is in chaos, with numerous small, but heavily armed groups looking to exploit instability.

"Meanwhile, large majorities in Jordan, Egypt, Turkey, and Saudi Arabia identify as anti-Israel. And there is always Iran, the biggest, meanest kid on that block, hovering in the background with arms folded, with the big Russian bear hovering behind them. Everyone involved is armed to the teeth."

"And our next steps?"

Kurt shook his head and shrugged his big shoulders. "Our next steps are to walk a fine line. The whole region is a minefield, and we need to be careful where we put our feet. Israel is one of our closest allies and an important strategic partner. They are really the only functioning democracy in the whole region. At the same time, Lebanon has been an ally and a partner of ours for a long time. Jordan and Turkey are allies of ours. We buy the bulk of our foreign energy supplies from Saudi Arabia. We also have a commitment to brokering peace between the Palestinians and Israel, and engineering the creation of a sovereign state in Palestine."

He nodded, as if to himself. "I'd say our job is to not inflame tensions any further, and hope this little flare-up turns out to be a nine-day wonder—or better yet, a nine-hour wonder."

Susan almost laughed. "In other words, we sit on our hands."

Now Kurt smiled. “I’d say we should sit on our hands. But right now our hands are tied behind our backs.”

CHAPTER SIX

December 12
1:40 p.m. Israel Time (6:40 am Eastern Standard Time)
Tel Aviv, Israel

The news was bad.

The young woman sat on the park bench, watching her little boy and girl, twins, play on the swing set. In the near distance was the tan apartment block, sixteen stories high, where the woman lived. There was no one around today, the park mostly empty.

It was unusual for an early afternoon in spring, but not surprising given the circumstances. Most of the country seemed to be inside somewhere, glued to their TV and computer screens.

Last night, Daria Shalit, a nineteen-year-old soldier in the Israeli Defense Forces, had gone missing after a skirmish with Hezbollah terrorists who had made a surprise attack along the northern border. The seven other soldiers in her patrol—all men—had died in the fighting. But not Daria. Daria was just gone.

IDF troops had pursued the terrorists back into Lebanon. Four more Israelis had died in the fighting there. Eleven young men—the cream of Israeli youth—all dead in an hour. But that was not what consumed the country.

The fate of Daria had become an overnight obsession. If the woman closed her eyes, she could see Daria's pretty face and dark eyes alight, smiling as she clowned around with a machine gun, smiling as she posed with friends in bikinis on a Mediterranean beach, smiling as she received her school diploma. So beautiful and always beaming, as though her future was assured, a promise she was sure to receive.

The woman did close her eyes now and let the tears stream down her cheeks. She put a hand to her face, hoping her children would not see her weep. Her heart was broken for a girl she had never met but somehow knew as well as if Daria were her own sister.

The newspapers were crying out for blood, demanding the complete destruction of the Lebanese people. There were violent arguments in the Knesset through the night, as the government issued threats, demanded the girl's release, but took no immediate action. A rage was building, ready to explode.

Hours ago, the bombing had begun.

Israeli jets were pounding southern Lebanon, the Hezbollah stronghold, and all the way north to Beirut. Each time the announcements came on TV, the woman's neighbors in her apartment building erupted in shouts and cheers.

"Kill every one of them!" an old man shouted in something that sounded like triumph, but of course could not be. His gruff voice was clear through the paper thin walls. "Kill every single one!"

The woman took her children outside after that.

Now she sat in the park, silently weeping, letting herself cry, getting it out, all the while her ears tuned carefully to the calls and shouts of her two children. Her children, innocents, would grow to adulthood surrounded by enemies who would gladly see their throats cut and their flesh bled white.

"What are we to do?" the woman whispered. "What are we to do?"

The answer came in the form of a new sound, low and far away at first, mingling with the sounds of her children. Soon it moved closer and louder, then louder still. It was a sound she knew too well.

Air raid sirens.

Her eyes popped open.

Her children had stopped playing. They stared across the playground at her. The sirens were loud now.

LOUD.

"Mama!"

She jumped from the bench and ran toward the children. There was a bomb shelter beneath their building—a quarter of a kilometer away.

"Run!" she screamed. "Run to the building!"

The children didn't move. She raced to them and gathered them in her arms. Then she ran with them held to her, one in each arm. For a few moments, she didn't know her own strength. She dashed across the pavement with these two precious packages, both crying now, the sirens around them shrieking louder and louder.

The woman's breath was harsh in her ears.

The building loomed, growing closer. Everywhere, people who were invisible just moments ago ran toward the building.

Suddenly, yet another sound came—a sound so loud, so high-pitched that the woman thought her eardrums would burst. She looked up and a missile streaked across the sky, coming from the north. It slammed into the upper floors of her building.

The earth beneath her feet shook from the impact. The world seemed to spin around her, even as the top of the building blew apart in a massive explosion, concrete masonry flying through the air. How many people in those rooms? How many dead?

She lost her balance and fell, spilling her two children onto the ground. She crawled on top of them, covering them with her body just before the shockwave came. Then a hail of debris from the explosion rained down, tiny biting pebbles and shards, choking dust, the remains of the old and infirm who could not leave their apartments in time.

The sirens did not stop. The deafening shriek of another missile came, flying just overhead, followed by the blast and rumble as it found its target not far away.

On and on and on raged the sirens.

Another missile shriek began to grow. It whistled in her ears. The skin on her body popped out in gooseflesh. She pulled her children closer, closer. The sound was too loud. It no longer made sense. It was beyond hearing, monstrous beyond all human comprehension—her systems shut down in the face of it.

The woman screamed in tandem with the missile, but she seemed to make no sound at all. She could not look up. She could not move. She felt its shadow above her, blotting out the light of day.

Then a new light took her, a blinding light.

And after that, the darkness.

CHAPTER SEVEN

6:50 a.m. Eastern Standard Time
The White House Residence
Washington, DC

The morning light was streaming through the blinds, but Luke did not want to get up. He lay flat on his back in the big bed, his head propped up on pillows.

Susan lay next to him under the sheets, the President of the United States, her head resting on his chest, her short blonde hair hanging loose against his bare skin. He noticed a few flecks of gray that her stylist had missed. Or perhaps that was on purpose—on a man, a little bit of gray would indicate experience, seriousness, *gravitas*.

She was breathing deeply.

"Are you awake?" he whispered.

He felt her smile against his body. "Of course I am, silly. I've been awake for over an hour."

"What are you thinking about?" he said.

"What are *you* thinking about? That's the important question."

"Well, I'm worried."

She pressed herself onto her elbows, turned, and looked at him. As always, he was astonished by her beauty. Her eyes were pale blue, and in her face he could see the woman who had appeared on magazine covers more than twenty years before. She was aging backward, moving in reverse toward that time. He would almost swear to it—in the short time they had been together, she appeared to grow a little bit younger nearly every day.

Her mouth made a half smile and her eyes narrowed in suspicion. "Luke Stone is worried? The man who takes down terrorist networks with a wave of his hand? The man who topples despotic rulers and stops mass killers alike, all before breakfast? What could Luke Stone possibly be worried about?"

He shook his head and smiled, despite himself. "Enough of that."

Truth be told, he was more than worried. Things were getting complicated. He was committed to putting his relationship back together with Gunner. It was going well—better than he could have hoped—but Gunner's grandparents still had custody of him. Luke was beginning to think that was for the best. A protracted custody battle with Becca's wealthy and hateful parents—it would be long, drawn-out, and ugly. And what would he win? Luke was still in the spy game. If he moved in with Luke, Gunner would end up spending a lot of time on his own. No guidance, no supervision—it sounded like a lousy arrangement.

Then there was the Susan situation. She was the President of the United States. She had her own family, and technically speaking, she was still married. Her husband, Pierre, knew about Luke, and apparently he was happy for them. But they were keeping this a secret from everyone else.

Who was he kidding? They weren't keeping anything a secret.

Her close security team knew about him—it was their job to know. And that meant it was already a widespread and growing rumor within the Secret Service. He passed through security to get in here late at night, two, sometimes three nights a week. Or he signed in as a guest in the afternoon, but never signed out again. The people who monitored the video surveillance saw him entering and leaving the Residence, and took note of when he did so. The chef knew he was cooking for two, and the servers who brought the food out were two heavyset older ladies who smiled at him, and bantered with him, and called him "Mr. Luke."

Susan's chief-of-staff knew, which meant that Kurt Kimball also probably knew, and God only knew where it went from there.

Every single person who already knew about him had family, friends, and acquaintances. They had favorite early morning breakfast joints, or lunch counters, or bars where they regaled the regulars with tales of life inside the White House.

The reporter's question yesterday suggested that the rumor had already broken out of the box. They were one leak, one disgruntled staffer's call to the *Washington Post* or CNN, from a full-blown, twenty-four/seven media circus.

Luke didn't want that. He didn't want Gunner subjected to that glare. He didn't want the boy in the custody of the Secret Service everywhere he went. He didn't want the media following him or staking out his school.

Luke also didn't want the attention for himself. It was better for his work if he could remain in obscurity. He needed the freedom to operate, both for himself and for his team.

And he didn't want the attention for Susan. He didn't want it for their relationship. Things were hot and heavy right now, but he couldn't imagine this thing lasting under constant scrutiny from the media.

It was impossible to raise these issues with her. She was an irrepressible optimist, she was already under the glare of the media anyway, and she was riding high on endorphins. Her answer was always some variation of, "Oh, we'll work it out."

"What are you worried about, Mr. Luke?" Susan said now.

"I'm worried…" he began. He shook his head again. "I'm worried that I'm falling in love."

Her thousand-watt smile lit up the room. "I know," she said. "Isn't it great?"

She kissed him deeply, then leapt out of bed like a teenager. He watched her as she padded across the room, nude, to her closet. She still had the body of a teenager.

Almost.

"I want you to meet my daughters," she said. "They're coming to town next week to spend Christmas."

"Terrific," he said. The thought of it made his stomach do a lazy barrel roll. "Who should we tell them I am?"

"They knew who you are. You're that superhero. James Bond without the clean shave or the fancy suit. I mean, you rescued Michaela's life just a few years ago."

"We were never properly introduced."

"Still. You're like an uncle to them."

Just then, the phone on the bedside table began to ring. It made a funny sound, not so much a ring as a buzz, or a hum. It sounded like a monk with a bad cold chanting in meditation. Also, it lit up in blue on each ring. Luke hated that phone.

"You want me to get it?" he said.

She smiled and shook her head. Now he watched her come back across the room, moving faster this time. For a brief moment, he imagined another world, one where they didn't have their jobs. Hell, maybe even a world where they were both unemployed. In that world, she could climb right back into bed with him.

She picked up the phone. "Good morning."

Her face changed as she listened to the voice on the other end of the line. All of the fun went out of it. The light in her eyes faded, and her smile dropped away. She took a deep breath and let out a long exhale.

"Okay," she said. "I'll be down in fifteen minutes."

She hung up.

"Trouble?" Luke said.

She looked at him, her eyes showing something—a vulnerability perhaps—that the masses never saw on TV.

"When isn't there trouble?" she said.

CHAPTER EIGHT

7:30 a.m. Eastern Standard Time
The Situation Room
The White House, Washington, DC

The elevator opened and Luke stepped into the egg-shaped Situation Room.

Big Kurt Kimball stood at the far end of the room, his bald head gleaming, and he spotted Luke right away. Kurt usually ran these meetings with an iron hand. He had such a deep, effortless, and encyclopedic command of world affairs that people tended to follow his lead.

"Agent Stone," he said. "Glad you could join us this early."

Was there a hint of hidden meaning, even sarcasm, in that statement? Luke decided not to touch it.

He shrugged. "The President called me. I got here as soon as I could."

He glanced around the room.

Ultra-modern, the place was much more than a conference room—it was set up for maximum use of the space, with large screens embedded in the walls every couple of feet, and a giant projection screen on the far wall at the end of the table. Tablet computers and slim microphones rose from slots out of the conference table—they could be dropped back into the table if the attendee wanted to use their own device.

Every plush leather chair at the table was occupied—a few military uniforms, several business suits. Most of the people were middle-aged and overweight—career government types who spent a lot of time sitting down in comfortable chairs and eating lunch. These chairs all looked like the captain's chair on the command module of a spaceship crossing the galaxy. Big arms, deep leather, high backs, ergonomically correct with lumbar spine support.

The seats along the walls—smaller, red linen chairs with lower backs—were filled with young aides and even younger assistants, most of them slurping from Styrofoam coffee cups, tapping messages into tablets, or murmuring into telephones.

Susan sat in a leather chair at the closest end of the oblong table. She wore a blue pinstriped pantsuit. Her right leg was crossed over her left, and she leaned in close to hear what a young aide was telling her. Luke tried not to stare at her.

After a moment, she glanced up and nodded to him.

"Agent Stone," she said. "Thanks for coming."

Luke nodded. "Madam President. Of course."

Kurt clapped his big hands, as if Luke entering was the cue he had been waiting for. The clap made a sound like a heavy book dropping to a stone floor. "Order, everybody! Come to order, please."

The place went silent. Almost. A couple of military men at the conference table continued to talk with each other, heads leaned in close.

Kurt clapped his hands again.

CLAP. CLAP.

They both looked at him. He raised his hands as if to say, "Are you done?"

The room finally went dead quiet.

Kurt gestured to a young woman sitting in a chair to his left. Luke had seen her before, many times. She was Kurt's indispensable aide, practically an extra appendage. She wore her auburn hair in a short bob cut like Susan's—short bob cuts like Susan's were all the rage with young women these days. Magazine editors and fluff news shows hadn't exactly overlooked this fact. Critics called it the Hopkins Bob if they liked it, the Hopkins Helmet if they didn't. They all seemed to be in agreement about what to call the women who styled their hair that way, however.

Susan's Army.

Luke enjoyed that one. He didn't wear a bob, but he supposed he was also in Susan's Army.

"Amy, let's see it," Kurt said. "Israel and Lebanon, please."

On the screen, blue and yellow icons that represented explosions began to appear across southern Lebanon, reaching as far north as the southern edge of Beirut, the explosions becoming sparser the further north they went.

"Hours ago, the Israeli air force began a bombing campaign, attacking the Hezbollah tunnel systems and fortifications along the Blue Line, as well as the Hezbollah-dominated neighborhoods of south Beirut. This is not a surprise, and in fact was telegraphed to us by Yonatan Stern's government last night."

On the screen, large red icons in the same shape as the earlier ones began to appear across Israel. There were maybe fifteen of them in total. A moment later, smaller red icons, tiny starbursts, began to appear in northern Israel. There were dozens of these.

"Soon after Israel began its air strikes, Hezbollah started to launch missile attacks into Israel. This is not unusual, especially when there is exchange of fire between the two forces. The 2006 war followed more or less this same trajectory. But a problem has arisen. In the intervening years, Hezbollah has obtained better firepower."

A photograph of a large missile on a mobile launch pad appeared.

"This is the Fateh-200 missile. It is an Iranian-built weapon system, long-range missiles with multiple warheads that pack a powerful punch. Launched from inside Lebanon, it can reach nearly anywhere in Israel, except perhaps the sparsely populated Negev Desert in the south. It has sophisticated control and guidance features that for the first time give Hezbollah precision-strike capability."

Kurt paused. "From what we can gather, it now appears that Hezbollah has obtained the Fateh-200. We believe they have launched anywhere from twenty to thirty of these missiles so far, each with as many as a dozen warheads. They targeted civilian and military infrastructure in population centers across Israel, including Tel Aviv, the western edge of Jerusalem, and the center of Haifa, among others. Israel's medium-range missile defense system, known as David's Sling, knocked perhaps half to two-thirds of these from the sky. But that wasn't good enough.

"Several civilian neighborhoods were hit and numerous buildings destroyed. A warhead landed within half a mile of the Knesset, the Israeli congress, while it was in session."

"What are the current casualties?" Haley Lawrence, the Secretary of Defense, said.

"Thus far, all we have are the official figures that have been released. More than four hundred civilians killed, thousands wounded, amid widespread destruction and panic. No figures on military casualties have been released, but the Israelis have mobilized for total war, calling for duty all reservists and able-bodied veterans of previous wars. They have intensified the bombing campaign in Lebanon dramatically, probably in an attempt to destroy any more Fateh-200s before they're launched."

"Has it worked?" Luke said, already knowing the answer.

Kurt shook his head. "We don't know. We doubt it. As we speak, Hezbollah is still launching small, unguided missiles and rockets into northern Israel, demonstrating that their response capability still exists. We believe they are holding back the Fateh-200s for the time being, but will resume those launches on a timetable of their choosing.

"Israel has publicly blamed the Iranians for providing Hezbollah with the new missiles. In all likelihood, this is an accurate assessment. Hezbollah is a cat's paw for Iran. Thirty minutes ago, Israel threatened to attack Iran if another Fateh-200 or similar missile is launched into Israeli territory."

Kurt paused. "Ten minutes later, Iran informed the Israelis that they will counter any Israeli attack by launching nuclear weapons. In the same statement, they indicated that any Israeli attack will be grounds for Iran to launch nuclear weapons at the American air base in Doha, Qatar, as well as the large American embassy complex in Baghdad."

The room went dead quite for several seconds. Luke, standing in a corner, watched the looks on the faces. Several people blushed, as if they were embarrassed. Others stared with wide eyes and mouths hanging slightly open.

"Iran doesn't have nuclear weapons," someone said. "They can't."

Kurt shook his head. "Every international agreement and accord states that Iran is not a nuclear-armed state, and is forbidden from becoming one. But that doesn't mean they haven't acquired nuclear weapons. Amy, give us Iran, please."

A new map appeared on the screen—Iran. The map gave Luke a sinking feeling. He had been to Iran. It wasn't his favorite place in the world.

"The Islamic State of Iran is a Shiite Muslim theocracy. We know that they have harbored an ambition to acquire nuclear weapons since at least the 1979 Islamic Revolution."

"But if they ever tested a nuclear weapon," Susan said, "we would know about it." It was the first time she had spoken since the meeting started.

"It would be nice if that were true," Kurt said. "Deep underground testing facilities are proliferating everywhere in the world—they are very difficult to find and map. Advanced radiation detection systems can account for, down to very small amounts, radiation released into the atmosphere. We can combine that with our ability to measure the force and direction of prevailing winds, and determine with a fair amount of accuracy where the radiation is coming from. But when I say a fair amount of accuracy, what I mean is to within several hundred miles. Given Iran's proximity to

Pakistan—which is a known and accepted nuclear-armed state—it's hard to pinpoint a radiation source and say for sure it's in Iran."

"But those tests have seismic signatures," Susan said. "They're practically like earthquakes."

Kurt nodded. "And that's what makes Iran doubly challenging. It is one of the most seismically active places on the planet. Earthquakes are common there, and frequently devastating. The most recent disaster was in 2003, when a 6.6 magnitude earthquake killed at least twenty-three thousand people in the city of Bam. But disasters aside, seismic activity in Iran is nearly constant. We monitor it on a daily basis. Listening for an underground rumble in Iran is like listening for waves to crash at the beach. It happens all the time."

"What are you saying, Kurt?" Susan said. "Just say it."

"Iran could build and test nuclear weapons," Kurt said. "And we might not find out about it."

Instantly, an idea occurred to Luke. It was just one of those things. There is a question, and your mind spits out the answer. You don't have to like the answer, but there it is in front of you.

"Why don't we send in a covert infiltration team?" he said. "They could go in and find out if this is a bluff or not. If it isn't a bluff, they discover the location of the nukes, and call in air strikes."

Admittedly, he didn't have the entire plan worked through, but once he said it out loud, he could see the wisdom in it.

"We don't have the necessary people in place for that kind of deployment," said a man in dress greens. "It would take weeks or even months—"

"General, I beg to differ," Luke said. "We do have the people in place. My own organization, the Special Response Team, is ready."

CHAPTER NINE

8:15 a.m. Eastern Standard Time
The West Wing
The White House, Washington, DC

"This is a disaster," Susan said. "It's crazy. I'm not going to allow it."

They were walking back through the West Wing to the Oval Office, three of them—Susan, Kurt, and Kat Lopez. Susan's and Kat's shoes clacked on the marble floor. Three big Secret Service men trailed them; two walked in front.

The double doors to the Oval Office were just up ahead, a large Secret Service man on either side. Susan and the swarm of people around her were all walking so fast, it felt like she was being sucked toward the office on a conveyor belt. She felt out of control. She did not want to have this meeting. A couple of months ago, sending her best agents on a life-threatening mission wouldn't have rattled her cage all that much.

"Susan, we have another problem," Kurt said.

"Hit me."

"The Israelis are no longer sharing casualty assessments with us, or keeping us updated on their plans. Yonatan Stern is furious. He wants to attack Iran immediately, and we have asked him to hold off from doing that. He is already pounding southern Lebanon to dust, but Hezbollah is still launching missiles. He calls these attacks, and the Iranian threat with no clear way to respond, a humiliation, and he blames us for it. He is ready to kick our ambassador out of the country. He wants to speak with you directly."

Susan shook her head. "This day keeps getting better and better."

They passed through the double doors and into the Oval Office.

"Do you want me to schedule a call with him?" Kat said.

Susan shrugged. "Sure. I'll talk to him. Kurt, can you have someone draft me my talking points? What am I supposed to tell him? Why can't everybody just be friends? Why don't you just bake those guys with the missiles a cake?"

"Of course," Kurt said, and peeled off into a corner of the office, already on his telephone.

Kat disappeared back out through the doorway.

Susan gazed around the Oval Office. In front of her, three tall windows, with drapes pulled back, looked out on the Rose Garden. Outside, it was a sunny day in early winter. There were several people in the room. Luke Stone sat in a high-backed chair in the sitting area. Beneath his feet was the Seal of the President of the United States. Sitting beside him was big Haley Lawrence, the Secretary of Defense, who looked like he had been gaining weight—the additional bulk somehow took on the appearance of baby fat, making a man well over six feet tall seem a lot like a little boy.

There were two other men in the room, both standing. They wore dress green military uniforms—men who Susan guessed were in their mid-fifties, very fit, with crew-cut hair. They could be twins—Tweedledum and Tweedledee.

"Madam President," Tweedledum said. He reached out a hand to her. "I'm General Steven Perkins with the Defense Intelligence Agency."

She nodded to him as his hand swallowed hers in a firm military grip.

"General."

Tweedledee also reached out for his shake. "Madam President, I'm Mike Sobchak with Naval Intelligence."

"Admiral."

She shook her head. "Okay, men, where are we on this?" Susan said. "What kind of scheme have you and Agent Stone cooked up?"

Kurt was back, having murmured into his phone for all of eleven seconds. "Please shut the door," he said to the Secret Service men.

"It's a highly classified mission," Haley Lawrence said.

Susan shrugged and made a spinning gesture with her hand. "I figured as much. So give it to me."

"We send a small team to Israel on a State Department plane," Kurt said. "We've already sent three State Department planes since yesterday, so to anyone watching it might seem like more of the same—crisis diplomats flying in to try to defuse the situation."

"I'm sure no one suspects that we're going to send spies in," Susan said.

"When the team arrives, it will be briefed by Israeli intelligence on possible locations of Iranian nuclear sites. The team will coordinate with the Israelis to design an infiltration, and then drop into Iran under cover of darkness. The team then makes their way, by whatever means available, to the most likely sites, and either confirms or discredits the existence of nuclear weapons at those sites. If weapons are found, they call in air strikes on those coordinates, which destroy the weapons in their silos."

"Air strikes by whom?" Susan said. "Americans or Israelis?"

"Americans," Tweedledum said. "By definition, those strikes will have to be powerful bunker busters dropped from high altitude. Most likely, MOABs dropped from B-52 bombers, and that's if we can even take out the bunkers with conventional weapons, which is not guaranteed. We don't believe the Israelis have those capabilities."

"We don't believe?" Susan said. "Don't we know?"

"We're dealing with Israel here," Tweedledee said. "They might have them, they might not. They're not always forthcoming with information like that. In any event, if the Israelis bomb Iranian missile silos, there's always the chance it will start World War Three. The Russians are close allies with Iran. Meanwhile, the Sunni countries hate the Iranian Shiites. But only until the Israelis bomb them. Then they're all fellow Muslims and Israeli aggression must be avenged. If we do the bombing…"

He shrugged. "I think we can find a way to placate the Russians about this. And the Sunni countries will live with it."

"Why don't the Israelis send their own spies in to look for the bomb?" Susan said.

"We talked to their intelligence people. They think the mission is a sure failure. They would prefer to bomb Iran indiscriminately and destroy all of Iranian military bases and infrastructure, in the hopes of hitting any nukes they might have. We are encouraging them—encouraging them very strenuously—to refrain from that course of action. Obviously, the risk of bombing Iran and leaving even one nuclear missile operational is too high to contemplate what…"

Susan looked at Luke. "Hello, Agent Stone."

He gazed directly into her eyes. This was the thing she hated, the thing she had been dreading. She wanted to stop time right here and not have him say another word.

"Madam President."

"Do you intend to take this mission?"

He nodded. "Yes. Of course. It was my idea."

"It sounds to me like a suicide mission, Agent Stone."

"I've heard of worse," Luke said. "In any case, it's exactly the kind of thing the new Special Response Team was organized to do.

I've already talked to my team. We can be ready to leave in a couple of hours."

She tried a different tack. "Agent Stone, you're the director of the Special Response Team. My records indicate that you're forty-two years old. Wouldn't this mission be better handled by a more junior operative from your agency? Someone a little younger, say? Someone a little more energetic?"

"I plan to go in with Ed Newsam," Luke said. "He's thirty-five. And anyway, I'm still pretty energetic for an old geezer."

"Agent Stone and Agent Newsam both have extensive operations experience in the Middle East," Tweedledum said. "Both are elite combat veterans, have been deep undercover, and are familiar with Israeli, Arab, and Persian culture. Both have some ability to speak Farsi."

Susan ignored him. She glanced around the room. Everyone seemed to be staring at her. They wanted to talk about the design of the mission, she knew. They wanted her to green light it immediately, so they could gather the resources needed, come up with contingencies in case it failed, develop strategies for plausible deniability in case it went public. In their minds, who was going was not even in play anymore—the issue had already been decided.

"Can you gentlemen give me a few minutes alone with Agent Stone?"

* * *

"Luke, are you out of your mind?"

The other men, and all of the Secret Service, had gone.

"I wouldn't send my worst enemy on this mission. You're supposed to parachute into Iran, and then wander around the country with people trying to murder you, until you find nuclear weapons?"

He smiled. "Well, I hope it'll be a little better thought out than that."

"You're going to get yourself killed."

He stood then, and went to her. He tried to hug her. She was stiff for a moment, then melted into his embrace.

"Do you know how ridiculous it looks for the President of the United States to be overly worried about the life of one special operative, who's been doing exactly this type of thing his entire adult life?"

She shook her head. "I don't care. This is different. I can't sign off on a mission where you might get killed. It's nuts."

He looked down at her. "Are you telling me that in order to be with you, I have to give up my job?"

"No. You're the head of your own agency. You don't have to take this on. You don't have to volunteer for this. Send someone else."

"You want me to send someone else even though you think this is a suicide mission?"

She nodded. "That's right. Send someone who I don't love."

"Susan, I can't do that."

She turned away then, and abruptly, miserable tears started to flow. "I know. I know that. But for the love of God, please don't die over there."

CHAPTER TEN

4:45 p.m. Israel Time (9:45 a.m. Eastern Standard Time)
Samson's Lair – Deep Underground
Jerusalem, Israel

"Tell them to shut up."

Yonatan Stern, the Prime Minister of Israel, sat in his customary chair at the head of the conference table in the Israeli crisis command center, his chin in his hand. The room was a cavernous egg-shaped dome. All around him, his military and political advisors were in a state of chaos, shouting, recriminating, jabbing fingers at one another.

How had it come to this? seemed to be the prevailing question. And the answer upon which most of these brilliant strategic minds had landed was, *It's someone else's fault.*

"David!" he said, staring at his chief-of-staff, a burly former commando who had been his right-hand man since their military days. David looked back at him, big dark eyes baleful, teeth biting the inside of his cheek, as he did when he was nervous or distracted. Once upon a time, the man would kill enemies with his bare hands, and yet somehow appear apologetic while he did so. He still looked apologetic now.

"Please," Yonatan said. "Bring the place to order."

David shrugged. He stepped to the conference table and slammed a giant fist down on its surface.

BOOM!

He didn't say a word, but brought his fist down again.

BOOM!

And again. And again. And again. Each time the fist landed, the room became a little quieter. Eventually, all the men in the room stood and stared at David Cohn, Yonatan Stern's organizer and enforcer, a man none of them respected intellectually, but also a man none would ever dare cross.

He raised his fist one last time, but now the room was silent. It paused in midair, like a hammer. Then it floated slowly back to his side.

"Thank you, David," Yonatan said. He looked at the other men in the room. "Gentlemen, I would like to begin this meeting. So please, take your seats and enthrall me with your acumen."

He looked around the room. Efraim Shavitz was here, always boyish, much younger than his years. People called him the Model. He was the Director of Mossad. He wore an expensive, custom-tailored suit and Italian black leather shoes with a high polish. He looked like he was heading out to a nightclub in Tel Aviv, and not currently overseeing the destruction of his own people. In a room full of aging military men and frumpy thinkers, Shavitz the dandy looked like some sort of exotic bird.

Yonatan shook his head. Shavitz was one of his predecessor's men. Yonatan kept him on because he came well recommended and seemed like he knew what he was doing. Until today.

"Efraim, your assessment, please."

Shavitz nodded. "Of course."

He pulled a remote control from his jacket pocket and turned to the large screen at the end of the conference table. Instantly, a video of a missile launch from a drab green mobile platform came on.

"The Fateh-200 has come to Lebanon. We have suspected this might be the case—"

"When did you suspect that?" Yonatan said.

Shavitz looked at him. "I'm sorry?"

"When did you suspect that Hezbollah had obtained the Fateh-200 weapon system? When? I have never read such a report, nor has anyone mentioned to me that such a report might be coming. The first I heard of it was when long-range, high-explosive missiles began toppling residential buildings in Tel Aviv."

There was a long, drawn-out silence. The other men in the room stared, some at Yonatan Stern, some at Efraim Shavitz, some at the table in front of them.

"In any event, they have them," Shavitz said.

Yonatan nodded. "Yes, they do. Now about Iran… what do they have?"

Shavitz pointed at Yonatan. "Don't conflate Hezbollah acquiring powerful conventional weapons with the Iranian nuclear threat, Yonatan. Don't do that. We've told you that the Iranians were working on nuclear missiles. We know the suspected locations. We know the people involved. We have a sense of the number of warheads. You've been warned of these dangers for years. We've lost a lot of good men to obtain this information. That you took no action is not my fault, or the fault of Mossad."

"There are political considerations," Yonatan said.

Shavitz shook his head. "That's not my department. Now, we believe the Iranians may have as many as fourteen warheads, salted in three locations, and likely fairly deep underground. They may not have any. It may be a lie. But no more than fourteen."

"And if they do have them, all fourteen of them?"

Shavitz shrugged. A piece of hair above his forehead slipped out of place, very uncustomary for him. He'd better comb it back before he reached the nightclub. "And they manage to launch them?"

Yonatan nodded. "Yes."

"We'll be annihilated. It's that simple."

"What are our options?"

"Very few," Shavitz said. "Everyone in this room already knows what they are. Everyone here well knows our own nuclear, conventional missile, and air force capabilities. We can launch a massive preemptive attack, all out, against all known Iranian and Syrian missile sites, and against all Iranian air force bases. If we act with total commitment, and with all of our forces in perfect concert, we can utterly destroy Iranian and Syrian military capabilities, and set Iranian civil society back to the dark ages. Those in this room with political considerations don't need me to tell them what the worldwide backlash would be."

"What about a lesser strike?"

Shavitz shook his head. "For what? Any strike that leaves Iran with missile capabilities, with fighters or bombers in the air, or that leaves even a single nuclear missile operational, will spell disaster for us. While some of us have been sleeping, Prime Minister, or rewarding our friends with government contracts, the Iranians have been working like termites, building an almost impossibly robust conventional missile arsenal, all of it with us in mind.

"The Fajr-3, with precision guidance and multiple reentry vehicles—nearly impossible to knock down. The Shahab-3 program, with enough missiles, enough firepower, and the reach to carpet bomb every square inch of Israel. The Ghadr-110, the Ashoura, the Sejjil, and the Bina systems, all of which can reach us, thousands of individual projectiles and warheads. And, while it hardly seems pressing at this moment, they are still working on the Simorgh satellite-launched missile, which is in testing and which we can expect to see operational with a year. Once that system is in place..."

Shavitz sighed. The rest of the room was silent.

"What about our shelter system?"

Shavitz nodded. "Sure. Assuming the Iranians are bluffing and they don't have any nuclear weapons, we can say with confidence that should they launch a major attack against us, some percentage of our people would make it to the shelters in time, some of the shelters would hold, and afterwards, a handful of survivors would crawl out alive. But don't think for a minute that they would rebuild. They would be traumatized and helpless, wandering across a blasted moonscape. What would Hezbollah do then? Or the Turks? Or the Syrians? Or the Saudis? Rush in to bring aid and comfort to the last remnants of Israeli society? I really don't think so."

Yonatan took a deep breath. "Are there any other options at all?"

Shavitz shrugged. "Just one. The idea the Americans have floated. Send in a small commando team to discover if the nuclear weapons are even real, and to determine their locations. Then the American forces come in and precision strike those locations, possibly with our participation, possibly not. If the Americans make a limited, precise attack, and destroy only the nuclear weapons, the Iranians may hesitate to respond."

This was an idea Yonatan hated. He hated it because of all the fruitless loss of life—the loss of highly trained and valuable agents—that had already come from previous infiltrations into Iran. He hated it because he would be forced to wait while the agents disappeared, with no idea if they might resurface and whether they would know anything when they did. Yonatan did not like the prospect of waiting—not when the clock was ticking and the Iranians could launch their own massive attack at any time.

Yonatan especially hated this idea because it appeared to have come from inside the White House of Susan Hopkins. Hopkins had no idea of the reality of Israel's situation, and she did not seem to care. She was like a parrot with a reluctant owner, who had only taught the poor bird one phrase.

The Palestinians. The Palestinians. The Palestinians.

"What are the odds that such a mission would succeed?" Yonatan said.

Shavitz shook his head. "Very, very slim. But attempting it would probably please the Americans, and demonstrate to them the restraint we are showing. If we made the whole thing time-limited, perhaps forty-eight hours, we might not have anything to lose."

"Can we afford that much time?"

"If we closely monitor the Iranians for any sign of a first strike, and immediately launch our own strike at forty-eight hours, we should be okay."

"And if the agents are killed or captured?"

"An American team, with perhaps one Israeli guide who has significant Iranian experience. The Israeli will be a deep cover operative with no identity. If anything goes wrong, we simply deny involvement."

Shavitz paused for a long moment. "I already have the perfect operative in mind."

CHAPTER ELEVEN

12:10 p.m. Eastern Standard Time
Joint Base Andrews
Prince George's County, Maryland

The small blue jet with the US Department of State logo on the side moved slowly onto the taxiway and made a sharp right turn. Already cleared for takeoff, it quickly accelerated down the runway, left the ground, and climbed steeply into the clouds. Within another moment, it angled sharply left toward the Atlantic Ocean.

Inside the plane, Luke and his team easily fell back into old habits—they used the front four passenger seats as their meeting area. They stowed their luggage and their gear in the seats at the back.

They were leaving later than he had intended. The holdup was because Luke had gone to see Gunner at school. He had promised his son that he would never leave without telling him face-to-face, and sharing as much as he could about where he was going. Gunner had asked for that, and Luke had agreed.

They had met in a small room provided to them by the principal's assistant—it was a place where they stored musical instruments, mostly old wind instruments, many of them gathering rust, by the looks of things.

Gunner had handled it pretty well, all things considered.

"Where are you going?" he said.

Luke shook his head. "It's classified, Monster. If I tell you…"

"Then I tell someone, and that person tells someone."

"I don't think you would tell anyone. But just knowing would put you at risk."

He looked at the boy, who was more than a little long-faced.

"Are you worried?" Luke said.

Gunner shook his head. "No. I think you can probably take care of yourself."

Now, on the plane, Luke smiled to himself. Funny kid. He had been through a lot, and somehow hadn't lost his sense of humor.

Luke glanced around at his team. In the seat next to him sat big Ed Newsam, in khaki cargo pants and a long-sleeved T-shirt.

Steely-eyed, huge, as eternal as a mountain. Ed was older now, certainly. There were lines on his face, especially around the eyes, that hadn't been there before. And his hair wasn't as jet black as it used to be—there were a few gray and white strands running around loose in there.

Ed had left the FBI Hostage Rescue Team for this gig. The FBI was moving Ed up the ranks—more seniority, more responsibility, more sitting at a desk, and a lot less time in the field. To hear Ed tell it, he was switching because he wanted to see some action again. But that didn't stop him from holding out for more money. It didn't matter. Luke had been ready to make the SRT budget cry out in agony if that's what it took to get Ed back on board.

Across from Luke and to the left, facing him, was Mark Swann. He stretched his long legs out into the aisle as usual, an old pair of ripped jeans and a pair of red Chuck Taylor sneakers there for anyone to trip over. Swann had changed, of course. Barely surviving his time as a prisoner of ISIS had made him more serious—he no longer joked about the danger of missions. Luke was glad that he had come back at all—there was a period of time when it seemed like Swann might become a recluse, and never emerge from his penthouse condo overlooking the beach again.

Then there was Trudy Wellington. She sat directly across from Luke. She had curly brown hair again, and hadn't aged at all. That made sense. Despite everything she had seen and done—her time as an analyst with the original SRT, her relationship with Don Morris, her escape from prison and her time in hiding—she was still only thirty-two years old. She was slim and as attractive as ever in a green sweater and blue jeans. At some point, she had done away with the big, round, red-rimmed owlish glasses she used to hide behind. Now her pretty blue eyes were front and center.

Those eyes were staring hard at Luke. They didn't look friendly.

What did she know about his relationship with Susan? Was she angry about it? Why would she be?

"Do you know what you're doing, man?" Ed Newsam said. He said it good-naturedly enough, but there was an edge, an undercurrent to it.

"You mean, with this mission?"

Ed shrugged. "Sure. Start with that."

Luke glanced out his window as he spoke. It was a bright day, but the sun was already behind them. In a little while, as they moved further east, the sky would begin to darken. It gave him the sense of events surging out ahead—a familiar feeling, but one of his least favorite aspects of the job. It was a race against time. It was *always* a race against time, and they were way behind. The war they were trying to prevent had already started.

"I guess that's what we're about to find out. Trudy?"

She shrugged, seemed noncommittal. She picked the tablet up from her lap. "Okay," she said. "I'm going to assume no prior knowledge."

"Sounds good to me," Luke said. "Boys?"

"Good," Swann said.

"Let's hear it," Ed said. He eased back into his seat.

"This is Israel and Iran," Trudy said. "It's not exactly a short story."

Luke shrugged. "It's a long flight," he said.

* * *

"Israel is a young country, existing only since 1948," Trudy said. "But the idea of the Land of Israel as a place has been sacred to the Jewish people since Biblical times, possibly as long ago as two thousand years before Christ. The first written reference to Israel as a place occurs around 1200 BC. The area was invaded, conquered, and reconquered throughout ancient times by the Babylonians, the Egyptians, and the Persians, to name a few. Through it all, the Jews persisted.

"In 63 BC, the Roman Empire conquered the region, transforming it into a Roman province. For almost two hundred years, it became the site of a violent struggle between the Jews and the Romans, which ended in widespread destruction, genocide, and ethnic cleansing. The final Jewish revolt against the Romans failed in 132 AD, and the majority of Jews were either killed or dispersed—many went north into modern-day Russia, northwest into eastern and central Europe, or directly west toward Morocco and Spain. Some went east into Syria, Iraq, and Iran. A handful might have headed south into Africa. And some stayed in Israel.

"Over time, the Roman Empire faded, and the region was conquered by Arabs in the middle 600s, who themselves had recently adopted the new religion of Islam. Despite frequent attacks by Christian Crusaders, the area remained mostly under the control of Muslim sultans for the next nine hundred years. In 1516, it was conquered again, this time by the Ottoman Empire. On Ottoman maps as early as 1600, the area we think of as Israel was referred to as Palestine. When the Ottoman Empire was destroyed in World

War One, Palestine came under the control of its next ruler, the British."

"Setting us up for modern problems," Ed said.

Trudy nodded. "Naturally. Throughout history, some Jews had remained there, and over the centuries, there were numerous idealistic attempts to have Jews from other parts of the world return. By the early 1900s, those efforts were picking up steam. The rise of the Nazis led to vastly increased numbers of Jews leaving Europe. At the end of World War Two, the population of Palestine was about one-third Jewish. After the war, a massive influx of Jews, survivors of the Holocaust, left their destroyed communities across Europe and made their way to Palestine.

"In 1948, the State of Israel was formed. This set off a series of violent conflicts between Muslims and Jews that continue to the present day. In the initial fighting, Egypt, Syria, Jordan, and Iraq invaded, joined by contingents of irregulars from Yemen, Morocco, Saudi Arabia, and Sudan. The Israelis fought them off. At least seven hundred thousands Arabs fled or were expelled by advancing Israeli forces to the areas now known as the Palestinian Territories—the West Bank and the Gaza Strip."

"See, here's the part I don't get," Ed Newsam said. "1948 is old news. Right now you have all these Palestinians locked up in Gaza and the West Bank. Why not just give them their freedom and let them become their own country? Failing that, why not just give them all citizenship and incorporate them into Israel? It seems like either thing might put the brakes on all this fighting."

"It's complicated," Swann said.

"Complicated, to put it mildly," Trudy said. "Impossible is more like it. For one thing, Israel was established as a Jewish state—a homeland for Jews all over the world. This is a project nearly two thousand years in the making.

"If Israel wants to remain a Jewish state, it can't simply incorporate the Palestinians into the country as citizens. It would set the clock ticking on a demographic time bomb, one which would go off sooner rather than later. The country has universal suffrage—every citizen gets the right to vote. There are roughly six and a half million Jews in Israel, and nearly two million Israeli Arabs, the vast majority of whom are Muslim. There are about four and a half million Palestinians in Gaza and the West Bank combined.

"If the Palestinians all became citizens, suddenly you'd have a society nearly split down the middle between Jews and Muslims, with a relative handful of Christians and others thrown in. Right away, Jews would no longer be the majority. Also, Israeli Arabs and Palestinians have higher birthrates than Israeli Jews, generally speaking. Within a couple of decades, Muslims would have a clear and growing majority. Would they vote to keep Israel the Jewish homeland?"

"Doubt it," Swann said.

"So give the Palestinians their freedom," Ed said. "Grant them nationhood. Open their roads, let them control their own airspace and coastal waters, and let them trade with other countries."

Trudy shook her head. "Also impossible. I rarely make absolute declarations about future events, but I've looked at these scenarios from every angle. No matter who says what during international negotiations, no matter how many times the United Nations general assembly votes its condemnation, keep your eye on Palestinian nationhood. It never comes any closer to fruition. And that's because Israel will never voluntarily allow it. The very idea is absurd. It's suicide.

"Look, Israel exists in a state of sometimes desperate conflict with the countries that surround it. Survival is always an open question. Security is the most important thing in Israeli society, and providing it is a major focus of the state. Israel is a tiny country as it is. If the West Bank were not there as a buffer zone, and in fact became a foreign country, the situation would instantly go from difficult to very, very dangerous. Untenable. The coastal plain of central Israel is a narrow sliver of land, from the West Bank to the sea, varying for much of its length from nine to eleven miles wide. The average person could ride a bicycle that distance in under an hour.

"Most of the civilian population, as well as the country's industrial and technology sectors—are located there. To make matters worse, the West Bank lands are hills that overlook the plain—there are places in the West Bank where you can easily see the Mediterranean. When extremists in Arab countries talk about driving the Israelis into the sea, the thing to remember is it's a very short drive.

"The Palestinians are allied with Iran, and many Palestinians are hostile to Israel's very existence. If you grant the Palestinians nationhood, what's to stop Iranian tanks, fighter planes, missile batteries, and troops amassing on your border? Not just on your border, but on the high ground above you? It's a nightmare scenario. Further, the West Bank highlands are the water source for the freshwater aquifers in coastal Israel. What's to stop a sovereign Palestine from trying to block this water supply?

"Even further, although Israel doesn't acknowledge its nuclear capabilities, it is widely accepted that they have anywhere from fifty to eighty nuclear weapons. Most of these are thought to be housed at the Zachariah Missile Base southeast of Tel Aviv, and others are housed in the southern desert. But some—perhaps as many as twenty or even thirty percent—are deployed in underground missile silos in the West Bank east of Jerusalem. These are 1970s and 1980s Cold War–era weapons, and are likely still operational.

"The expense, the transportation logistics, and the public outcry would make it nearly impossible to move the silos back into Israel, and there is no way the Israelis are going to allow the Palestinians to administer those weapons. As I said before, Israel doesn't even acknowledge the weapons exist."

"So what are you saying?" Luke said.

"I'm saying that Israel faces an existential crisis no matter where they look. If they grant the Palestinians citizenship, the very concept of Israel gets voted out of existence. If they let the West Bank become sovereign Palestine, the country of Israel gets bombed out of existence. So they pursue a third path, one that is fraught with danger, but offers some chance of success. That's the path of never-ending tension and conflict with the Palestinians, Hezbollah, Iran, and whoever else decides to join in. It may seem extreme, imbalanced, and highly emotional from the outside, but it is actually simple, hard-headed, rational decision-making. Develop and maintain technological superiority at all costs, mobilize the entire population militarily, and never let your guard down, not for one second."

"But that only works for as long as you have technological superiority," Swann said. "Once your enemy catches up to you…"

"Right," Trudy said. "Then you've got big problems. And it looks like the Iranians have just caught up."

"Have they caught up?" Luke said. "Do they have nuclear weapons?"

Trudy looked at him. "Yes. I'm almost certain that they do."

* * *

Luke pulled down his window shade.

He had been staring out into the vast darkness until he realized there was nothing to see but his own face, wreathed in shadow.

The Lear jet was going east, and if Luke had to guess, he'd say they were over the North Atlantic, nearly as far as Europe now—

they'd been flying for hours, and had hours more to go. This was a long trip.

Luke looked at Trudy, who sat across the aisle from him. She was the only one besides Luke who was still awake.

Behind her, Swann lay curled in a ball across two seats. He was fast asleep. In the row behind Swann, Ed Newsam was doing the same thing. Ed was rock solid, of course. But Luke had some reservations about Swann. It wasn't Swann's fault—he had been traumatized by his time in ISIS captivity. He had changed. He was not the same wisecracking, sarcastic idiot he had once been. He was more reserved now, more careful. He spoke a lot less. On the surface, that might seem like a good thing—wisdom, maybe, or maturity. But Luke suspected it might be lack of confidence.

Swann had been rattled to his core. When the heat came, when the stress level amped up, it remained to be seen how well he would perform.

Luke looked across at Trudy. She had been asleep for a little while, curled into a ball. Now she was awake again, gazing out her dark window. From here, all Luke could see was a blinking light on the wing.

"Dark out there," Luke said. "A whole lot of nothing."

"Yes."

"What are you looking at?"

"Exactly that. Nothing."

He paused. It was awkward between them. He supposed it always would be. He didn't want to get into it with her now, their shared time together, because Swann and Ed were here. Swann and Ed were not involved in this, and he didn't want them to wake up in the middle of it.

"I remember the last time we went on a long flight together," Luke said.

She nodded. "So do I. Korea. You guys had just broken me out of prison. That was a crazy time. I thought my life was over. I didn't realize it was just beginning."

"How was your time on the run?"

She shrugged. She did not seem eager to look at him. "I wouldn't choose to do it again. But all in all, it wasn't terrible. I learned a lot. I learned not to get so attached to a specific identity. Trudy Wellington, who is that? One possibility out of hundreds. I dyed my hair blonde, just like you suggested. I also dyed it black. At one point, I even shaved my head.

"You know I fell in with a bunch of left-wing protestors in Spain for a while? I really did. I learned Spanish in high school, and

Spain was a safe place to disappear. No one had any idea who I was. They sent me for EMT training, so I could become a street medic. People get hurt at these protests a lot—usually minor things, but the ambulances can't get to them. Street medics are right there, in the middle of the action. I saw quite a few broken limbs and cracked skulls. I thought of Ed the whole time I was doing it—I always had a lot of respect for his medical skills. Even more so now."

She turned and faced Luke. "I learned a lot about myself, things I needed to learn."

"Name a big one," Luke said.

She smiled. "I learned that I don't need to give myself away to older men anymore. What was I looking for, protection? Approval? It was a silly, little girl habit. I've been sticking with men my own age or younger the past couple of years, and it's been pretty nice. I've decided I prefer men who aren't trying to teach me anything."

Ouch. Now Luke smiled. Words, however, seemed to escape him.

"I also learned I was a survivor."

"That's big," Luke said.

"Yeah," she said. "But not as big as the man thing."

CHAPTER TWELVE

1:45 p.m. Eastern Standard Time
The Situation Room
The White House, Washington, DC

"What time is it there?" Susan said.

Kurt looked at his watch. "Ah, about a quarter to nine at night. We're scheduled to talk to him at nine."

Susan nodded. "Okay. Give me the elevator pitch."

She looked around the room, packed as usual. Kurt stood at the far end of the oblong table, in his customary position. Haley Lawrence sat at the table among a sea of generals and admirals, a few of them women, Susan was gratified to notice. The edges of the room were full of aides and assistants.

"We've got a crisis unfolding," Kurt said. "And we've got to step carefully. That's the message."

Susan made a spinning motion with her hand, as if to say, *Get on with it.*

"As most people here will know, Israel has been a strategic ally of ours since its founding in 1948. In a constantly changing world, only a handful of countries—England, Canada, France, India, Saudi Arabia…"

Kurt waited and rolled his eyes as a few people booed the mention of the Saudis.

"…Morocco, a few others—have been with us longer. As a relatively small country in a volatile region, Israel's position is tenuous at best, and over the decades tensions have repeatedly erupted into open conflict with a host of regional actors. In the early days, these conflicts were the result of attacks by neighboring countries such as Egypt, Jordan, and Syria. In more recent years, the conflicts have focused on the plight of the Palestinians who were displaced when Israel was created, and who live in a sort of political limbo in the West Bank and the Gaza Strip, lands that Israel seized during the Six Day War in 1967. Every international body, indeed every country on Earth besides Israel and United States, considers Israel the occupying power in these territories.

“Islamic terrorist organizations have been using this situation as a fundraising tool for two generations. Also, Muslim countries can whip up anti-Israel sentiment any time it fits their purposes, as long as the Palestinians remain in limbo.”

“What is our policy on this?” someone along the back asked.

Kurt nodded. “Sure, good question. Just so we’re all clear. Our official policy is that there is an ongoing negotiation, the result of which will be that the West Bank and Gaza eventually become a country, probably called Palestine, and that Palestine and Israel will co-exist peacefully and may even become regional partners. In the meantime, we recognize Israel’s right to secure its borders and prevent attacks by Palestinians on Israeli civilians. We do not recognize Israel’s right to build so-called settlements in Palestinian territory, nor do we recognize Jerusalem as the capital of Israel. We consider it a partitioned city—the western half in Israel, the eastern half in the West Bank.”

“And Yonatan?”

Kurt glanced at a sheet of paper on the table in front of him. “Yonatan Stern. Sixty-three years old. Married, father of five, grandfather of eight. As a young man, he was a commando with the elite Sayeret Matkal unit of the Israeli Defense Forces. In 1976, he was one of the leaders of the successful raid on Entebbe Airport in Uganda, where Israeli commandos rescued more than one hundred Israeli hostages taken from a hijacked plane.

“Since he left the military, he has spent almost his entire adult life in Israeli politics as a war hawk and a hardliner. At the moment, he appears to sit atop an unassailable majority in the Knesset. His vulnerability is that he is currently the subject of at least four separate police investigations into corruption—ranging from receiving hundreds of thousands of dollars’ worth of gifts from wealthy supporters, all the way up to doling out preferential no-bid government military contracts and manipulating the Israeli telecom industry on behalf of friends.”

Kurt shook his head and whistled. “Stern is in legal jeopardy. It’s real, and it has been consuming much of his attention in recent months. He’ll be lucky to stay out of jail. And he has problems on the diplomatic front as well. While traveling in Europe three weeks ago, he was caught speaking into an open microphone, joking about the idea of a two-state solution with the Palestinians, seeming to dismiss it out of hand. Apparently, he didn’t know the mic was on, and he said the European Union was crazy—yes, he used the word crazy—for worrying about the Palestinians. You can imagine how well this little faux pas has played in European capitals and among the Israeli left wing."

He looked at Susan. "To be clear, Yonatan Stern is not an ideal partner. But I think we also need to recognize that he isn't Prime Minister for life, and there are many, many elements in Israeli society that are seeking a peaceful solution to the ongoing problems. Israel has been, and continues to be, an important ally of the United States, and their civilian population is under attack. There is no telling at this moment what the extent of that attack is likely to be. But if Iran has nuclear weapons, as they claim..."

Susan nodded. "Of course. My problem isn't with Israel. I understand the relationship is much larger than Yonatan."

"Good. All we need from him at this moment is restraint, which is not necessarily his strong suit. He's a hammer, and everywhere he looks, he sees nails. But he has to give us time to find and eliminate those nukes. Shall we talk to him?"

She shrugged. "Let's do it."

* * *

"I hope you're happy."

Yonatan Stern's deep disembodied rumble came over the black speakerphone device at the center of the conference table. "I hope this pleases you."

Susan looked at Kurt and shook her head.

"Why would this please me, Yonatan?"

"I think it should be obvious," he said.

"It isn't."

"Your country, at your personal urging, sought an appeasement with Iran, continuing to allow them to refine uranium. The Europeans went along with you. And this is the result—an Iran that is willing to claim it has nuclear weapons, in defiance of all international agreements. An Iran that is happy to put the most advanced conventional weapons it has into the hands of terrorists—maniacs who are accountable to no one."

"Yonatan..." Susan began.

"There are hundreds dead here, Susan. Perhaps thousands. We don't even know yet. Residential buildings have been completely destroyed, and rescuers can only slowly dig through the rubble for fear of further collapses. There was a firestorm in a neighborhood in Haifa. The hospitals everywhere are overwhelmed."

Susan shook her head. "I'm very sorry."

It was as if Stern hadn't heard her. "We are facing, perhaps for the first time since 1973, the question of annihilation. Now, I'm sure you think that the situation is more complicated than what I describe. Isn't that what the Americans always say? Oh my, Israel and Iran, Israel and Hezbollah, what a complicated situation! But it's not complicated. It's simple. You have unleashed Iran upon us. You did it. And now you ask us to hold back our response. For decades you have tolerated a failed state in Lebanon and called it your ally. Lebanon is a launch platform for Iranian terror attacks—nothing more, nothing less. It is not a country. And yet you ask us—"

Susan tried again. "Yonatan—"

His deep voice rose an octave. "Listen! Please listen to me. Will you listen? It's not your cities being bombed. It's not your friends and loved ones crushed under rubble or burning in fire. You do not know what is happening here."

"Yonatan," Susan said, "I've been burned in fire and crushed under rubble. I've seen my friends and colleagues burned alive in a firestorm. One of my best friends was shot and killed in front of my own eyes. I've been shot myself. I know what is happening there. I wish I didn't."

There was a pause over the line.

"Yonatan?"

"Okay," he said. "Okay."

There was another long pause. In the background, Susan could hear people in the room with Yonatan, speaking to each other in Hebrew.

"We can put the genie back in the bottle," she said.

"How can we do that?"

Susan took the plunge. "A unilateral ceasefire," she said, knowing how that would sound. But she had to start somewhere. "It will put pressure on both Hezbollah and Iran to stop the hostilities."

She could almost see him shaking his head.

"Impossible. My hands are tied on that score, even if I wanted to do it, which I do not. There is no pressuring Hezbollah, as you seem to believe. The only pressure they understand is force. We cannot stop while they continue to launch missiles into our territory. We cannot stop while they hold Daria Shalit. We cannot stop while our cities burn. There is such a thing as public opinion here, Susan, and I was elected because I pledged to protect my people."

"You're not going to win this by attacking Hezbollah," Susan said. "And if you attack Iran, all bets are off. Listen, we have sent you two of our best covert operatives, along with members of their intelligence team. There is a plan being cooked up between Mossad, the CIA, and my own Special Response Team."

She did not say, *"The man I love is going to risk his life for you."*

"I am aware of the plan," Yonatan said. "I must tell you that I am very skeptical of it. We have sent many undercover operatives into Iran, and we have lost—"

Susan did not want to hear that. "If the operation is successful, we will discover the location of the nuclear weapons, if they exist. Then we will go in and destroy them. We will inform that Russians and Chinese of our intentions to do so, and invite them to participate with us. As you know, all parties have agreed that Iran is not to have nuclear weapons. Those agreements are still in force."

"Susan, I wish I shared your enthusiasm for international agreements, and for secret missions. In Israel, we have some of the best, most highly trained covert operatives on Earth, and our secret missions fail as often as they succeed."

"Will you do it, though?" Susan said. This was where she normally excelled—the closing. "Will you wait? No matter what happens, no matter what they hit you with, will you hold off an attack, and give the mission a chance?"

Yonatan spoke in Hebrew to someone in the room with him. The man responded at length. Yonatan spoke again. The man responded again.

"Yonatan?" Susan said.

"I will," Yonatan said, "take your idea under advisement."

CHAPTER THIRTEEN

December 13
4:45 a.m. Israel Time (9:45 p.m. Eastern Standard Time on December 12)
Tel Aviv, Israel

"I don't know if anyone is going to believe that we're diplomats," Swann said. He hovered over Luke, holding a smartphone near his face. Luke could barely focus on it. He glanced up at Swann, with his crazy glasses, his ponytail, and his black RAMONES T-shirt. Was this what diplomats looked like?

"Yeah? Why's that?"

"Almost the entire embassy staff has just received evacuation orders. They're going to Cyprus, beginning in an hour from now."

Luke smiled. He looked around at the rooftop bar at the Hilton Tel Aviv. The place was hopping.

It didn't matter that it was nearly five in the morning, and the first pink light of the sun was beginning to appear. It didn't matter that the law technically forbade serving alcohol this time of day. It didn't matter that there was a war on.

Indeed, this last was the reason the place was still going. War correspondents liked to drink, and they didn't like it when the bars closed. The roof, which was normally a good place to catch views of the sea a few blocks away, and the mountains to the east, was now a good place to catch the light show to the north. It looked like the Fourth of July up there. Whether it was Israeli northern towns getting hit, or southern Lebanon Hezbollah bunkers and gun emplacements, was impossible to tell from here.

Several TV news people had already filmed segments standing in front of the railing at the north side of the balcony, with explosions going on behind them. Most of Europe was asleep right now, but back in the United States, it was still prime time.

Luke sat at a table with Trudy, picking over a plastic plate with falafel, hummus, French fries, and a salad made of finely diced tomato, onion, cucumber, and chili peppers, with lemon juice and olive oil. It was a frustrating delay. As tired as Luke was, he was anxious to get a move on. He had yet to go on a mission that benefited from waiting around.

Ed and Swann were nearby, standing at the bar amidst the flak-jacketed reporters, cameramen, and various other war junkies. The set-up here was pretty good. The food wasn't bad. This high up, the sea breeze was very nice. You could just hear the rumble of the explosions in the distance. A few of them—the closest ones—shook the building.

"Don't worry," he said as he noticed Trudy's eyes widen. "Israel is prone to earthquakes. Modern buildings like this one have to meet stringent codes."

"I'm not worried about the building falling down from a tremor," Trudy said. "I'm more worried about a missile hitting it."

Luke nodded. "There is that possibility."

On the drive here, they had seen the damage sustained from yesterday's missile strikes. A few buildings were still on fire. Streets were destroyed—giant klieg lights illuminating the rescue efforts as crowds of soldiers and construction crews dug through the rubble, looking for survivors. Ambulances sped down city streets, sirens roaring, bringing people pulled from the earth to the hospitals. Police checkpoints were everywhere. Candlelight vigils—prayer circles—were nearly as common.

Luke had taken a Dexedrine a little while ago, swallowing it with a beer, and its effects were starting to kick in. That, combined with the food in his stomach and the little bit of beer he had sipped, was having an effect on his mood.

He was starting to feel good.

"Luke, I want to ask you something," Trudy said.

He shrugged. "Shoot."

It felt a little odd to be here with Trudy. She was the best in the business at what she did—intelligence gathering and scenario spinning. She brought a sort of freewheeling creativity to it that most other people did not. People got hemmed in by data—what it said, what it didn't say. Trudy wasn't like that. She took leaps of faith. He liked that about her. She was…

Indispensable.

If that weren't true, he probably would have kept his distance from her. She certainly wouldn't be here with them now. Given all her baggage, and their history together, he might not even have hired her again.

"Are you sleeping with the President of the United States?" Trudy said.

Luke shrugged. "What could possibly give you that idea?"

Trudy nodded. "So you are. Okay. I'm not jealous, if that's what you think. I just worry about you."

Luke looked at her. She was beautiful. As beautiful as Susan Hopkins was at her age? Maybe, maybe not. But Luke tended to think that parsing gradations of beauty was a lot like trying to split strands of hair lengthwise with a large knife.

"I get that a lot," Luke said. "People worrying about me. What makes you worry?"

"You've spent most of your life in secrecy, Luke. In recent years, people in the wider world have begun to know who you are. But you're a hundred miles from being famous, and you're on the other side of the galaxy from the kind of fame Susan has. Just about everyone on Earth knows who she is."

Luke nodded. "True enough. Susan is one of the most famous people in the world."

"Right," Trudy said. "She might even be number one. And she's been famous since she was a teenager. She's used to that kind of scrutiny. But you aren't. And you've been involved in a lot of operations, some of which…"

There was a long pause as she seemed to search for the right words.

Luke shrugged. "Just say it. I don't get my feelings hurt that easily."

"Some of which could be considered war crimes," she said. "Some of which could be considered extrajudicial murders. Torture. Actions, like mock executions, that are against the Geneva Conventions. Insubordination. Impersonations. Actions that exceeded your authority. Actions that subverted the chain of command. Actions where there was significant collateral damage. Actions that… well, let's put it this way: you carried out at least one high-level assassination that was not ordered by anyone, and could have destabilized an entire region."

Luke sighed, just a touch under his breath. He launched into the official explanation, the one Trudy well knew. "Uh, generally speaking, I've been granted wide latitude to take actions that produce results in line with the…"

Trudy shook her head. "You don't get it, Luke. I'm not criticizing you. I know why you do the things you do. But if they ever came out, it would look bad. Really, really bad. Most Americans don't know what the government does in their name, and most don't want to know."

"Why would they have to know?" Luke said. "Those are classified operations."

Trudy shook her head again, more forcefully this time. Then she rolled her eyes. "Because if it gets out that you're the President's boyfriend, or whatever you are to her, you will become a household name overnight. That's going to lead to newspaper and TV coverage. Which is going to lead to people digging into your past. Just for fun, a few days ago I decided to see how hard I would have to work to come across classified information about you, to which I'm not supposed to have access. Do you know how hard it was? Not very hard at all."

"Trudy, you're an intelligence agent, trained to dig up information."

"Reporters are trained to dig up information."

Luke shook his head. "Not like you."

"And what if an intelligence agent decided to leak the information to the press?"

Now he really looked at her, as if seeing her for the very first time.

"What are you saying, Trudy? That you would—"

"No. I would never do that. But I have to tell you something that you don't seem to realize. Not everybody loves you, Luke. Some people think you're bad news."

Luke sat and chewed on that for a moment.

He glanced around at the crowd. A young man—short, balding, dressed in a suit that seemed too big for him somehow—wound his way through the crowd. He glanced down at his telephone, then made his way over to Luke.

"Mr. Montgomery?" he said. His accent said he was an American.

Luke nodded. "Yes. I'm Mr. Montgomery, and I'm with the State Department."

"I'm Steve Becker. I'm your liaison from the embassy. Are you and your team ready for your first meeting?"

Luke looked at the light, which was now filling the sky. Trudy had just given him an earful—in all his worries about shielding Gunner, and not letting his identity become too well known, he had never considered all the things that might leak out. Would he want Gunner to know these things?

Absolutely not. Not like that. One day, he might choose to tell Gunner himself. Then again, he might not. Also, declassified information about the events of his life, the actions he had taken part in, the opinions and recommendations that had been added to his file over the years, might raise questions about his fitness as a father.

And what about Susan? Did he want her to know these things?

She was the President. She could access that information any time she wanted. But something told him that she had chosen not to do so.

What if it was thrown in her face?

Luke didn't want to think about it. He stood.

"We are more than ready for our first meeting."

* * *

They didn't go to the embassy.

And they didn't go with Steve Becker. The driver was an Israeli—he wore a yarmulke, black pants, and a black vest over a white dress shirt. In marked contrast to Becker, his clothes were well tailored to his small, muscular frame.

He took them in a black SUV to a nondescript, squat, two-story cinderblock warehouse in an industrial district near the far eastern edge of the city. The neighborhood was a wasteland of similar warehouse-type buildings, fenced-in empty lots, and tract homes. A sign hung on the warehouse, in Hebrew, Arabic, and English letterings.

Resnick Quality Meats.

Nice. They were meeting at a slaughterhouse.

As they entered the gate to the yard around the warehouse, a corrugated steel door slid slowly open, allowing the car to enter the building. The SUV pulled into an empty chamber. There was nothing at all in the warehouse. No refrigeration units. No freezers. No cars or trucks parked. Just a large, two-story space, which looked like it had been swept clean with a broom. There was a small office that overlooked the warehouse, but there was nothing in there, either, and the lights were off.

"No meats here," Ed said.

"No."

The driver got out and opened the rear door. "Gentlemen," he said, "and lady. Please come with me."

Next to the empty office was an elevator. The door was open, and instantly the elevator began to drop rapidly into the Earth. Within seconds, they reached their destination. The door slid open without a sound.

It opened to an operations control room, a conference room much like the Situation Room at the White House, or the new one at SRT headquarters. Several men in uniforms stood there along with a few in street clothes. All of them stood ramrod straight, and stared at the newcomers with hard eyes. Luke stared back at them.

He tried to imagine what they were seeing as they watched the cream of American espionage arrive. He saw alarm bells ringing in their minds when they looked at Mark Swann. Luke almost turned and glanced back at Swann himself.

No matter. Swann wasn't a hard case like these men were. Neither was Trudy. But Ed Newsam would more than make up for whatever Swann and Trudy lacked in the hard case department.

A man, Luke guessed in his fifties, wearing a blue business suit, stepped up and offered Luke his hand. His skin was tan. His hair was impeccably neat, not a strand out of place. His teeth were blindingly white. Luke knew that his comrades called him the Model for his good looks and the way he presented himself. He was the director of the Mossad, in English, "The Institute." It was the Israeli intelligence agency, this country's version of the CIA.

"Luke, I'm Efraim Shavitz," he said.

"I know," Luke said. "I'm Luke Stone, as I see you've guessed. This is Trudy Wellington, my science and intel officer, this is Mark Swann, my technology officer, and this… well, this is Ed Newsam. Weapons and tactics."

Shavitz shook hands with each person in turn.

"We are here," Luke said, "to do whatever we can to help."

Shavitz nodded. "Good. Shall we begin?"

He indicated four seats at the long rectangular table, all in a row. Luke and his team took their seats, Swann immediately opening his laptop and Trudy placing her tablet within reach on the table in front of her.

"As you know," Shavitz said. "We are at war, and the very survival of our country, and our people, is at stake. It has become apparent that the Iranians have provided Hezbollah with new weaponry—Iranian-made and possibly Russian-made—that is nearly as advanced as our own. We are well used to the towns and cities of the north being targets of rocket attacks from Lebanon. We are well used to the towns of the south being targets for rocket attacks by Hamas from the Gaza Strip. But we cannot allow Hezbollah to possess advanced missile systems. We will scorch the very Earth to keep this from happening. We will destroy Lebanon utterly, leave not one building or tree standing, if need be, to root out the location of these weapons."

He gazed at Luke and his team, his eyes like those of an eagle, perhaps trying to discover if there was any doubt in their minds about the need to do this.

A middle-aged man in a military uniform halfway down the table spoke up. He had a flattop haircut, clean-shaven face, and chiseled features. He reminded Luke of the nickname often hung on US Marines back home—jarhead.

"We are surrounded by seven countries within a hundred miles, all of whom would see us destroyed. That doesn't even count the various terrorist and militia groups. We must—*must*—have military superiority. We cannot have advanced weaponry on our borders, in the hands of our enemies. Do you understand?"

Luke nodded. "Of course."

"Good," the man said. "Sometimes the things we hear from across the ocean… the newspaper reporting, the easy rhetoric that gets thrown around… it can seem that we have no friends."

"Oh, we're your friends," Mark Swann said.

The man gazed at Swann for a long moment.

"I cannot tell you enough how encouraging I find that."

"Can we continue?" Luke said.

"Of course," Shavitz said. "At the head of the table is Dr. Abram from the Institute for Counter-Terrorism at the Interdisciplinary Center in Herzliya. He is one of our foremost researchers into the Iranian nuclear threat. Dr. Abram?"

The man stood. He was clearly not a military man. He was overweight—portly trending toward obese—and wore thick glasses that tended to slide to the end of his nose. His hair stood up in thick tufts on either side of his head. Behind him, the large monitor screen came to life. A map of Iran appeared. The man picked up a pointing stick from the table. This was going to be a real university-style lecture.

"Agent Stone, my other American guests," he said, "welcome. As you must know, despite international sanctions, Iran long ago developed the medium-range ballistic missile capability to reach Israel. It is likely by now that they have developed the capacity to reach major cities in Western Europe, should they desire. It is not entirely out of the question, though they are unlikely to announce such a thing, that they have the ability to reach America."

Luke glanced at Trudy. She gave a small head shake, as if to say, "Not a chance."

The professor noticed the head shake, said nothing.

"In any event, what they have not done, perhaps until now, is develop the ability to build nuclear warheads that might ride on such missiles. That missing piece has led them to refrain from using their missile capacity because they know that any counterattack from Israel, Europe, or the United States would be completely devastating to them.

"However, we have been concerned for the past several months that they were racing to complete the development of this capacity. We believe they now have the weapons, and we believe they will launch as they indicate. Iran, for all its myriad other failings, is not a country that makes a lot of idle threats."

On the screen, icons appeared on the map of Iran. The professor pointed to each of them in turn. "Here you see Tehran, the capital city, located in the north central area of the country, just below the mountainous region of the north. Although there are dozens of underground military facilities in Iran, we believe there are just three such locations where the nuclear warheads could be located."

He indicated a red square with his pointer. "This is the massive military complex of Parchin, just east of the capital. Much of it is underground, and much is deeply buried. The Iranians claim that their facilities are as deep as five hundred meters, which would be impossible to penetrate with conventional weapons. However, because of the terrain, their technological limitations, and the ever-present threat of earthquakes, we believe this is not true. We think Parchin goes as deep as two hundred meters, perhaps a little more. That's deep, but not impenetrable."

Trudy raised her hand. "Doctor, what do you base your suspicions on? Why would the nukes be at Parchin, say, instead of somewhere else?"

Dr. Abram indicated two icons near the one for Parchin. They were the international symbol for radioactivity—three upright black triangles, embedded with three upside down yellow triangles.

"These are the nuclear enrichment facilities of Fordo and Natanz. Fordo in particular interests us because it is just outside the Muslim holy city of Qom, where a great deal of archaeological activity has taken place. Both facilities can enrich uranium to a concentration of twenty percent, and in all likelihood to a weapons-grade concentration of ninety percent.

"Iran is monitored very closely by international satellite surveillance, and of course the Iranians know this. In the normal course of business, materials from the uranium mines at Saghand and Yazd, which you see further to the south, are trucked to the enrichment facilities at Fordo and Natanz. This is witnessed from the sky on a regular basis. But both Fordo and Natanz, and especially Fordo, are close enough to the military complex at Parchin that you could build a tunnel and bring the enriched uranium, and potentially the nuclear warheads themselves, the rest of the way underground."

He let that sink in. A nuclear enrichment facility operating openly, but moving weapons beneath the earth to the missile sites nearby.

"Parchin is the most likely suspect to house the Iranian warheads. We believe that they would have enriched enough uranium by now for eight, or possibly nine warheads. Not much, when counted against the thousands held by the Americans and the Russians, and also not much when counted against the number held by Israel—"

"How many warheads would you say Israel has?" Swann said.

Dr. Abram gave Swann a pained smile. "Enough, I suppose."

"What if you're wrong?" Ed Newsam said. They were the first words he had uttered since the meeting began. "What if the warheads aren't there? What next?"

The doctor nodded. "It's a good question. We believe the next most likely military bases are located at or near the enrichment facilities at Bushehr, on the Persian Gulf coast, or Isfahan in the center of the country, in that order. Both are large enrichment facilities, both capable of producing weapons-grade material. Both are located near military bases. We believe the Bushehr facility is the more likely of the two because of its proximity to Saudi Arabia, just across the Gulf here. A missile attack from Bushehr would reach its target in Saudi Arabia, if that were the target, within a few minutes of launch, with essentially no warning for the targeted population."

"Your concern for the Saudis is heartwarming, Doctor," Swann said.

Abram smiled again, this time with a little more mirth than before. "Please understand. I don't care about the Saudis. I would just as soon have a world with no such place as Saudi Arabia. But I must consider all contingencies. And missiles targeting Riyadh can very easily be retargeted to hit Tel Aviv or Eliat, or Haifa or Nazareth. I do like to think they would spare Jerusalem."

"Those bases look pretty far apart," Luke said, indicating the map. "And we need to talk about how well fortified those places are. Can we get in? Can we get out?"

Shavitz spoke up. "It is a difficult mission, but not impossible. There is an informant in Tehran. Naturally, he fears for his life. He will not communicate, except in person. We believe he can either get you the information you need, or put you in touch with people who can give you that information. In other words, if you can confirm the existence and location of the weapons from someone who has high-level access to intelligence, you may not need to infiltrate the bases themselves."

He paused.

"Of course, what would be better than any of this is if you can secure proof that the entire thing is a hoax, and the weapons do not exist."

"It's going to be hard to prove a negative," Luke said.

"Harder still is going to be getting out," Shavitz said.

"Tell me," Luke said.

"Time is of the essence," Shavitz said. "The clock is ticking, and Iran could attack us at any moment. Whether they have nuclear missiles or not, Iran's conventional missile arsenal is incredibly robust. We cannot let too much time elapse. We cannot wait until they attack us. Forty-eight hours after you enter Iranian airspace, you must be at the rendezvous point in the Caspian Sea port of Rasht."

"What happens if we aren't?" Luke said.

"If we haven't obtained specific intelligence on the nuclear weapons by then, we will commence our own attack, which will be very comprehensive. Once it begins, we will not be able to get you out."

"You might even call the attack indiscriminate," the jarhead from earlier said.

"We will hit every military base, every known and suspected missile site, civilian and military infrastructure and communications, electricity, water supplies. The idea is to cripple Iran's ability to respond."

Trudy raised her hand. "Uh, with all due respect, that's a terrible idea. You will cause massive suffering among civilians, and you will never completely destroy their ability to respond. I've studied Iran extensively. It's too big for what you describe. There are too many places to deploy their missiles. They're too sophisticated. They hide everything, even from themselves."

Shavitz shook his head. "This isn't my decision. The Prime Minister's war cabinet has decided to give this mission a chance to work. But they will not wait forever. Too much is at risk."

"Forty-eight hours, though?" Luke said. "It sounds a bit arbitrary. It might take us a week to get in there and—"

"You won't survive a week in Iran, Luke. I wouldn't even entertain that idea. They are on high alert. The police and the Revolutionary Guards are everywhere. Neighbor informs on neighbor. Anything out of the ordinary is reported. If you stay too long, they will catch you. Being captured in Iran is one of the most unpleasant things I can think of. The best thing is to get in and get back out as fast as you can."

Luke stared at Shavitz. It sounded like the Israelis weren't fully invested in this—not if they wouldn't give it the time it needed. Luke had been under deep cover in worse places than Iran, for longer periods, and survived.

"Is the legendary Luke Stone worried?" a man in the corner said.

Luke glanced at him. He was young, very fit, not big but wiry, with a close-cropped light-colored beard. He had a rude shock of yellow blond hair on his head—it looked fake, like he had poured it from a bottle. He also had blue eyes.

He slumped insouciantly in his chair, away from the conference table. He was one of the few people in the room in neither military nor business-type dress. Instead, he wore a blue T-shirt, blue jeans, and an oversized pair of Timberland work boots, with the laces untied.

"Could it be that the American is afraid?"

Luke felt nothing about the man's interruption. Emotions ran high sometimes, and maybe this was some young hot dog who had been passed over for the mission. In Luke's experience, hot dogs and talkers might last a mission or two, depending on the abilities they brought to the table. But then they got killed. And sometimes, they took everybody else on their team down with them.

"Can I help you?" he said.

The guy shook his head and looked away. "I don't think so."

"We know that you like to work small," Shavitz said. He indicated a spot on the map. "The plan is a night drop from high altitude along the border here with Iraq. The border is porous, with Kurdish and Shiite militias, as well as nomadic tribes passing back and forth all the time. There are a lot of air patrols in that region. You jump right at the limit of Iraqi airspace, and drift perhaps thirty miles east into Iranian territory, helped by prevailing winds."

He indicated a point inside Iran. The map zoomed in and Luke could see the curve of a road.

"You make your way by morning to this rendezvous point, where a truck with one of our people will take you into Tehran. He will take you to see a person in Tehran, a double agent we have been working with. We believe this person is reliable, and may know the location of the warheads."

"Sounds a little iffy," Ed said.

Shavitz shrugged. "There are people in our government who believe this operation is a waste of time. How would you say it? It's like searching for a needle in a haystack. Nevertheless…"

Luke stood and walked over to the map. He put his finger on the border region on the screen. Touching it made it zoom in even further, showing a topographical map and indicating high mountains. "Both Ed and I have been inside Iran, but neither one of us has been in this area. We don't know this terrain. The odds of us dropping in at night, getting our bearings, and then walking overland to that rendezvous point before daylight…"

Shavitz nodded. "That's why you're going to drop in with one of our best men as your guide. He has traversed that region numerous times."

Ed shook his head. "People die when they ride with us. You should know that upfront. This looks pretty dicey. Don't send anyone you can't afford to lose."

"You should do a better job protecting your people," the young guy with blond hair said.

Ed turned and looked at him. "That's not what we're there for. We move fast, and we hit hard. Hard, you dig? People sign on, they need to keep up. And they need to keep their heads down."

The young guy looked at Shavitz. "How can this man infiltrate Iran? A giant, hard-hitting black man with an American accent? Who is going to believe this? He is like a character from Sunday morning cartoons."

"There are black Persians, of course," Shavitz said. "Descendents of slaves from many generations ago. And there are descendents of more recent nomadic Muslim tribes from Africa. A black man can pass in Iran."

The kid looked at Ed. "Do you even speak a word of Farsi?"

Ed shrugged. He stared back at the kid. "*Bibito gaeidam,*" he said in perfect Farsi, no American accent at all.

The kid scowled. "*Madar ghende.*"

Now Ed smiled. "*Kir to kunet.* If you don't shut your mouth."

Luke looked at Swann and Trudy, who were watching the exchange in bafflement. Luke shook his head and smiled. "You don't even want to know what they're saying."

The kid rose from his chair. He was tall and slim. His body seemed to vibrate with electricity. "I'll wash your mouth out with soap."

Ed didn't budge. He just shook his head. "You don't want to dance with me, little man."

"I also don't want to take you into Iran."

Luke turned to Shavitz. "You've got to be kidding me. This guy?"

Shavitz nodded. "Agent Stone and Agent Newsam, meet Agent Ari Meil of Mossad. Former captain with the Sayeret Matkal. Infiltration and intelligence-gathering are two of his many skills. He is among the best we have. If his work weren't so secret, he would be a national hero."

Shavitz paused. "He can get you in there. And he can get you back out again alive."

Luke stared at the kid. The kid stared back, eyes fierce.

"The question is," Ed said, "if we have to listen to this guy run his mouth for two straight days, will we even want to go on living?"

CHAPTER FOURTEEN

9:45 a.m. Israel Time (2:45 a.m. Eastern Standard Time)
Tel Aviv, Israel

"Sayeret Matkal," Trudy Wellington said.

They were all sitting in Luke's hotel suite at the Hilton. The room was on the fifteenth floor, and the balcony had a panoramic view of the Mediterranean Sea. The accommodations were good. The bed was king-sized and comfortable. Within minutes of entering the room, Swann had found a listening device inside one of the table lamps. Luke was sure there were others.

"Watching me, watching you," Swann had said, before reassembling the lamp.

Luke shrugged. It didn't matter. Who was the enemy around here, anyway?

They had ordered up some room service, and once again the food was okay—hotel food, sort of Israeli, sort of American, sort of nothing at all. Ed had eaten four eggs, potatoes, and a quarter-pound cut of steak. It wasn't on the menu—he just asked them if they had it, and they said yes.

Watching Ed put food away was like watching an ice shelf calve away from Antarctica. It was like watching a giant tornado demolish a trailer park in Oklahoma. It was like watching a killer whale chow down on a group of baby seals. It was a force of nature, a thing unto itself.

Luke sighed. The jump wasn't until late tonight. True, it was from Iraq, but they probably wouldn't even leave here until this afternoon at the earliest. And he was tired. It was time to get some sleep.

"Sayeret Matkal," Trudy said again. She was holding her tablet, waiting for their attention.

"Yes, please enthrall us," Swann said.

"It's the special forces unit of the Israeli Defense Forces. Primarily an intelligence-gathering unit, conducting deep reconnaissance behind enemy lines, and modeled after the British Army's Special Air Service. This is right down to the SAS's motto, 'Who Dares, Wins.'"

"Nice," Ed said. "I've always liked that one."

"No need to make up your own if there's already a good one you can take off the shelf," Swann said.

"The unit is also roughly analogous to the United States Army's Delta Force."

Ed made a mock gasp. Both he and Luke had come through Delta Force. Luke pictured the vetting process he had gone through to join Delta. He pictured the training he had gone through after he was accepted. Brutal. Absolutely brutal. If the kid had done anything like that, he couldn't be all bad. And he was younger, much closer to those days than either Ed or Luke.

"Members are chosen from the IDF, and they are the best soldiers physically, intellectually, and psychologically that the IDF has to offer. The selection process is called Gibbush, and is notorious for putting soldiers through several days with no sleep, over a course that is physically and mentally grueling."

"Okay," Luke said. "It sounds like something Ed and I are familiar with. If the kid could be a little less… himself, let's say, we can find a way to mesh with him. They probably gave him to us because he's good. Because he has Iran experience. Because he's cool under fire. Because they expect us to run into some hotspots, and he has combat experience."

"Or for some other reason that they're not sharing," Swann said. "Turns out they didn't even tell us his name."

Trudy smiled. "Swann's been doing oppositional research."

"Tell me," Luke said.

Swann took his laptop off the table. He glanced at the ceiling light and looked at Luke.

"It's okay," Luke said. "We know they're listening. And they know that we know. There are no secrets between friends."

Swann shrugged. "Ari Meil," he said. "Born twenty-nine years ago in the Jewish Quarter of East Jerusalem. His father was a Syrian Jew who emigrated to Israel in the 1960s. He owns an electronics store in Jerusalem to this day. His mother was the daughter of Dutch Jews who survived World War Two hidden in basements and attics by members of the Dutch Resistance. She is a midwife.

"Meil was an honor student and standout basketball player in high school, and joined the IDF just after his eighteenth birthday. He was recruited into Sayeret Matkal at nineteen. Married his high school sweetheart, an Israeli Arab—interesting—and had two children. During the 2014 Israel-Gaza conflict, Captain Ari Meil led a group of commandos on a helicopter drop to kidnap two high-ranking members of Hamas. The intelligence was wrong, or it was a trap—there was no Hamas meeting at the site, and the building was wired to explode. Four members of the infiltration team died, including Captain Meil, who was crushed under a collapsing cinderblock wall."

Luke rubbed his face and yawned. "Are there any other Ari Meils in the phone book? Maybe our Ari isn't really dead."

Swann nodded. "Yeah. There's a guy who runs a fruit and vegetable stand in Ramla. He's sixty-three years old. There's also a guy who does wedding photography. He's based out of Nazareth, but he's willing to travel pretty much anywhere, from Haifa in the north to as far south as Beersheba. Sound like your man?"

"Sounds like my man is a ghost," Luke said.

Just then, his satellite phone, which was sitting on the end table, began to ring. It was a friendly-looking phone, white with big orange buttons, and its ring was a neutral hum. Even so, the phone made him jump just a little.

He glanced at the number.

"Guys, I need to take this," he said.

"Is it your girlfriend?" Ed said.

Luke shook his head. "It's your boss."

The three of them stood to leave.

"Stone," he said into the handset.

A deep male voice came on the line. "Hold for the President of the United States."

Trudy went out and shut the door behind her. Luke glanced around the room, at all the places Israeli listening devices, and tiny video monitors, could be hiding. This was going to be awkward.

Her voice came on. "Luke?"

"Madam President," he said, and headed for the door to the balcony. Hopefully it was windy out there.

CHAPTER FIFTEEN

12:15 p.m. Israel Time (5:15 a.m. Eastern Standard Time)
The Western Wall
The Old City, East Jerusalem

She was afraid.

Her name was Miryam, though no one here knew that. These were her last moments alive. No one knew that, either.

Her body trembled as she passed shoulder to shoulder with the other women beneath the stone archway of the ancient Dung Gate. The procession made its way through the Old City of Jerusalem, many marchers—young women, old women, and girls—who were coming to the Western Wall to pray for an end to the fighting, and the safe return of Daria Shalit. The narrow streets were crowded—packed—and despite the chill in the air, she felt flushed and hot. She felt like she might pass out.

L'vado y'imlokh nora, the women sang. Their breath rose in white plumes.

(In majesty He still shall reign)

V'hu hayah v'hu hoveh

(And He was, and He is)

Miryam knew all these words by heart.

The air was full of noise—the singing of the women, the screaming and shouting of the others. The Orthodox men and boys did not want them there. They pressed in on all sides, white shirts, black hats, beards—held back by Israeli police in blue uniforms. There were pitched battles to reach the women.

But still they sang:

V'hu yih'yeh b'tif'arah

(And He will be in glory)

Miryam had been through this many times. Previously, it had seemed like a charade, a stage play acted out, live, on the streets. The men didn't really want to attack the women—they just wanted to shout their displeasure, and feel, afterward, that they had done something. The police didn't really try that hard to hold them back.

But today was different.

As Miryam watched, up ahead, two young men broke through the lines. One was dragged down by police almost instantly. The other grabbed at an older woman, tearing away her prayer shawl—her *tallit*—and pulling her to the ground.

"Oh my God," Miryam whispered under her breath. All her formal prayers were forgotten, so she just talked. No one could possibly hear her, anyway.

"Oh my God, Allah, please accept my sacrifice. Please open your Heavenly gates to me this day, and hold me to your..."

A much older man loomed in front of her. An ancient. He wore thick glasses and a long white beard. The police probably did not tackle him because he was too frail. He raised a long bony finger, like a schoolteacher admonishing a misbehaving student. The other women streamed around him, ignoring him, still singing.

"You will not!" he shouted. "You will not commit this sin on this day! Not this day, the day when the very fate of God's holy land hangs in the balance! Go home! Go home to your husbands and fathers and renounce this!"

Miryam pulled her *tallit* close around her as she passed him. She hugged her Torah scrolls. The Orthodox men hated the Women of the Wall, she knew. To the Orthodox Jews, women could not wear the *tallit* or the *tefillin*, the small black leather boxes containing scrolls of parchment inscribed with verses from the Torah, or read from the Sefer Torah scroll.

That modern feminist women would dare to do these things, and while standing at the Western Wall of the Temple, was more than an affront, more than an offense. It was a sin. It was a threat. It was to tear at the fabric of everything these men knew to be true.

"You will beg before too long!" the old man screamed behind her. "You will beg His forgiveness!"

But this was not Miryam's fight. She was not a Jew, after all.

She was a Palestinian. She had been born in Gaza seventeen years ago, and had grown up in the rubble of streets and buildings that had been bombed, and partially rebuilt, and then bombed again. She had grown up in a city with electricity three hours a day. She had lived in an apartment on the fifth floor, where every day, men carried two buckets of water up the stairs to meet her family's needs for the day.

Three years ago, her ten-year-old brother Hashan had been shot down while throwing bottle bombs at an Israeli tank. She had died inside that day. Last year, her lover Yasser had been blown apart while attempting a rocket attack on an Israeli helicopter. Whatever little thing that still lived within her, whatever tiny flame that flickered, went out. There was no hope. There was no reason to continue this life.

She would give what remained of herself to Allah. She would die in jihad.

She had prayed for almost a year, that her sacrifice would be acceptable to Him. She had prayed that when she died, she would do so surrounded by the ruined corpses of her enemies.

The procession passed through the police checkpoint now, at the entrance to the great plaza that opened before the Western Wall. Thousands of people were here—too many to count. Before her, in the crowd, hundreds of blue and white Star of David flags waved. Dozens of people held aloft banners with the smiling face of Daria Shalit.

So many people, so many...

Miryam walked through the metal detector holding her breath, though she knew the bomb sewn inside her garments was made entirely of plastic, and the kitchen matches she would apply to the detonating chemical were made of light wood.

Nothing happened. Her last hope, the last hope of everyone, was that some Israeli policeman would have been suspicious of her as she passed through the checkpoint, or some piece of metal on someone else—a clasp, a buckle—would set off alarms and they would all be pulled aside for further searches.

Why? Why would they search these Jewish women on their way to the Wall?

They wouldn't.

Miryam felt dizzy, her head starting to spin. She stumbled on an uneven stone, and a firm hand from the woman behind her steadied her.

"Careful, my girl," the woman said. "Stand tall. Be proud. Reject their shouts and their catcalls. This is the work that God calls us to do."

They had been so kind to her! These Women of the Wall were so kind. They were so beautiful. They thought she was a young Sephardic Jew from Greece named Helena, who was alone in Israel. She had infiltrated their ranks six months ago, and they had accepted her and loved her as one of their own. They had clothed her and fed her. She had sung with them and danced with them, and prayed with them. They had children, they had men in their lives, they had work. They were committed to this path. And she had become one of them.

Sometimes, she could almost convince herself...

But no. She was not a Jew. The Jews had killed her brother, and the man she would have married, and loved.

She almost screamed then.

"Why? Why weren't you kind before? Why did your tank kill Hashan?"

The tank… Oh my God, the tanks were so big.

She couldn't breathe.

These beautiful women, who had been so kind, so gentle. The screaming men, surging around them again, held back by the police. Throngs of people—people from all walks of life, filling this plaza.

The Wall loomed up ahead. It was gigantic, reaching to the sky, the large, ageless stones dwarfing the people that swarmed in front of them. The women were never going to make it to the Wall—there were too many people between here and there.

They were jostled again, the crowd pushing and shoving. Miryam tripped and fell to the ground. Others stumbled over her, on top of her. The Orthodox men had broken through the police line. A chain reaction happened, and dozens of people fell. Women, men, police, all falling into a twisting, thrashing pile.

Now. Do it now.

Now was as good a time as any, before she was crushed to death.

She dropped her Torah scroll, reached down to her pants, and ripped the light material of her clothes, pulling out the plastic canister.

It was a clever device—about the size of a small flashlight, with two interior chambers. The larger chamber was packed with more than three hundred grams of one of the most powerful explosives known to man—a highly stable compound that could not be ignited by a mere open flame. In the smaller chamber were fifty grams of a lesser chemical, often called Mother of Satan. Mother of Satan was very unstable—stray sparks or lit cigarettes often caused firestorms in the kitchens of the men who worked with it.

A tiny wick extended from the device. A small flame would ignite the Mother of Satan. The Mother of Satan would detonate, igniting the more powerful chemical, setting off the reaction that would make a very large explosion. These were the things that had been explained to her.

She pulled the box of wooden kitchen matches from her pocket. Her hands shook, and the first match went out instantly. She lit another. It stayed lit for a few seconds, not long enough for her to hold it to the wick.

She lit another.

She glanced around her. A woman was there, lying on the ground with her, perhaps five feet away. Her name was Faye. She was an older woman, in her fifties. She had gray hair and glasses, and was a little overweight. Her glasses were gone now, fallen off in all the commotion. But still she could see. Well enough, she could see.

"Helena?" she said. "What are you…"

Miryam looked away. She was not Helena. She had never been Helena.

To her right was a young police officer. He had tackled a full-bearded Orthodox man, and was struggling to handcuff him using a thin plastic zip tie. In the midst of his struggle, his eye caught hers. He looked at the flame. He looked at the plastic canister.

His eyes went wide. Circular eyes, large round eyes.

He forgot about the man he was trying to arrest. He crawled over the man, squirming like a snake, trying to reach her. The Orthodox man continued to fight, delaying the policeman, wasting one precious second.

"Wait!" the policeman shouted. "Stop!"

"I'm sorry," Miryam said, and touched the flame to the wick.

Then the policeman was there with her. He easily pulled the canister away. She didn't resist him at all. He held it up and gazed at it. The wick was already lit. He tried to squeeze it out with his thumb and forefinger, but the flame had gone into the canister.

It was inside. It was too late to stop whatever came.

She was surrounded by her enemies—hundreds of them, thousands of them. Many were the women who had been so kind, so beautiful—these devout women of God, these women who would fight for women.

She tried to think of Allah then, that he would accept her sacrifice, and find it pleasing. She looked and Faye was crawling to her.

"Helena, no!"

Miryam tried to think of Allah, but could not.

"Faye," she said, shaking her head, the tears streaming now. "I'm so sorry."

Then the light came, and the heat, and in that instant she thought:

It doesn't hurt.

And in that same instant, before the darkness came, she also knew:

It's the same God. It's all the same God.

CHAPTER SIXTEEN

12:40 p.m. Israel Time (5:40 a.m. Eastern Standard Time)
Tel Aviv, Israel

Something terrible had happened.

Luke woke to shouts and screams somewhere nearby. His eyes popped open and he sat straight up in his hotel bed. The bed was large—king-sized—and he had fairly melted into it. Funny. Now that he was awake, there didn't seem to be any sound at all.

Ed Newsam sat to his left in a chair, near the door to the balcony, calmly sipping from a white coffee cup. He was wearing shorts and a black T-shirt tight to his chest, and he seemed completely relaxed. His eyes watched as Luke adjusted to his surroundings.

The flat-panel TV directly across from the foot of the bed was on, the sound muted. It showed drone footage taken from above some kind of disaster—bodies and parts of bodies were strewn all over a plaza. The flagstones were dark red with blood. Flashing lights were everywhere: People ran back and forth with stretchers. Others simply writhed on the ground. As the drone circled overhead, Luke noted the Western Wall with the Temple Mount behind and above it, the Al-Aqsa Mosque complex with its golden dome coming into view.

The caption on the TV was in Hebrew. Just below it was the English translation:

Dozens feared dead in Western Wall suicide bombing.

"Oh no," Luke said.

Ed nodded. "Yeah."

"When did it happen?"

Ed glanced at his watch. "Maybe fifteen minutes ago."

"Was there screaming?"

"Here in the hotel? Oh, yeah. Screaming, wailing, gnashing of teeth—the whole nine yards. I thought it would wake you, but it didn't. You were out cold."

"I heard it in my sleep. What are they going to do?"

Ed shrugged. "Them? Same old. Settlers in the West Bank have already started the reprisal attacks. It is what it is, man. You got all these people over here, he said, she said, acting like a bunch of unruly kids. I don't think we have a dog in that fight. I'm here to do a job, which is to find Iranian nukes and put them out of business."

"Why are you in my room?"

Ed smiled. "The TV is better in here."

Luke stared at him and rubbed his eyes.

"Nah. Not really. I was going to wake you up soon. We just got the word a little while ago. We're taking off from an airbase in the Negev Desert. We're supposed to meet the mysterious Mr. Wonderful down there. We'll fly over the Gulf of Aqaba, across Saudi airspace to Iraq, then land outside Basra. That's where we'll take off from for the jump. The long and the short of it is, we're on the move soon, and we need to get on the same page with Trudy and Swann before we go."

"Have you given any more thought to that kid?" Luke said.

"You mean our guide? The ghost?"

"Yes."

"Yeah, I have. I've never met an honest to God covert operator with such a big mouth. Personally, I don't think he's the hot shot they say he is. Oh, I'm sure he's tough enough in a gunfight, but that's not what we need. I think they gave him to us because he's expendable."

Luke nodded. "Which in turn makes us…"

Ed took a sip of his coffee. "Expendable, yes."

"That's not too good," Luke said.

"Well, I could be wrong about him," Ed said. "I was wrong about something once before. But I'll tell you this. When I see him again, I'm going to find out who he is, even if I have to give him a talking to."

Luke smiled. "Especially if you have to give him a talking to."

Ed shook his head, but seemed to suppress a smile. "I ain't on a suicide mission, brother. If this guy's a throwaway, we need to know that going in."

"And if he is?"

Ed shrugged. "You're the boss. You tell me. You want to die because the Israelis aren't invested in this, they think this is an American thing, and so they gave us a cocky kid with one foot already in the grave?"

"I don't want to die for any reason, brother," Luke said.

Ed pointed at him. "Now that's my kind of leadership."

The door to the room opened and Trudy came walking in, followed by Swann. "I thought you were going to get him up," Trudy said.

"I did get him up."

"I meant all the way up, as in standing on his feet."

"Well, if you want something like that, you need to specify."

Trudy looked at Luke. She seemed fine—awake, energetic, refreshed. Her eyes squinted in concern. "You look like hell," she said.

"I'm tired," Luke said. What he almost said was *"I'm old."* Too old for a suicide mission? Yes. Almost certainly.

There was no age young enough for a mission like that.

CHAPTER SEVENTEEN

1:10 p.m. Israel Time (5:10 a.m. Eastern Standard Time)
Beit Aghion – the Prime Minister's Residence
Rehavia, Jerusalem

His confidence was shattered.

For the first time he could remember, perhaps for the first time in his life, he did not know what to do next. He spoke into the telephone, perhaps too harshly, to a young aide. The Americans were trying to schedule another call with their President Hopkins, and the aide had probably drawn the shortest straw—the one to ask Yonatan Stern when would be a good time to speak with the President of the United States, the so-called leader of the free world.

"No," he said into the handset. "I will not talk to her until this crisis is over. And you tell them this for me, please. I want you to speak it word for word. Are you ready?"

The young voice murmured its assent.

"You tell them, the Americans always lecture me about the narrow road to peace. How can there be peace? How can there be peace when these terrorist monsters train children to blow themselves apart, killing countless innocents who have gathered to pray for this very same peace of which they speak? How can there be peace when nowhere is safe, and nothing is sacred? What peace is this they are trying to obtain for us? Is it something we should want? Is it something we should wait for, this peace that never comes?"

There was silence on the other end of the line.

"Okay? Did you get that?"

"Yes."

"Good. Tell them all of it. I want her to hear it all."

He placed the phone in its cradle. He sat back in the chair and took a deep breath. This was his study, a beautiful, comfortable room. Weak winter light came in through the windows—it was bleak and overcast today, fitting weather for a day such as this one. The rug beneath his feet was decades old and Persian—a gift from Israel's one-time ally, the Shah of Iran. Flames crackled in the fireplace. The walls were lined with bookcases, the shelves groaning under hundreds of books—few knew that the Israeli bogeyman was a voracious reader.

The classics of the ancient world—not just the Torah, but also Aristotle, Plato, and Homer, the Greek myths, the Epic of Gilgamesh, the Bhagavad Gita. He knew the Hindu gods, not as well as he knew his own God, but certainly as well as almost any outsider could. He knew the Gospels as well as any Christian. He had read the Quran cover to cover five times.

Confucius, the *Tao Te Ching*, *The Art of War*. He had worked his way through Shakespeare, but also James Joyce. The Enlightenment philosophers. Kahlil Gibran? Naturally. Who could live in this region and not read Gibran? He had read at least a hundred biographies and memoirs of great men and women, or people who had lived through extraordinary circumstances. Another hundred on military strategy.

The Devil Wears Prada? God forgive him, but yes. Harry Potter. *The Lord of the Rings,* of course. Isaac Asimov. Noam Chomsky and Howard Zinn. Karl Marx and Adam Smith and Charles Darwin. Paul Krugman. Sigmund Freud. Carl Jung.

He shook his head. He was the man who knew too much. He had read everything, and he knew everything—everything except how to make this stop.

He was clever, he supposed. Clever, but not smart. A tactician but not a strategist. He could outwit his political opponents, outflank the ones who would attack him from his right, while marginalizing the ones who criticized him from the left.

He could secure another trade deal, or a new weapons system. He could use Israeli technological goodies to bribe Jordan, Saudi Arabia, and Egypt into uneasy friendships, if you could even call them that. All the while, Hezbollah grew in strength, the Iranians acquired nuclear weapons, the Russians helped Assad re-impose his will in Syria, and the Palestinians became ever more restive, ever angrier, ever more radical. The Egyptian government had feet of clay, and could topple at any time—the Muslim Brotherhood waited and watched in the shadows, with knives out. The Turks gave aid and comfort to ISIS, and slipped weapons into Gaza on speedboats under cover of darkness.

Everywhere, they encircled him, the noose tightening.

At amusement parks, in the video arcades, they had a game where the player held a soft, fuzzy hammer. He was confronted by a wide surface full of round holes and every second or two, a mole would pop up from a hole, then drop back down again. The object of the game was to whack the moles on the head as they appeared.

Yonatan Stern played this game endlessly, with human lives at stake. He whacked harder and harder, as more moles popped up everywhere he looked. He needed more and better hammers. He needed more and bigger hands with which to hold them. Stronger, faster arms. Better vision. He needed to string razor wire over the holes to keep the moles underground. He needed to sterilize the moles so they would stop proliferating.

He looked up. His wife was here. She stood near the door, watching him, the eyes behind her glasses sad and concerned. When had she entered? Had she always been here? Had she heard his phone call? He didn't know.

He saw her the way a man of almost seventy sees the woman with whom he has spent half a century. He sees the young woman he lusted for and fell in love with. He sees the old woman slowing down and fading. He sees all the women in the middle. He sees all of it, and none of it, at once. Mostly he sees his beloved.

"Sarah," he said. "If you had asked me this morning, I would have told you we were winning. Slowly but surely, we were gaining the upper hand."

"What would you tell me now?"

"We are lost. Win or lose, we are lost."

He closed his eyes for a moment and felt the tears streaming from them. God. He hadn't cried in how long? He didn't remember.

When he opened his eyes, she was there before him. He wrapped his arms around her waist and pressed his head to her stomach, like a small boy might do to his mother. She wrapped her arms around his head, the way a mother might do to a small boy who was in distress.

"The Wall," he said. "Oh my God. It will never be the same. It will never be a safe place again. It will never be sacred again."

Instantly, she corrected him. "It will always be sacred."

He did not respond, realizing the truth in what she said.

"What will the Americans do?" she said.

He shook his head. "Nothing. We are alone, once again."

"They didn't offer anything?"

"They sent us two commandos and an intelligence team. The commandos will slip into Iran, work their way across the country, and find the nuclear silos. They will assess their vulnerabilities and readiness, and then call in air strikes to destroy the weapons."

"That's something, isn't it?"

He shook his head. "It will never work. The men will be killed. Or they will be captured and languish as hostages in some hellhole Iranian prison. Or, if they are lucky and very, very good at what they do, they will somehow escape from the country with their lives, but without ever finding the weapons."

"Then why do they go, if those are their only options?"

He shrugged. "Elite commandos are a different breed. They are crazy, in a sense. They live for excitement. They need adrenaline like normal people need oxygen."

"Was that why you once went on these missions? Because you craved excitement?"

For a few seconds, he caught the image of an airport lounge, old and outdated even for the times. He moved through it, as though watching the scene unfold on black-and-white 8-millimeter film. He was running, his men beside him, shooting down hapless Ugandan soldiers in uniform. A small bomb went off. Smoke poured from somewhere. People were screaming, somewhere up ahead. There was no time to waste.

He shook his head. "No. I never craved excitement. I was terrified the entire time, but pretended I wasn't. I did it for Israel, because it was my duty, and because God called me to do so. I did it to protect people who could not protect themselves, who could not do the things that I could."

"Then why," she said, "do you assume these men do it for a different reason?"

He looked up at her. He thought of the men who had come here—who were they? Why had they come? Who and what did they leave behind? He had thought so little of this mission, of its chances of success, and he'd had so many other pressing issues to deal with that he hadn't even bothered to meet them when they arrived.

"Because I'm an old man and a fool," he said. "That's why."

"What do you think now?" she said.

"I think that you should run the country."

"Darling," she said. "Don't you know? I already do."

CHAPTER EIGHTEEN

2:15 p.m. Israel Time (7:15 a.m. Eastern Standard Time)
Masada Air Base
Negev Desert, Israel

"Amazing," Luke said.

The desert was like the surface of the moon.

He gazed out at it from the tarmac of the airstrip runway. The bleak land went on as far as the eye could see—mostly pale shades of yellow, red, and orange, undulating hillsides, craggy promontories, high plateaus, all of it seemingly lifeless, except for some scrub brush that dotted the ground and clung to vertical cliff faces.

With nothing to stop it, the wind howled across the vast landscape. It blew fine sandy grit into Luke's face—his aviator sunglasses blocked it from getting in his eyes. A black bandana covered his nose and mouth.

"It's nice to look at," Ed said. "But I'll take the sand at Miami Beach over this anytime."

Luke smiled and shook his head. He glanced at Ed, who was sitting on their gear. The gear was piled near the cargo door of the plane, a small, fast unmarked four- or maybe six-passenger jet, which was probably meant to look like the private plane of some up-and-coming corporate oil titan.

Luke and Ed hadn't loaded up yet for a very specific reason. They were waiting for the man called Ari Meil.

Across the runway and the aircraft taxiway, the control tower stood. Beneath it was a long, low-slung series of corrugated steel huts. It wasn't much of an air base, if that's what it really was. As Luke watched, a figure appeared over there, walking toward them. He was tall and upright, with a bag slung over one shoulder, and carrying another one with his opposite hand. He walked fast, but at the same time, seemed in no particular hurry.

"Here he comes," Ed said. "The man of the hour."

As the kid approached, Ed slowly stood. Luke followed the big man's movements out of the corner of his eye. Ed rolled his shoulders a few times. He did a few deep knee bends and loosened his hamstrings just a bit. He reached to the sky, getting up high on his tippy-toes. He put his right arm in the air, then behind his back, and pushed down on the elbow with his left hand. Then he switched arms.

"I'm a little tight," he said.

The kid came across the last runway. His light blond hair was gone—now it was dark brown, maybe black. His clean-shaven face was also gone—replaced by a full beard. Luke noticed that tinted contact lenses had turned his blue eyes brown. It was quite a transformation, from a European to a Middle Easterner in a few hours.

If an elite soldier carrying fifty or sixty pounds of gear could saunter, that's what the kid was doing.

"Hello, dummies," he said. "Ready to die?"

"Seems like it's been going around," Ed said.

The kid nodded. "A lot of innocent people died today."

"Yeah," Ed said. "People are dying. Which is something you and I need to talk about."

The kid slung the bag on his shoulder to the ground. "Talk away."

"I don't ride with ghosts," Ed said. "Never have, and I'm not going to start now. An operation like this has more than enough unknowns. The identity of the people involved isn't going to be one of them."

The kid shrugged. "You know who I am."

Luke shook his head. "No. We don't."

The kid dropped his other bag and looked at Luke. A sound escaped his mouth—it was halfway between a grunt and a laugh. He smiled and shook his head. "You guys. A couple of practical jokers, right? You heard what the Director said. My name is Ari Meil. I was a captain in Sayeret Matkal. I was recruited into Mossad and—"

"And you died four years ago," Ed said.

The kid stopped and stared at Ed. His body was suddenly tense. He seemed to think carefully about his next words.

"You know what a Golem is, big black man? A Golem is not quite dead, not quite alive. A supernatural being, the protector of the Jewish people. It is brought to life from the mud of the land itself. It has no past. It has no future. That's me."

Ed shook his head. "Not good enough." He tilted his head from side to side, the ligaments crackling as he did so.

"It'll have to do," the kid said.

"It won't."

The kid held an arm out toward Ed. "You don't want to test me. Because I'll surprise you. I bet you're not half as bad as you think."

Ed wasted no time. He stepped up and landed a hard right cross to the kid's face. It was a bone-cruncher. And it was fast, a blur, so fast it was almost like it hadn't happened. Except the kid's head snapped around, followed an instant later by his body. He seemed to spin in slow motion, like a ballet dancer. His feet left the ground. But somehow, when he landed, he was still standing, bent over with his hands on his knees.

Wow. Tough kid. Luke had seen one shot from Ed's right hand put people to sleep—on the ground, snoring, body twitching. Good night.

Ed seemed a little surprised himself.

Suddenly, the kid spun, delivering a hard kick to Ed's ribs.

Ed backed away, a hand to his side. Now he seemed very surprised. Not only had the kid not gone down, he still had some fight left in him. It was an affront to everything Ed knew to be true, and all he held dear. His eyes suddenly went to that crazy place.

"Oh, he does want to dance after all."

The kid went into a fighting crouch as Ed moved in. Luke noticed the kid already had a cut beneath his eye. That eye was going to swell.

"I like dancing," the kid gasped.

Luke stepped between them, his hands in the air. "All right, all right. That's plenty." He pushed them further apart, and neither one resisted.

"Guess who's going to Iran tonight? Me, that's who. Also both of you. Now guess who's the boss of this dangerous little expedition? Also me. And guess who doesn't need his people in traction when he goes? Can you guess?"

They stared at him.

"Don't make me pull rank, all right? That's not how this is going to work."

Ed's body relaxed a bit. He looked at the kid.

"Okay. You probably don't like me very much right now. I can tell you, the feeling is mutual. But I want us to be friends, and I can't be your friend if you don't tell me your name. See how easy that is? We can be best friends with just two words from you."

"Ari Meil," the kid said.

Ed shook his head. He half-smiled. "I'm gonna break you, man."

"So do it."

As Luke watched, a convoy of black SUVs passed through the gate to the airstrip. The sun glinted off the windshield of the first one. The Mercedes logo gleamed almost like a large mouth.

"Ed," Luke said. "We got company."

Ed turned, saw the speeding cars, and forgot about the kid

The cars pulled up right in front of them. A handful of bodyguards in suits climbed from the cars, a couple of them holding Uzis tight to their chests. The rear door of the middle SUV opened and a thick older man in a black pinstriped suit clambered out. His hair was silver and combed over the top of his head. His ears were unusually large. His cheeks were wide and prominent—chubby, almost. His eyes were alert and intelligent.

Luke recognized him instantly. He was Yonatan Stern, leader of the raid on Entebbe many years ago, and now the Prime Minister of Israel.

He extended a hand to Luke. "Agent Stone."

"Prime Minister Stern," Luke said.

"*Brukha haba'ah le Israel,*" Stern said. "Welcome to Israel. I'm sorry I wasn't available to greet you earlier."

"Thank you, sir. I understand how busy you are."

Stern glanced at Ed and Ari. They stood some distance from each other. Ari's eye was already swelling. The gash below it was bleeding just a bit.

"Is everything all right?" Stern said.

"Ah, everything's fine," Ed said. He extended a hand. "I'm Agent Edward Newsam of the Special Response Team. Former Delta Force operator, former FBI Hostage Rescue Team. I work with Agent Stone."

The Prime Minister shook Ed's big hand. Ed's knuckles were raw and scraped.

"Your President tells me you gentlemen are the best of the best."

"We work very hard, sir," Ed said.

Stern looked at the kid. "Agent…?"

"Prime Minister," the kid said, "my personal name is classified information. I am Agent K57. Sometimes referred to as Ari Meil. Sometimes referred to as the Golem."

Stern almost seemed to do a double take. He looked the kid up and down. He focused on the kid's eye.

"You… are the Golem?"

"Yes."

"And you're fit for duty?"

The kid nodded. "Of course."

"You are a great credit to your people," Stern said. "Believe me when I say that your work, and your sacrifice, has not gone unnoticed."

The kid nodded. "Thank you, sir."

He looked at all three of them now. The desert wind made his suit ripple, and his hair blew sideways. Behind him stood three large men with Uzis, impassive, their eyes hidden beneath dark aviator glasses. Behind them, the strange, endless desert.

"These are the darkest days Israel has faced in many years. The forces that would destroy us have become unspeakably strong. When I was young, I was a soldier like yourselves. I understand what you face, and I pray for you, both that you succeed in your mission, and that you come home safe."

Stern paused.

"I am very glad, and very proud, to know each of you. I hope we can meet again in happier times."

CHAPTER NINETEEN

7:31 a.m. Eastern Standard Time (2:31 p.m. Israel Time)
The Oval Office
The White House, Washington, DC

"He just called," Kurt Kimball said. "He says he's running about fifteen minutes late." Kurt hung up his telephone and looked at Susan.

Susan sighed. It had been a long sleepless night. Early this morning, she had summoned Gholam Rahmani, the Director of the Iranian Interests Section, to a meeting with her. There were no diplomatic ties between Tehran and Washington. The Iranian Ambassador to the United Nations was not in the country. Rahmani was the closest thing she had to an opposite number—he ran his office out of the Pakistani Embassy.

They had set the meeting for 7 a.m. Then his office had called and asked could it be 7:30. Now it looked closer to 7:45, or even 8 a.m.

"Does he know he's meeting with the President of the United States?" she said.

Kurt just smiled.

"Give it to me again, Kurt."

Kurt shrugged. "Not much to say. Gholam Rahmani, fifty-six years old. Master's degree in International Relations from the University of Tehran. Career diplomat, with numerous posts in various parts of the world. Fluent in English and French, passable in half a dozen others. More of an administrator than what you might call a negotiator."

"And Iran?" Susan said. "One more time."

Kurt shook his head. "Complicated. Mostly bad stuff since the 1979 Revolution and the Hostage Crisis. We openly backed Saddam Hussein against them in the Iran-Iraq War from 1980 to 1988. More than a million people died in that war, nearly constant atrocities committed by both sides. At the same time, the Executive Branch and CIA were secretly selling them weapons to fight Saddam, while funneling the profits to the Contras in Nicaragua."

"Playing both sides," Susan said.

"Yes," Kurt said. "Very cute."

"What else?"

"Iran has long backed terrorist groups throughout the Middle East, and to some extent the world. They supported the PLO for many years. They are the primary supporters of the Assad regime in Syria, Hezbollah in Lebanon, and Hamas in the Palestinian territories. We believe that for two decades, Iran has allowed Al Qaeda militants to traverse their territory unimpeded. One of Iran's stated goals is to destroy Israel. They have never backed away from or softened this stance, not once, during any international negotiations.

"Since 2010, they have shot down at least half a dozen American spy drones flying in or near Iranian airspace along the border with Iraq. In one case, they claimed that their cyberwarfare department commandeered an RQ-170 Sentinel operated by the CIA and brought it safely to the ground in Iranian territory."

"Did they?" Susan said.

Kurt nodded. "Yes. As far as we can tell, they did. As a result, existing drones in that series had to be redesigned and redeployed elsewhere."

He went on.

"For thirty years, they have threatened to mine the Strait of Hormuz into and out of the Persian Gulf. Tankers from a host of oil-producing countries travel through there. Iran controls the high ground to the north of the Strait, though they have never attempted to mine it. US Naval assessments, and assessments by international intelligence organizations, have often been conflicting as to whether they could close the Strait, and if they did, how long they would manage to keep it closed. The general consensus now seems to be that yes, they could close the Strait, but that it would cost them dearly in blood and treasure. The time frames I've seen extend from fifteen days on the low end, up to a hundred thirty or more days on the high. Needless to say, if Iran somehow managed to close down oil shipping in the Persian Gulf for more than four months…"

"Economic collapse," Susan said.

Kurt nodded. "At least." He glanced down at his notes.

"From 1995 until 2015, we implemented a trade embargo against them, which covered most items except foodstuffs. Trade between the two countries dropped off a cliff. Unfortunately, this hurt American manufacturers much more than Iranian manufacturers, since historically we export far more products to Iran than we import from there. When we concluded the nuclear deal with them, we lifted the sanctions in exchange for their promise not to pursue a nuclear weapons program."

Kurt paused. "Which brings us to where we are today."

"Nowhere good," Susan said.

"Our best hope is that they're bluffing."

A Secret Service man popped his head inside the door. "The Director of the Iranian Interests Section is undergoing a security check at the West Wing entrance. He should be here momentarily."

Susan nodded. "Thank you."

She looked at Kurt. "What do I want from him?"

Kurt shook his head. "I don't think he can give you anything. He's not empowered to do so. But he will talk to people upstream from him. All you can do is pass on our message in the most emphatic terms possible. They need to stop this. They need to back all the way up. And they need to start over from the beginning. If they have nuclear weapons, that's not a status quo we can live with. They must surrender them and allow in international inspectors."

A few moments passed. The doors opened again. Susan and Kurt both stood as a small man in a suit passed through. He was heavyset, with a receding hairline up top and a thick salt-and-pepper beard, and he wore glasses. A young woman trailed behind him.

"Madam President," he said, and held out a thick hand to her.

"Director Rahmani," she said. "Thank you for coming. This is my National Security Advisor, Kurt Kimball."

The two men shook hands.

"And this is?" Susan said, indicating the woman.

"That is my assistant, Ms. Ahmad. She will be taking notes, if you don't mind. I want to make sure I represent our conversation correctly to my superiors."

"Of course." Susan offered the young woman her hand, which the woman accepted, hesitantly, eyes watching her boss.

"Welcome," Susan said. "Won't you both sit down?"

Rahmani sat. His assistant remained standing.

"You're probably aware that I summoned you here for a reason," Susan said.

Rahmani nodded. "Of course. Things are… difficult."

Susan nodded. She almost laughed. The man had a gift for understatement. "That's one way to put it," she said. "And I'm afraid that your country is making it more difficult. Your sudden declaration that you are a nuclear-armed power, and your threats against Israel, have put my country in an awkward position."

"You are in an awkward position because you are the protectors of the Zionists," Rahmani said. "I'm not sure what you expected to happen, given whom you choose to share your bed with."

"For one, I expected you to honor your agreements."

Rahmani shrugged. "Our enemy does not honor agreements. When Israel was created, the rulebook was shredded."

Susan decided to try a different tack. It was clear that this man had received orders from his superiors. Toe the party line. Do not apologize for anything. Blame Israel for everything.

"The policy of the United States is that any further attacks on Israel will be considered an attack on America. Do you understand this policy?"

Rahmani frowned. "Perhaps. I'm not sure. It would hardly matter to me, since Iran has not attacked Israel, and has no plans to do so. We merely stated the truth, which was if attacked by Israel, we will counter with overwhelming force, including nuclear weapons. We stated this *after* we received a direct threat from Israel."

"Sir, you are playing a very dangerous game. Earlier today a suicide attack at the Western Wall killed hundreds of people."

Rahmani waved that away. "An attack by a Palestinian from Gaza, not by an Iranian. We have nothing to do with—"

"Do you deny that Iran funds and controls Hamas?" Susan said.

Rahmani stared into her eyes. His eyes were hard. "Madam, I don't confirm or deny anything. I spend my days providing aid to Iranian travelers in America. We help people obtain duplicate passports and receive medical care. We repatriate people who are in trouble of one kind or another. Does Iran fund Hamas? I should think not. Hamas is a Sunni organization, and Iran is a Shiite country. The Sunnis have sworn to destroy us. Would we pay them to do this?"

He paused.

"And whether Iran funds Hamas or not, I know that we do not control them, as you suggest. No one controls Hamas, not even their own leaders. It must be so. I cannot think of a group as poorly organized, and which brings more routine disasters down upon their own heads, and upon the heads of their people, than Hamas. They would benefit from a certain amount of outside control."

Susan shook her head. "I don't think you're hearing me."

"Then please explain in simpler terms," he said. "Perhaps my English…"

"We hold you responsible for the attack at the Western Wall," Susan said.

"For an attack by a teenage girl who never set foot in Iran, and who probably never met an Iranian in her entire life?"

Susan nodded. "Yes. And we hold you responsible for the missile attacks by Hezbollah. We hold you responsible for providing Hezbollah with advanced weaponry. And I can tell you in no uncertain terms, should you use nuclear weapons—"

"Only in defense, Madam. Only if Israel attacks us."

"If you use them at all, you will bring the entire might of the United States down upon your own heads."

Rahmani shook his head. "Like the Israelis, we are not without powerful friends. Both the Russians and the Chinese have pledged to come to our defense."

Susan shook her head.

"Don't fool yourself. They won't risk World War Three for Iran. It's not worth it."

Rahmani raised a finger and wagged it at her. "And if you believe that, then you are the one playing a dangerous game. You are the one fooling yourself."

He rose to leave. "Are we done?"

"Not quite," Susan said. "Here's what's going to happen. You will immediately agree to dismantle and surrender your nuclear weapons, under the supervision of international observers, including ones from the United States. The process will begin with a reasonable timeframe, not more than thirty days from now. If you cannot agree to this, we will be forced to destroy the weapons ourselves. Afterwards, you will be subject to frequent inspections to determine that you have not restarted your weapons program."

Rahmani smiled. "Good luck to you, Madam President." He glanced at Kurt. "And good day to you, sir."

After he left, Susan looked at Kurt. "What did you think?"

Kurt rubbed his forehead. "I thought you guys really hit it off."

CHAPTER TWENTY

5:45 p.m. Tehran Time (9:45 a.m. Eastern Standard Time)
The Ministry of Intelligence of the Islamic Republic of Iran
Tehran, Iran

"Is that all she told him?"

The man stared out a large bay window at the snow-capped peaks of the Alborz Mountains. To the west, the last of the day was fading, the weak yellow light playing on the white of the snow and ice.

His name was Mohammed Younessi. He was tall and thin, completely bald, and bore more than a passing resemblance to the famous actor Yul Brynner. His title, translated into English, meant Director of Accountability. It was not internal organizational accountability, however, that he was in charge of.

"No," the man behind him said. "He also said she told him that America would destroy the weapons themselves, if we won't do it."

Younessi smiled. It would be a tall order for the Americans to destroy the weapons, if they existed. First, they would have to find them. Their location was one of the most closely held secrets in all of Iran—Younessi himself did not know where they were, or if they had ever been built in the first place. It would take a very skilled spy to unravel these secrets.

"Have there been any infiltrations?" Younessi said.

"None that we are aware of."

"That we are aware of?" Younessi did not like it when underlings spoke in a way that lacked certainty.

"Forgive me," the man said. "There are American unmanned drones patrolling at the edge of our territory twenty-four hours a day. A few have strayed into our airspace, then quickly exited again, likely testing us. But we are monitoring them closely. The Shiite tribes move back and forth across the border with Iraq, but they are tight-knit and it is very unlikely there are infiltrators among them. We watch the mountains to the north and the Caspian Sea approaches. Our ground checkpoints on the border of Kurdish-held territories are very tight. The east is secure. Is it possible an infiltrator could slip in? Difficult, I would say, but not impossible."

Younessi shrugged. “And of course we know who the suspected collaborators are.”

He did not turn around, but he could tell the man behind him nodded. “Of course.”

“Watch them carefully,” Younessi said. “If any activity seems strange, or even slightly unusual, eliminate them. But keep them alive long enough to set a trap for their friends from abroad.”

“Yes, Director,” the man said.

“And watch the skies. Double our jet patrols along our western flank.”

An idea occurred to him then. The situation with Israel and America was tense, high pressure. But there might be a way to raise the stakes even further. He thought of imagery from the old times, 1979, when the students stormed the American embassy and seized the hostages. In his mind’s eye, he could see the Americans with blindfolds on their faces, being led in front of the cameras.

“If at all possible, I would like to capture an American or Israeli spy. I would like to parade such a person in public for the world to see.”

“Captured alive?” the man said.

Younessi nodded. “Yes. With a written confession that they can recite on television and radio.”

“And if no such spy becomes available?”

Younessi shrugged. “A collaborator will do. Even someone already in prison.”

“Of course.”

Younessi spun around. He pointed at his employee. “But don’t discount the possibility of a spy. To destroy the weapons, they must find them. To find them, they must infiltrate. Spies are coming, if they aren’t already here.”

“Yes, Director.”

Younessi smiled. He cracked his knuckles. He enjoyed hurting people—it was part of his job. It would be a tricky thing to do to an American, because of all the international organizations watching. But there were ways of hurting people that did not leave lasting physical marks. Then it was your word against theirs. And if the person was a deep cover spy, and your enemy America denied that person’s very existence?

My, my, my. Then you could do anything you wanted.

Younessi stared hard at his underling, the man who worked for him. “If you catch a spy, bring him to me first.”

CHAPTER TWENTY ONE

9:45 p.m. Tehran Time (1:45 p.m. Eastern Standard Time)
The Skies above Eastern Iraq

Luke breathed pure oxygen through a mask affixed to his face.

He sat on a long bench inside the plane. At one end of the bench sat a young man, who for lack of another name, Luke was starting to think of as Ari Meil. At the other end sat Ed Newsam.

The two hadn't spoken again since their fight at the secret Israeli airbase. Indeed, during their stopover at the American base in Basra, while Luke and Ed went into the PX for a bite to eat and took naps in a guest barracks, the Israeli disappeared again.

It wasn't good. Luke was going to have to find a way to bridge the gap between them. Not just between Ed and the kid, but between Luke and the kid as well.

Luke checked the altimeter on his wrist. They were flying at close to 29,000 feet, not far from the border between Iraq and Iran. They would drop another few thousand feet before they made the jump. They were visible to the Iranians up here, without a doubt. But the sky was full of planes and drones patrolling this airspace, so this one plane shouldn't be that obvious. And when they jumped, they'd be too small to pick up on radar.

The jump door was closed, but it didn't matter. Luke was cold, despite the special polypropylene jumpsuit that covered him nearly head to toe. Outside the door's window, it was full-on dark. Away on the northeast horizon, there was a glow of light coming from the ground. He didn't even have to guess—that was Tehran. It was a big city.

He stood and stepped over in front of Ed.

Ed leaned back on the bench, resting against the wall. His eyes were closed, and his face was covered by an oxygen mask, same as Luke.

His giant combat pack was belted to the front of him, his legs spread out around it. Ed had been busy acquiring weapons in Iraq. He had an MP5 submachine gun belted to one side of him. Strapped to his other side was his favorite weapon—the M79 grenade launcher. There were handguns mounted to his waist. Ed was strapped with guns, just the way Luke knew he liked it.

Luke himself was going skinny on this trip—a couple of handguns, a couple of knives strapped to his calves, a few Israeli grenades. They were going to be sneaking around. It was probably better to be quiet than loud. Whatever other weapons Luke might need, he would try to acquire as he went.

He smiled down at Ed—with his eyes closed, he looked a lot like the little boy he once must have been. The guns were his security blanket.

"Ed."

He gave Ed's leg a light kick.

Ed's eyes opened.

"Almost there, man. You want to do your checklist?"

Ed nodded.

Luke knew the list by heart, but he pulled a small piece of paper from his breast pocket. It was hard to handle the paper with his thick gloves on, and he had left it hanging half out of the pocket. That way he could at least get a grip on it.

Luke began the protocol. "Altimeter?"

Ed patted the fat watch on his wrist.

"What's your reading?"

Ed tapped a button on his watch and looked at the reading.

"Twenty-seven and change."

Luke glanced at his own altimeter and got the reading: 27,348. They were dropping. They had told him to expect a jump at just below 26,000 feet.

"Check."

"Parachute."

Ed touched the parachute on his back. "Check."

"Helmet."

Ed tapped himself on his hard, molded-plastic head. "Check."

Luke went through the list, working his way carefully to the end. Each time he mentioned an item on the list to Ed, he let that serve as his own check.

"How's your breathing?" Luke said.

"Feels good."

"Dizzy, any nausea or tingling sensations?"

"No."

"Exhaustion, sleepiness, unexplained tiredness?"

Ed shrugged. "I left the US twenty-four hours ago. I've been sleeping in two-hour increments. I might be a little tired."

"Anything that will affect your jump?"

"No, man. I'm good."

"This is a HAHO jump. High altitude, high opening. How do you feel about that?"

"I love it."

Luke smiled. "When we jump, we're going to pull cords at twenty seconds. We're still over Iraq, but very close to the border with Iran. We're following the kid's lead. I know you don't love that, but it's what we've got. We're steering east and north as much as we can—we're hoping prevailing winds will push us east. We're shooting for at least twenty miles in country before we land. As always, no lights, no sound. No radio contact. It's going to be dark out there, so keep your eyes open. Got it?"

Ed nodded. "Got it."

"If the bad guys spot us and we take ground fire, or God forbid, aerial fire, we cut our primaries, drop hard at terminal velocity, and open our secondaries low. Watch for eighteen hundred feet, then pull. If that happens, the trip is scuttled. When you land, don't wait around. Head west into Iraq by any means necessary. No prisoners, brother. Just make it home alive."

"Roger that," Ed said.

Luke nodded. He tapped Ed on the helmet. "Cool. Good man."

He made his way to the other end of the bench. The kid was here, sitting across from the closed jump door, staring at it. His pack seemed huge between his legs.

"Ari."

The kid looked up. Through his oxygen mask, Luke could barely see his face. All that was visible were his eyes.

"You want to run a checklist?" Luke said.

Ari shook his head. "Not necessary. I've done this many times."

"Suit yourself."

"I will."

Luke sat down, a few feet away and just across from them. In a moment, he would have to go and strap his own combat pack on. For now, he made a triangle with Ed and Ari, in a spot where both of them could hear him.

"We need to work together on this thing," he said.

The kid shrugged. "You guys do your job. I'll do mine."

Luke looked at him, then looked at Ed. He paused for a moment. The kid gave him second thoughts about this whole mission. The kid was a second thoughts factory, generating new second thoughts around the clock, three shifts a day.

"You have a lot of friends back home… Ari? People enjoy this attitude of yours, do they?"

The kid shook his head. He stared at Luke, then looked down the bench at Ed. "You guys don't get it, do you?"

Ed shook his head. "No. We don't."

"I don't have any friends. I don't have a family. No parents, no siblings, no wife and daughter. I don't have a name. I don't have a home. I can't have these things. It's too dangerous. Not for me. For them. You don't know my name, not because I don't want to tell you. If you were captured and tortured—and rest assured, in Iran you would be tortured—they would get my name from you. That can't happen. Because my family would die. Security is paramount in Israel, but believe me, the Iranians can reach inside when they want to. And if they find out who I am, they will want to."

"What have you done?" Luke said.

"I've killed people."

Luke shrugged. "We've all killed people."

The kid was quiet.

"You're an assassin," Ed said. It wasn't a question.

The kid stared at the closed doorway.

"I am a member of Kidon," he said.

Kidon, Luke knew, was the most secretive branch of Mossad. These were the killers, the ruthless, the merciless, and the most capable people in Israeli intelligence.

"Tell me," Luke said.

"Hassan al-Laqis was considered the father of Hezbollah's missile program. He convinced the Iranians to trust Hezbollah with increasingly advanced weapon systems. He also raised money through Hezbollah's drug trafficking, and purchased heavy anti-tank gunnery, and chemical weapons, from a Russian arms dealer. The Iranians don't approve of chemical weapons, so he went around them. He was a very dangerous man. He was gunned down on a Beirut street corner two years ago. The case was never solved."

Luke and Ed said nothing.

"Mohammed Ali Sistani was a radical cleric in Iran. He had a large following among Shiites, and he hated Jews with a passion that can only be thought of as psychotic. He had a radio program that was heard throughout Iran, as well as in eastern Iraq, western Afghanistan, and Pakistan. He had opened a school for jihad, where young students were trained to commit suicide attacks. Two of his graduates destroyed a beach resort popular with Israelis outside Dar es Salaam, killing twenty-seven people besides themselves and injuring hundreds. Three other students of his attacked an Israeli youth hostel in Bangkok, killing fourteen people, including ten guests, and the owners, a couple in their early thirties, along with their two young children. When the Thai police arrived, the attackers detonated explosives, burning the building to the ground. Sistani, left to his own devices, would have continued to encourage these types of attacks, both at his school and to his large audience of listeners."

"What happened to him?" Luke said.

The kid shrugged. "He died six months ago. Stabbed in the back as he left his radio studio in Tehran late one evening. His two bodyguards had their throats slit. They bled out very quickly. Sistani died more slowly, in an alleyway among garbage bins, and in quite a bit of pain. He was an old man and he was afraid to die. He wept, and he prayed, but he did not beg for his life. Give him credit for that."

"Any others?" Luke said.

The kid nodded. "Yes. It's my job."

Suddenly Luke was suspicious. "Is this mission a front? Is it really an assassination?"

The kid stared at him. "No. Weren't you at the briefing? We're not killing anyone unless we have to. We're looking for nuclear weapons. It just so happens that I'm the best we have at infiltrating Iran, so they sent me."

The kid looked at Ed. "Are we good?"

Ed shrugged. "I guess we're good. If you can't tell us, you can't tell us." He reached a heavy gloved hand across and Ari tapped it with own.

At that moment, a buzzer sounded and a green light came on above the door to the closed door to the cockpit.

"That's the cue," the kid said. "We're here."

He worked his way to his feet as Luke went back to strap on his pack. Luke watched as the kid waddled to the door with his heavy combat pack between his legs. He wrenched open the door, then turned and looked back. He stared at Ed, who was already moving toward him.

"Hey, big man!" the kid shouted. "Ready to dance?"

Then he dove out and was gone.

Luke sighed. He looked at Ed. Ed just shook his head as he waddled past toward the open door.

"After you," Luke said.

CHAPTER TWENTY TWO

2:50 p.m. Eastern Standard Time
The Situation Room
The White House, Washington, DC

"Iran is one of the oldest civilizations known to man," Kurt Kimball said, his voice a deep monotone that threatened to put his audience into a coma.

"For thousands of years it was known to outsiders as Persia—the word Iran appeared in writing for the first time in the 200s AD. Iran's fortunes have ebbed and flowed throughout history. Six hundred years before Christ, Persia was probably the greatest empire the world had ever seen."

Susan was barely listening. She tried to think of where Stone might be at this moment. Was he safe? Was he injured? Was he dead?

She looked around the egg-shaped room at the tired, sallow faces. It was a packed house. Another day, another crisis.

Susan had not made a substantial public statement yet. The cable news shows were starting to say that she was dithering—fiddling while Rome burned. Israel and Iran were having a nuclear standoff. Israel and Hezbollah were in the midst of a hot war along the Lebanon border. Nearly three hundred people had died in a terror attack at the Western Wall. Israel was bombing Gaza and the West Bank. The Palestinians were launching rockets into Israeli settlements, and into towns in southern Israel.

There was no end in sight, Susan was worried sick about Luke Stone, and Kurt was giving them all a history lesson on Iran.

Susan shook her head. She should never have allowed Stone to go on this mission. She should never have allowed the Special Response Team to regroup. If Stone came back from this alive, she was going to fire him.

Fire him? She was going to kill him.

Kurt droned on. "Iran was a center of science, culture, and art during the Islamic Golden Age, while Western Europe was mired in the Dark Ages. This reached its peak in the 900s and 1000s—many of the most important scientific, medical, philosophical, historical, and musical works of the era were written in Persian."

"Kurt?" Susan said.

"Yes?"

"I know this is important information, crucial to have and fascinating to hear. But I'd like to fast-forward past the next nine or ten centuries and get to the present day. We have decisions to make here, and the Middle Ages might not have that much bearing on them. Also, I want to get a status report on our current activities, if we have one available."

Kurt put a hand up. "Okay, Susan. Okay."

"I don't want to ruin your doctoral presentation," Susan said.

Kurt smiled and shook his head. He sifted through some papers in front of him.

"May I continue?"

"Please. By all means."

"Modern Iran," Kurt said, raising his index finger, "is one of the most important geostrategic places on Earth. It has the largest proven natural gas reserves, and the fourth-largest proven oil reserves, in the world. It straddles the line between the Middle East and Asia, and has hundreds of miles of coastline along the Persian Gulf—including the narrow Strait of Hormuz, which requires a constant American military presence so Iran's military can't use it as a chokepoint to cut off the flow of oil from other Gulf countries.

"When it comes to human rights violations, Iran is practically in a league all its own. George Orwell would have been proud to know them. Arbitrary detention and imprisonment, disappearances, a kangaroo court system where death sentences are often decided in minutes, torture techniques left over from medieval times, public hangings—these are just a few of the arrows in their quiver. The nightmare begins immediately. Many prisoners freed later describe their initial questioning as having been absurd, illogical, or consisting entirely of physical abuse, screaming, loud noises, and accusations. This is, of course, by design. Our own CIA experiments have determined that nonsensical, violent interrogations break the typical prisoner's spirit very quickly."

Kurt looked up. "It might be needless to say, but the health of Iranian political prisoners tends to deteriorate rapidly."

"Are they worse than the Saudis?" someone said.

"The Saudis have a bad record on human rights. The difference in Saudi Arabia is that there are rules. Everyone knows what they are. You might not like the rules, they may be unspeakably backward, but you are aware of them ahead of time. In Iran, many people find themselves in prison for years, being tortured routinely, and they have no idea why it's happening. Meanwhile, their families don't know where they are. Often enough, the first official acknowledgment a family will receive from the government is a letter informing them their loved one has been executed for treason."

This kind of talk wasn't setting Susan's mind to rest one bit. If Stone got captured by the Iranians during a black operation…

"And the current conflict?" she said.

Kurt nodded. "Iran provides weaponry to its allies among the Shiite tribes in Iraq, to the Assad government in Syria, Hezbollah in Lebanon, and the Palestinians. Iran does not recognize Israel, and is the primary supporter of attacks against Israel in the world. In general, Iran is regionally powerful, both economically and militarily. It is well protected, both by its own military, as well as by its relationships with Russia and China. It projects its own power, and as a cat's paw for Russia, into Middle Eastern conflicts. If it has indeed emerged as a nuclear-armed power, it will be a major destabilizing influence throughout the Middle East, and by extension, the world."

"What would be the effect of a nuclear war between Iran and Israel?" Susan said.

Kurt shook his head. "It's really too horrible to contemplate."

"Well, it seems like we're stuck contemplating it at the moment."

"Yes we are. And we estimate that Iran probably has enriched enough nuclear material for anywhere between eight and fourteen nuclear warheads, each with an explosive potential perhaps twenty times the size of the Hiroshima bomb. They have hundreds of missiles that are capable of carrying nuclear warheads. We can assume that because of Israel's missile defense system, Iran would launch a massive attack with both nuclear and conventional weapons, all at once. Israeli missile defense would quickly be overwhelmed—there would be no way to guess which incoming missiles were the nukes and which weren't. Under such a scenario, we estimate that at least five nuclear warheads would reach their targets. Israel is tiny—depending on where the missiles hit, five should be enough to utterly destroy the major population centers in the middle of the country, wipe out communications, critical infrastructure, the electrical grid, food storage and provisions, and in all likelihood, access to clean water and sanitation.

"More than half of the Israeli population would be killed immediately, or would die soon afterward. Ninety percent of the population would be dead within a year. Much of the Palestinian population would die off as well. It would be difficult for the international community to organize relief because of the radioactivity. In the days and weeks that followed an attack, winds from the Mediterranean Sea would blow a toxic, radioactive cloud eastward into Jordan and Syria, then Iraq, and then back into Iran itself, although this would be mitigated somewhat by the Zagros Mountains along Iran's western border. The death toll from the toxic cloud alone would likely be in the hundreds of thousands. Syria and Iraq are already collapsed states and humanitarian disasters—add poisonous radioactivity, and you're looking at a very volatile mixture."

"How would Iran fare?"

"Iran is a country of eighty million people, and is physically much, much larger than Israel," Kurt said. "But Israel has a larger and more powerful nuclear arsenal. We don't know for a fact, but we believe they have at least fifty nuclear missiles capable of reaching Iran. Most of these are ballistic missiles deployed in underground silos, but some are also bombs deliverable by airplane. If Israel finds itself under nuclear attack, they will have no reason to hold back.

"Iran has limited missile defense capability. As a result, most of what Israel launched would hit its targets. This would result in widespread death and destruction, including the complete destruction of Tehran, a city of eight million people. We can assume that at least thirty to fifty million people would die immediately. It would cause a total collapse of the Iranian economy and infrastructure. It would create a shock to world oil and natural gas supply, and precipitate skyrocketing prices as the Chinese and Indians seek to get their energy from other markets. Those shortages alone would likely cause runaway inflation and a worldwide depression. It gets worse, because if Iran sees its own imminent destruction, there is no reason for them to refrain from bombing the Saudi oil fields and closing the Strait of Hormuz—two things they have long threatened to do. If they managed that, worldwide oil consumption would drop overnight to levels not seen since the 1950s. This might sound like a good thing in some abstract way, but it isn't. It is a very, very bad thing. The world economy is dependent on oil.

"Meanwhile, the toxic cloud from fifty or more nuclear explosions? It would drift east from Iran into Afghanistan and Pakistan, destabilizing already unstable societies. Pakistan is a nuclear-armed power, and there is no telling what they might do in response, especially if their fragile government collapses. Within a couple of weeks the toxic cloud would reach India, a country of nearly a billion people, the majority of whom already live in abject poverty, and have limited access to clean air and clean water to begin with."

Kurt looked up from his paperwork again. "The thing to realize is that in the event of nuclear war between Iran and Israel, what I just shared with you is basically a best-case scenario. It describes the fallout from a limited war that only includes those two countries. The two of them would likely manage to destroy each other, taking out the world economy, and probably half a dozen other states while they were at it. We could anticipate reprisal terror attacks against the Jewish population here and in Europe, and I assume that with Iran out of the picture, Sunni Muslims would feel free to attack and slaughter Shiites anywhere they found them.

"Radioactivity would eventually find its way around the world, contaminating air, water, crops, and livestock populations. The Chernobyl disaster was thought to have caused hundreds of thousands of cancer deaths worldwide over the following two decades. This event would be a thousand times as large as the Chernobyl disaster. It would unleash a host of ills that are hard to anticipate—crop failures, starvation, widespread radiation sickness among vulnerable populations, civil unrest, refugee crises on a scale never seen before, government collapses, and additional wars. A major danger is that it would destabilize the already fraught relationship between India and Pakistan, causing a second nuclear war, this time between those two countries."

"Is there any possible good that might come from it?" a military man in dress greens, a four star general, said.

Kurt looked at him. "I can't think of any. Can you?"

"Well, as you mentioned, it would get Iran out of the picture."

Kurt switched his gaze to Susan. "Let's take a break, shall we?"

CHAPTER TWENTY THREE

December 14
1:05 a.m. Tehran Time (5:05 p.m. Eastern Standard Time on December 13)
Zagros Mountains
Ilam Province, Iran

The night was bitterly cold.

They had landed hours before, on a plateau beneath the slopes of a steep, snow-covered mountain. The ground was hard, and it took over an hour to bury their parachutes, taking turns breaking the frozen earth with the small fold-up shovel Ari had brought.

At some point during the jump, Luke had come to think of the guy as Ari. Somehow, it sounded better to his ears than the Golem. If that's who the man wanted to be, then okay.

It was time to get started. Forty-eight hours? And they had already burned two of them. There really wasn't any time to waste.

Luke stared out into the darkness from the high plateau. The winds howled along the peaks above them, the trees rustling and shaking. Far below them, deep in a valley, there appeared to be the lights of a village.

"Are we hiding from people on this trek?"

Ari shrugged. "This region is sparsely populated. The Iraqis bombed here mercilessly in the 1980s. Many people fled. The ones who remain are farmers and animal herders. They go to bed when the dark comes, and rise before first light. Hopefully, we will reach the road while they sleep. Anyway, they are mostly Kurds, plus a few nomadic tribes. They have no love for the Iranians."

He paused. "But yes. We will avoid them. You never know who is indebted to the regime in one way or another."

They made their way down. It was a long, difficult hike through a trackless wilderness. Here and there, Ari found a path they would follow for a while. Mostly, they blundered ever downward over loose rocks and scree, and through dense underbrush. The wind would shake the trees above their heads, bringing a gentle dusting of snow.

They barely spoke, moving in single file, Ari in the lead, checking his compass every few minutes, followed by Luke, and then Ed. Hours passed in this formation. Late, a bright half moon came out from behind the clouds, and Luke could make out the towering peaks of the mountains high above them.

They were standing in a small, dense forest. Ari pressed himself against a thick tree. Luke and Ed did the same. Ari indicated the area just ahead of them.

Perhaps fifty yards away, and three stories below them, there was a break in the trees. A narrow ribbon of roadway cut through the forest. A truck was parked down there, along the side of the road, its hazard lights flashing in the dark. Two men worked with flashlights, trying to fix something—perhaps changing a flat tire.

"That's our ride," Ari said. Steam rose from his mouth.

He looked at Luke and Ed. His eyes were serious. "The men will ignore you. Do not speak to or acknowledge them in any way. Simply go to the back of the truck, walk up the ramp and into the trailer. A few minutes after we are in, they will finish their repairs, close the gate, and off we go. It's a long drive to Tehran—this will be a good time for sleep, if you can manage it. There will be plenty of straw bedding. It's not very comfortable, but I imagine you've slept on worse."

Luke looked at him. *Straw?*

Ari dug into the breast pocket of his coat. He came out with small Styrofoam ear plugs. They were the cheap, squishy kind—they would expand to fill your ear canal. People often stuffed them in their ears at shooting ranges.

He handed two to Ed and two to Luke.

"Is it going to be loud?" Ed said.

Ari shook his head. "No. It's going to smell." He held up his own plugs. "Put them in your nose."

They hiked down to the truck, doing exactly as Ari had instructed. Once on the roadway, the walked past the two men, ignoring them as if they weren't even there. The men didn't look up or appear to notice them. The two groups were like spirits to each other, inhabiting different dimensions.

Luke climbed up the steel ramp into the back of the truck. The trailer was separated into pens, each pen filled with about a dozen brown sheep. The sheep were thick with their winter coats.

Ari squeezed into a pen, patted a couple of sheep, and immediately lay down on the straw-covered floor.

"The Iranians love their sheep," he said. "If you're lucky, these sheep will lay down with you and give you their warmth."

"Wool?" Luke said.

Ari shook his head. "Meat. You never had sheep's head soup? Kaleh pache, they call it. They put the whole head in—eyes, tongue, brain, everything. Also the hooves. Very nice for breakfast—it will keep you full all day. Perhaps we'll get some at a bazaar stall in Tehran. After the mission is over, of course."

"Okay," Luke said. "Once we find the nukes and call in the air strikes, we'll hang around for a couple of days, relax and eat strange food. That sounds like fun. I'm sure the Revolutionary Guards will be delighted to host."

Behind him, the metal gate to the trailer clanged shut. The man padlocked it closed. Up front, the truck's engine roared into life.

Ed was pushing his way into a pen with the sheep. He had a considerably harder time squeezing between the metal rails than Ari had. After a moment, his giant bulk was surrounded by fuzzy, bleating livestock.

"I didn't know this was going to be a pleasure trip," he said.

CHAPTER TWENTY FOUR

8:35 am Tehran Time (12:35 a.m. Eastern Standard Time)
Tehran, Iran

"No war! No nukes! No war! No nukes!"

The young woman raised her fist in the air as she shouted the words. All around her, on the campus of the University of Tehran, and spreading out into the surrounding streets, thousands of students chanted the same slogan.

She had come because enough was enough. She had come because this time, the students really were going to seize power.

The government leaders, the ayatollahs, the clerics, the secret police, the Republican Guards—they had gotten away with too much for far too long. They had squashed dissent in the name of policing public morality. They had imprisoned, tortured, raped, and murdered those who would dare question them.

Now they claimed they had built nuclear weapons, despite every agreement to the contrary. They were threatening to launch a devastating war with Israel—a war Iran could not possibly win. Even if Israel were totally destroyed, Iran would be as well. Who would benefit from such a disaster?

What was the obsession with Israel? There were more people in the city of Tehran than in the entire country of Israel. Let them work out their own problems. Let us work out ours. We have enough problems right here to keep us busy for generations.

It was time. If no one else would stand up and put a stop to the lies, put a stop to the madness, the students would before it was too late.

"No war! No nukes!"

Up at the front, there was a makeshift stage. Some student leaders stood on the stage with megaphones, leading the chants. Suddenly, they seemed disturbed. They were looking at something to their left, away across the vast crowd.

And their chant changed.

"Resist!" a young woman on the stage shouted. "Resist!"

Without warning, she removed her dark hijab, letting her hair flow free. She waved the hijab like a flag. A roar swept through the crowd. Instantly dozens of young women and girls followed suit. Then hundreds did. Then, perhaps, thousands.

A sea of hijabs waved.

Was it too much? No! They could not punish us for showing our hair. Those days were over. Today was a new day.

But… something was happening. A commotion far to the right, coming this way.

"Resist!" the girl screamed from the stage, her voice breaking now.

Gunshots rang out. The girl onstage was shot down, with a dozen others. Were they rubber bullets? Were they real? There was blood on the stage. The dark hijab took wing like a kite, fluttering on the breeze.

People started to run. People started to scream.

The commotion was coming. It was the police. Large armored vehicles pushed slowly through the crowd, driving it forward, separating it. The vehicles had plows on mounted on the front, like snow plows. A phalanx of helmeted policemen followed the vehicles, carrying clear plastic shields, clubbing the protestors with batons.

Protestors fell before the batons. They fell under the wheels of the armored trucks.

From the left, another wave of trucks and policemen came.

The crowd was squeezed between the two approaching fronts. A giant mass of people surged backward, trying to escape it. People fell and were trampled.

The young woman fell. Someone stepped on her stomach.

She looked up at the stage. No one was there anymore. No one held a megaphone. No one shouted "Resist!" No one shouted anything.

Closer by, people screamed in fear and pain.

Far away, against the bleak overcast sky, a dark object flew, blown about by the wind. For a moment, it looked like a bird. Then it looked like what it really was—just a cast-off piece of rag.

Everywhere, people were falling. She could not rise—too many people were on top of her. She crawled a small amount, and fell under the crushing weight. Then there were new screams, louder, more urgent.

She turned. An armored vehicle was here. It moved implacably through the writhing mass of demonstrators, shoveling them to the sides like snow. She tried to crawl again. She fell, lying on her side now. She could not move. She was pinned.

In seconds, the front tire of the giant vehicle was in front of her. It was monstrous. It smelled like burning chemicals. It stopped, hesitated, reversed, then rolled forward again. The thick, notched rubber was an inch from her face.

Her entire being rebelled against what was about to happen. She screamed, louder than she had ever screamed before.

"No!"

Her scream was lost in the wall of sound around her.

She felt the heavy truck tire roll on top of her head. There was a pause—the briefest of moments—when it seemed as if the tire would just roll over her head and leave it intact. This gigantic, infernal machine—many thousands of pounds—was perched on top of her skull.

It was a miracle! She was going to survive!

And when the truck tire dropped to the ground, crushing her head—even then, for a split second, it seemed to her that she was still alive.

CHAPTER TWENTY FIVE

3:05 a.m. Eastern Standard Time
The White House Residence
Washington, DC

The clock on the kitchen wall was an ornate holdover from an earlier time.

Made of wood, its face covered in rounded glass, the numbers in Latin. It had a pendulum of yellow metal that hung down beneath the face, and which swung back and forth, softly but incessantly.

Tick, tick, tick...

A moment ago, when the clock struck III, a single gong sounded. The clock always gonged once, no matter what the hour.

Now the seconds were racing by again, the pendulum swinging, as the short, slow hour arm began its inevitable descent toward IV.

The clock was the only sound in the room.

Susan sat alone at the alcove table in the family kitchen, eating a 3 a.m. snack. Organic chocolate ice cream with frozen organic strawberries and blueberries. Plus the kind of whipped cream that sprayed out of a metal canister. That one wasn't organic. She wasn't even sure if it was really cream. But it tasted good.

She had never slept well in this old house, and tonight was no exception. Too many ghosts around every corner. True, the place had been entirely rebuilt, but the ghosts were still here. For a little while, since Stone had been staying over, she had begun to experience what she might describe as real sleep. But now?

Stone was gone. She had no idea if he was alive or dead. The world was spiraling out of control, and she was here worrying about Stone. She felt a little bit like a teenage girl—head over heels, confused, and ultimately, ineffectual.

She needed to get her head together.

The phone at her elbow rang. She looked at the number and picked it up.

"Pierre. Darling. Thanks for calling me back this late."

Susan pressed the phone to her ear as she talked. She had changed into a pair of old blue jeans, faded and ripped and perfectly fitted to her contours. She wore a light blue hooded sweatshirt that said THE BIG BOSS across the front of it. She wore big fuzzy bunny rabbit slippers. She felt like a teenager, and she was dressed like one.

She was stuck alone in this big scary house for the night, so she might as well be comfortable.

"Sweetheart," he said, and all the old feelings for her husband came flooding back. Different feelings from the ones she had for Stone, deeper, less intense, a lifetime of feelings. They had been together twenty-five years. They had two beautiful twin girls together. There was a lot of water under the bridge.

Susan stared at the clock on the wall. But it was almost as if she were looking through the wall, back into the past, to the early times she spent with Pierre. She could picture him when they met—the twenty-nine-year-old billionaire. He was beautiful, with a skinny body and big brown eyes. He looked afraid, like a deer in the headlights. His dark hair always flopped down in front of his face. He was hiding in there. It was cute.

She had made a lot of money in her career as a fashion model, several million dollars. Financially, she had been very, very comfortable. But suddenly money was no object at all. They traveled the world together. Paris, Madrid, Hong Kong, London... they always stayed in five-star hotels, and always in the most expensive suite. Astonishing views became the backdrop to her life, even more so than before. They married, and they had children, two wonderful twin girls. Then the years began to pass, and slowly they grew apart.

Susan became bored. She looked for something to do. She got into politics. Eventually, she ran for United States Senator from California. After she won, she spent much of her time in Washington, sometimes with the girls, sometimes not. Pierre managed his businesses, and increasingly, his charitable efforts in the Third World. Sometimes they didn't see each other for months.

Almost ten years ago now, Pierre called her late one night and confessed something she supposed she already knew. He was gay, and he was in a relationship.

They stayed married anyway. It was mostly for the girls, but for other reasons as well. For one thing, they were best friends. For another, it was better for both of them if the world thought they were still a couple.

The truth was, Pierre was the deep relationship of her life. She loved him totally. What was wrong with that? He was her partner. And she was his. He was a wonderful father. He was caring. He was in touch with his emotions. He was probably the smartest man she had ever met. There was nothing about their relationship that concerned her.

His boyfriends came and went. He was discreet about it, and apparently they were too. She never even knew about them.

She sighed again. Then the scandal came. Her own political party had obtained photos of him with a young man, poolside at their Malibu house. In an attempt to destroy her, they had leaked the photos to the media.

She and Pierre had weathered even that.

They were rock solid. It was more than a relationship. It was more than a marriage. It was an alliance. Pierre was completely supportive of her relationship with Stone. He was the only person she had told about it.

"It's not that late," Pierre said. "It's only midnight here."

Susan smiled. Pierre had always been a night owl. He was probably just getting revved up.

"How are you doing?" he said. "How's your man?"

"He's gone," she said.

"Oh? I'm sorry to hear that. Where did he go?"

She sighed. "Uh, I can't say."

"Meaning you don't know?"

"Meaning I can't tell you."

"Does it have something to do with… everything that's been going on?"

"I can't tell you that, either."

He paused. "Are you worried?"

She nodded. Suddenly she felt like she was ready to cry. "Yes."

"Oh, Susan."

"I know. It's stupid. He's a grown man. It's what he does. I knew that going into this. I just never really thought about…"

"It's not stupid," Pierre said. "It just isn't. You care about someone, and I'm guessing he may be in danger."

"I think he is."

"Then it's not stupid to worry. Of course you're worried."

"It's making it hard to do my job."

"What job? Oh, that President thing? Well, take a week off. Tell them you need some me-time. It's not like they're going to fire you. Nobody else wants that job."

She laughed. The past few weeks with Stone had been some of the only me-time she'd had in years.

"I've got a lot on my plate right now."

"I know you do. I've got the TV news on right now."

She didn't like the sound of that. She had unplugged from everything hours ago. No one had called her down to a meeting, so she had assumed that the situation was status quo. It was the middle of the night! Couldn't everyone just stop for a little while?

"What is it showing?"

"Students, mostly. Young people up in arms, just as they should be. We should really hand the whole thing off to them. They're ready, they're confident, they have weeks of life experience to draw on. We're just making a mess of things."

"Come on, Pierre. Tell me. I don't want to have to turn it on."

"Well, out here, we've got campus sit-ins and protests at Berkeley and USC. They've got bottle-throwing riots up in Portland and Seattle. As I mentioned, it's early. These things could go all night."

"What are they protesting?"

"Oh, you know, Israel."

"Israel?"

"Yeah, the students want the universities to divest their endowment funds from anything having to do with Israel. No Israeli companies, no American companies that do business in Israel, no Israeli bond issues, no Israeli real estate trusts or Israeli investment managers. The rioters want Portland and Seattle, not to mention Oregon and Washington, to do the same, only with their pension funds."

Susan shook her head. "Israel's under attack, last time I checked."

"In more ways than one, I'd say."

Susan let out a long breath. "Okay. That's okay. The kids are letting their voices be heard."

"That's not all."

"Tell me." She caught herself using Stone's little catchphrase.

"There was a large antiwar protest at the University of Tehran. It started a couple of hours ago. It's daytime over there. The police and Iranian military broke it up. Seems like a number of the kids got killed, either shot by the cops or trampled in the ensuing melee. Hundreds of people were arrested."

Susan put her head in her hands. She thought of the conditions in Iranian prisons Kurt had been talking about earlier. She thought of how the kids over here were protesting against Israel, while the Iranian kids were protesting against their own government. Whose side was anybody on? She thought of how Stone was somewhere in Iran at this moment. Would the unrest help him or hinder him? She had no idea.

"Listen, how are the girls?" she said, changing the subject. She couldn't think about these large-scale problems right now. They always came back to Stone somehow.

"Beautiful, of course."

"What are they up to?"

"Well, they're getting ready for their big DC Christmas trip. And they're thinking they want to get into modeling. Just like Mom."

Susan's hands rubbed her forehead. "Oh God, Pierre. They're fourteen years old."

"Mom was fifteen when she started. So I keep hearing."

"It's an evil business. I can't…"

"Times have changed."

"Pierre!"

"Hear me out on this, Susan. It's not like when you were a kid. They don't have to go anywhere. They don't have to deal with anyone. We let them create an Instagram account. My people monitor the account, vet the comments, delete anything problematic. Watch for stalkers. We run everything by the Secret Service. The girls wear nice clothes, nothing too sexy. They take selfies, so we don't even need a photographer. They're beautiful girls, and they're the daughters of the President. Can you imagine how many followers they would get? Can you imagine how many designers would love to hang their new products on them? I'll handle any contracts that might come up. It'll be a good experience. They think they can make money at this, and I think they're right."

"They don't need money, Pierre."

"Everybody needs money, Susan."

Susan shook her head. Another thing to worry about. Another thing to obsess over. Was he crazy? He must have gone insane. "Honey, I hate this idea. Okay? I hate it. Michaela was kidnapped less than three years ago. Can we please just—"

"I promise there is no danger. And I think the idea will grow on you."

She nodded. "It will grow on me. Like a fungus. Like a toxic mold. It is going to grow on me and infect me, and make me deathly ill."

He seemed to hesitate.

"Pierre…" she began.

"I already told them yes."

CHAPTER TWENTY SIX

4:45 p.m. Tehran Time (8:45 a.m. Eastern Standard Time)
South Tehran, Iran

"He is being watched, so we must be careful."

They moved down an alleyway in the darkness, three big shadows. Luke and Ed followed Ari. The days were short this time of year. The sun had dropped behind the mountains to the west nearly an hour before, so it was already like night.

They had spent the day inside the truck, parked among dozens of similar trucks, near a slaughterhouse on the outskirts of the city. Luke's straw bed had been plenty comfortable—with the cool early winter air blowing through the slats of the trailer, and the body heat given off by the sheep, it had been the best rest he had gotten in a while.

Now they were in a residential district in an older part of the city, a crowded slum. The city streets were on lockdown—military vehicles everywhere, checkpoints set up at major intersections. Ari had navigated here almost entirely through back alleyways—using a map of the city that existed only in his mind.

He stopped and turned to face them.

He spoke barely above a whisper. "This is it. When we go in, you just want to stay quiet. He will not trust you. Also, my Farsi is quite good, but I need to listen carefully. I can't have three conversations going on at once."

"Your gig, boss," Ed said.

Luke nodded. "Got it."

The kid was good. He was smoothly efficient, confident, highly skilled. He had gotten them inside Iran, halfway across the country, then through a locked down city, all without a hitch. He didn't seem to bear a grudge about the fight. And the man they were meeting here was his informant. As far as Luke was concerned, their job was to stay out of his way until he needed them.

"Watch how I go, then follow behind me. Don't stay out here. It's much better to be inside."

"Of course."

There was an iron fence near them, with vertical bars topped by sharp points. Ari turned and went up the fence, using his arm strength. When he reached the top, he stepped across the points, lightly, like a dancer, until he reached the bricks of the building next door. Then he went up the brick face like a spider, his fingers finding holds where none seemed to exist. There was a half open window on the second floor. He slid inside of it and was gone.

Luke looked at Ed.

Ed shook his head. "Man, those spikes are gonna go right through my feet, I know it. I outweigh that boy by at least sixty pounds."

"Let's go," Luke said. "I'll try to open that window for you a little more."

Moments later, they were inside as well.

It was a dark apartment, lights off and cold inside. The place was a warren, cluttered with bookcases and furniture, stacks of boxes and old magazines. Luke and Ed wound their way through the shadows and gloom.

Up ahead, in front of a window facing the street, Luke spotted Ari's silhouette. He stood next to an armchair, itself facing out the window.

"Ari?" Luke whispered.

"Yes. Here."

"Where's the informer?"

"He's here, too."

Luke moved through the dark to the armchair, Ed two steps behind him.

The man was leaning back in the chair, his head tilted way back, his throat slit from ear to ear. The skin of his face had turned black. His wrists and forearms were bound to the arms of the chair with some kind of wire. Luke looked at it closely. The wire was sharp, and had cut through the man's shirt sleeves and through the meat of his lower arms. Red slices crisscrossed his forearms—the blood had dried some time ago.

"Ed?"

"Yeah."

"How long has he been dead?"

Ed shrugged. "Without any gear with me, and in the dark like this, it's hard to say. The body is stiff, with pronounced discoloration of the face and hands. No obvious putrefaction at this time, but the cold air in here has probably slowed that down. This place is like an icebox. Twelve hours, at a broad guess."

"He was a good man," Ari said. "He wanted to change things."

"What does that time frame mean to us?" Luke said.

"It means they killed him before we got here."

"Did they know we were coming?"

Ari shook his head. "Not necessarily. A man like this has probably been under suspicion a long time. They may have killed him just to be on the safe side."

"What do we do now?" Ed said.

Ari shrugged. "I don't know. He wasn't supposed to be dead."

"You *don't know*? Is there anyone else we can talk to? Or is this the only one?"

Luke didn't like the idea of this. They had done a high altitude night jump into Iran, sneaked their way across the country in a truck full of sheep, to talk to a guy who was dead? With a nuclear war looming?

"There is one other," Ari said. "If anything, he would know much more than this man. But he's locked away in prison."

"All right," Ed said. "I guess we're going to prison then."

"How do we get inside?" Luke said.

Ari shook his head. "We don't. It's impossible."

Luke pulled out his satellite phone. "Nothing is impossible."

CHAPTER TWENTY SEVEN

4:03 p.m. Israel Time (5:03 p.m. Tehran Time, 9:03 a.m. Eastern Standard Time)
Tel Aviv, Israel

"It's called Evin Prison," Luke said through Swann's headset. "I need a layout, I need a way inside, and if possible I need to know a prisoner location."

Swann and Trudy were sitting in Swann's hotel suite at the Hilton. The room was on the tenth floor, and had sweeping views of the Mediterranean out the bay windows. The sun was already far to the west, slowly sinking into the sea.

"Evin Prison," Swann said to Trudy.

They had set up Swann's room as a makeshift command center. A bank of three laptops sat on a long fold-out table against the wall. Their rig was on the Internet through an encrypted satellite link-up that Swann had designed himself. Outside of the electricity, they were dependent on nothing from the hotel. If they had to, they could run on batteries. Swann had swept the room three times for bugs as much as was feasible. He had taken all the listening devices he found out onto the balcony and dropped them ten stories into the empty pool.

The detritus of food containers littered the areas around the computers. He and Trudy had taken all of their meals here, waiting for a call from Luke.

Stone's satellite phone used a voice scrambler at his end, then bounced up to a black satellite, back to earth at a CIA undercover op site in Pakistan, then around the world—China, Japan, New Zealand, Brazil, Morocco, and finally here, before the voice was unscrambled. Anyone who keyed in on Stone in Iran and managed to trace the call would think he was calling Pakistan, and they wouldn't be able to make out what he was saying. The security measures created an odd delaying effect, and made Stone's voice sound like a robot calling from the bottom of a tin can.

Before Swann had done anything, Trudy had already pulled up the name of the prison.

"Evin Prison?" she said. "He wants to go into Evin Prison?"

Swann was on his computer. "What's the location?"

"North Tehran. In a neighborhood called Evin. Right up against the foothills of the Alborz Mountains, and just north of Sa'adat Abad."

"Got it."

She turned her monitor toward him. The monitor showed him a bleak image of sheer gray walls, four stories high, with looping razor wire running along the top. She showed him another image of a similar wall in a different location. She showed him an image of the main entrance—a steel gate with a manned checkpoint and machine gun pillboxes on either side.

"It's the place they send political prisoners to be tortured," Trudy said. "Everything I'm pulling up makes it sound straight out of *Midnight Express*."

"Uh, Luke? At first blink, it doesn't look good."

"Keep blinking," Luke's robot voice said. "Until it starts looking better. I also need information on a man named Hamid Bahman. He's inside that prison, and I need to know where. We don't want to be wandering around the hallways, calling out his name."

"Hamid Bahman," Swann said.

"Who is he?" Trudy said.

He shook his head. "I don't know. That's for you to figure out."

"What's the place look like from the sky?" Luke said.

"I don't know, Luke. You have to give me a minute."

"Okay. But one more thing. I have an idea. I need to know if people hang glide around here, and if they do, where they buy their gear."

Swann looked at Trudy. His shoulders slumped. She wasn't wearing his headset, so she had no idea what Luke was saying.

Trudy was scrolling through a wall of data and shaking her head. "Yeah, he doesn't want to go in there. This is the list of people executed inside those walls. It's a long list. Here's an account of the various tortures used. It's pretty long, too. Whipping of the soles of the feet."

"Ouch," Swann said. He didn't really want to hear about the tortures. It cut a little close to home for him.

"Whipping of the back," Trudy said, beginning to move through the list in a kind of singsong, matter-of-fact way. "Submersion in water. Electrocution. Crushing of the hands and feet. Cigarette burns. Flaying of the skin. Rape. Forced confessions broadcast on TV and radio. Forced participation in the execution of other prisoners. Mock executions."

Swann felt the goose bumps rise along his back.

"Hmmm. In terms of actual executions, they apparently just did away with stoning in 2010. No rush. They still throw prisoners off the roof and into the streets surrounding the prison, though. Four stories ought to do it. Firing squads are still done. Hmmm. Sometimes they hang especially well-known prisoners from gallows above the prison walls. You can see the body hanging from the streets below. Here he is, guys."

"Trudy, are you done?"

She nodded. "Yeah. It's just interesting."

"Luke, I'm going to call you back," Swann said.

"Okay, but don't take your time."

Swann nodded. "I wouldn't have it any other way."

* * *

They worked steadily, barely speaking. Within fifteen minutes, they had put it all together.

"Hamid Bahman," Trudy said. "Fifty-two years old. Former nuclear physicist. I say former because I don't think he'll be going back to work. He's been sentenced to life in prison. Suspicion of treason. He's been inside for three years. Eighteen months ago, Amnesty International announced concern for his welfare, claiming that their information suggested his health was faltering rapidly."

"Where is he?"

"The notorious Section 209. That's the torture wing. My data suggest he is in cell C31, where he is kept in solitary confinement."

Swann nodded. "Good. I've got a layout. I see 209 here, though I can't see the cell numbers. They'll just have to find that cell when they get inside."

The satellite phone rang. Swann pressed the answer button.

"I thought you were going to call me back," Luke said.

"I was. We weren't done yet. Where are you?"

"Walking through alleyways, trying not to stay in one place for any length of time."

"I've got the layout for you," Swann said. "A layout of the larger prison, along with one of Section 209, which is the wing you're looking for. But you'll need a way to receive it, like a smartphone. Obviously one that's operational on an Iranian network, but also that no one has ever used before. When the layout comes in from a satellite link, I'm guessing that phone is going to become hot rather quickly."

"No good," Luke said. "It's not like we can walk into a store and buy a cell phone. We don't exist, and we don't want to call attention to ourselves. Anyone on the street we steal a phone from, eventually the government will trace it, and we'll bring the ayatollahs down on the heads of some innocent person. I'll have to call you from there, and you'll just have to guide me through."

"Okay," Swann said, anticipating Luke's next thought. "About the roof, it could work. It's a large building, with as many as fifteen thousand prisoners at any one time. The roof is long, with several stairwell doors that open out to it, including one above Section 209. And people do hang glide in Tehran, it turns out. They do it all the time. One place they jump from is the mountain cliffs above the North Shahran neighborhood, less than three miles west of the prison. And I've got a list of adventure outfitters you could hit that carry that kind of gear. I don't understand how you plan to land, though. I mean, the guards are bound to spot hang gliders coming in low like that, aren't they?"

Luke's tinny robot voice sounded far away. "We're not going to come in low."

"What? I don't know what you—"

"You ever been hang gliding… Albert?"

Swann nearly laughed. Luke had called him by his old alias, Albert Helu. During Swann's paranoid days, he had started insisting on it.

"Yeah. I have. Quite a few times, actually.

"Well, I thought of a new way of doing it."

"Luke…"

"Don't worry," Luke said. "Just leave that part to me."

CHAPTER TWENTY EIGHT

9:20 a.m. Eastern Standard Time
The Situation Room
The White House, Washington, DC

"Agent Luke Stone is alive and has infiltrated Iran."

Susan had walked into the room moments before, and Kurt had just called the meeting to order. The morning had been quiet so far. The fighting in Israel continued apace. The riots in Berkeley and Portland had spun out of control, but the one in Seattle had ended peacefully. The Iranians had crushed their own dissenters, and had imposed martial law across the country.

Susan had barely slept. The heavy paper cup in her hand was her third dose of java in the past half an hour.

Kurt had been going through a list of updates. Susan had been sipping her coffee. Aides and staffers were scrolling through websites and shuffling pages. Haley Lawrence was whispering to a young aide. Kat Lopez had been here a moment ago, giving Susan the rundown on the day's schedule, but now she was gone.

"Israeli troops have penetrated Lebanon to within twenty miles of Beirut," Kurt said. "Significant losses on both sides, and still no sign of the missing soldier. Hezbollah has managed to continue rocket attacks against northern Israel, despite heavy aerial bombardment by the IAF. Hamas is launching homemade rockets from Gaza, with little effectiveness. All border crossings from Gaza and the West Bank have been sealed by Israel, Jordan, and Egypt. Also, as you know, Iran has issued a threat against the American airbase outside Doha, in Qatar, as well as our embassy in Baghdad. Those are important and we need to get to them. I recommend putting that—"

Susan looked up and raised her hand.

"Kurt, what did you say about Luke Stone?"

Kurt looked at Susan, perhaps a few seconds too long. There was something in his eyes, but Susan couldn't say what it was.

"We received a status report from his intelligence team in Tel Aviv. Stone and two other operatives, one American and one Israeli, have successfully infiltrated Iran, and made their way to

Tehran. They have been in touch. The Israeli asset in Tehran they were going to meet is dead, probably murdered by the regime. Stone requested further information from his intelligence people, and apparently move on to question another possible source within Iran."

Kurt paused.

"Who is the source?" Susan said.

Kurt shook his head. He glanced around the room. "I don't know if this is the venue."

"Out with it, Kurt," Susan said. "There aren't any loose lips in here."

Susan looked around herself. Most people in the room seemed tired, distracted, just waking up or pulling themselves together.

"Hamid Bahman," Kurt said. "Former physicist for the Iranian regime, and one of the architects of the Iranian nuclear weapons program. He's been in Evin Prison for the past three years. Amnesty International and Human Rights Watch have both issued official communiqués, condemning his treatment and sounding the alarm for his well-being. No one has any idea if he's even alive or dead. The Iranians haven't presented evidence that he's alive for more than eighteen months."

"Where do they plan to interview him?" Haley Lawrence said. "In prison?"

Kurt nodded. "Yes."

"I meant that as a joke," Lawrence said.

Kurt shrugged. "I know. But we're talking about Luke Stone."

"Is it dangerous?" Susan said. "What Stone is doing?"

She felt like a fool saying these things in front of Kurt, and in front of all these people. She felt like a schoolgirl with a crush. She felt too distracted to make sense of anything that was happening.

Kurt raised his hands. "Susan, with all respect, we have other, more pressing agenda items to attend to. Yes, it's dangerous. It's insane, actually. If he's alive, Bahman is being held at Evin Prison, which is one of the facilities Iran uses for torturing dissidents. No one has ever broken out of Evin Prison, and while we don't have any hard data about it, I'd be willing to bet that no one has ever successfully broken in there, either."

Susan stared at him. She was still relieved to know that Stone was alive—so relieved, in fact, that most of what Kurt had just said went in her right ear, passed straight through her head, and exited out her left ear.

Stone. He had made it into Iran. Now he was going inside a prison. It didn't make sense! People didn't break into prisons.

Kurt continued. "Susan, I'd like to redirect this conversation. I think we need to focus on a contingency plan for if Iran carries through on its threat to attack Doha. We have ten thousand servicemen and women stationed at the air base there, along with another twenty thousand family members living on the base and nearby."

A man in dress greens, a three-star general, raised a hand. Normally, generals from the Pentagon sat straight upright, like they had an iron rod inserted in their backs, but this man slouched to his left, his chin in his hand. His other hand held a Styrofoam cup of coffee. In fact, he was the most unstraightened general Susan had ever seen.

"General Kirby?"

"Madam President, I'm Nat Kirby, United States Army Intelligence."

"General, thanks for being here."

"Oh, you're welcome. And nothing against Stone—I knew him when he was a young man in Delta Force. He was an excellent soldier, one of the best, and I'm sure he's still an exceptional covert operator. But he's on a fool's errand and a suicide mission. Breaking into Evin Prison? Stone was always a little bit of a cowboy. One of these days he's going to get himself killed. With that in mind, I'd suggest that we do two things. One is to put a plan in place for plausible denial of Stone's operation, in the very real eventuality—"

"That's been done," Kurt said. "The Israeli commando on Stone's team has no identity—a so-called ghost in spy craft parlance. For Stone and his partner Ed Newsam, we've planted false DNA and fingerprint data with the Pakistani ISI, the Egyptian secret police, and Interpol—the three likeliest places the Iranians will turn for information. If the Iranians bother to look, they will discover that Newsam and Stone are private intelligence contractors, seeking inside information on the Iranian energy industry."

Susan didn't like the sound of this. Stone hadn't mentioned anything about a cover story in case he was captured.

The general nodded. "Good. Second thing is rather than wait for Iran to attack Doha, or to fire nukes at Israel, we need to start talking about a preemptive strike. We can't wait around for Stone to find out if Iran has nuclear weapons. We should just assume they do, worst-case scenario, and consider engaging them with a massive, overwhelming attack, or a decapitation strike aimed at their leadership."

He raised a bound sheaf of paper from the table in front of him.

"I've brought an intelligence assessment of both options. I'd like to summarize its findings, if I may."

Kurt looked at Susan.

"Susan?"

Susan shook her head. "I'd like to ask a question of the general."

"Of course."

She looked at him. Stared at him, in fact. She tried to make her eyes hard. She tried to frighten him, though she knew it wouldn't do any good. Kirby knew the deal about Susan—they all did. The generals she'd fired, the time she put the Chairman of the Joint Chiefs of Staff in prison for treason. Kirby didn't care. He was slumped so low, and leaning so far to one side, that his face seemed ready to slide off sideways onto the floor.

"Are you really in the United States Army?" she wanted to say. *"I've never seen anyone in the Army with such bad posture."*

She kept that in check, however.

"Tell me something," she said instead. "This is where you inform me that we have no good options, right? That we should bomb them back to the stone age when they least expect it, killing tens of millions of people, but they'll get some of their own missiles out anyway, killing a few million Israelis and everyone at Doha, and the Persian Gulf will become a lake of fire for the next seven generations. Is that about it?"

Kirby looked at the report on the desk in front of him. His fingers did a funny sort of dance across its surface, like five stubby ballerinas.

"I commend your acumen, Madam President. You're not that far off, actually. It's really not an ideal situation."

Susan felt the anger rising inside of her. She resented this. The constant drumbeats for war. All the countries with all their endless battles with each other. The generals with their dispassionate reports concerning abstract future bloodbaths.

"General," she began, "why is it that every time we have a crisis, someone comes in here from the Pentagon, waves a booklet in my face, and tells me we need to start bombing people? Why don't you guys ever have a report to share about a possible negotiated settlement?"

He shrugged. He didn't seem the slightest bit nonplussed, or even surprised, by her question. He didn't attempt to sit up straight. In another minute, if the trajectory of his slouch continued, he might disappear under the conference table.

“Madam, we’re the military. Bombing people is our job. We’re very good at it. If you want to send the Iranians flowers, I think you’d better call a florist.”

CHAPTER TWENTY NINE

7:30 p.m. Tehran Time (11:30 a.m. Eastern Standard Time)
Evin Prison
Tehran

Ed had never been hang gliding before.

That turned out to be just as well because there were only two gliding rigs to steal from the adventure store. The shop, which had closed at 5 p.m. (and which they had entered through a back door fifteen minutes after the owner had locked up), was like a hopeful combination of Eastern Mountain Sports and some church basement fundraising sale—they had plenty of outdoor gear you could buy, but a lot of it seemed left over from back when Junior was in middle school.

They did have parachutes, though, a whole mess of them.

They had carried the whole mess up into the foothills above a modern college campus in the North Shahran neighborhood. It had started to snow, a wet early season precipitation—heavy, almost as much rain as snow. Luke gazed out at the lights of the vast city. Visibility was dropping. He couldn't decide if that was good or bad.

"What did you say you weigh again?" he said.

Ed shrugged. "Two-forty, let's say."

Luke calculated his own 195 and Ed's alleged 240. He didn't even count the guns Ed was carrying, or the rolled-up fire ladder Luke had inside the gear bag strapped to his back. "Four hundred and thirty five pounds, that's heavy." The hang gliding rig was old. It was very heavy, yet somehow flimsy and rickety at the same time.

"Two-forty? You sure?"

"Call it two-fifty."

Luke shook his head. Icy granules were clinging to his beard. The wind seemed to slip straight through his windbreaker jacket. "This is going to be a short flight."

To their right, the kid was ready. He was staring at them.

"Laurel and Hardy, am I right? That was the old American comedy team."

Luke looked at Ari. "You know where this place is?"

Ari nodded. "I know exactly where it is."

"You know the deal? Come in off the city streets pretty high—twenty-five hundred feet. When you get over the roof, unclip from your rig, ditch, wait a beat, then throw your parachute. You will come down hard. Twenty seconds max, if my calculations are right, probably less than that. These chutes aren't for jumping—they're for saving your neck when all systems fail. With any luck, when you hit the roof, you won't go right through it."

"Where are you going to be?" Ari said.

"Right behind you. When we see you jump, we're going to do the same thing five seconds later. We'll try not to land on your head."

Ari smiled. He looked at the two of them, sharing a glider. "What if you crash into the side of a building?"

"Keep going. Infiltrate the prison, do the interview, and when you get back out, come peel us off the bricks."

"With pleasure. I will use a pressure washer."

Abruptly, Ari lifted his rig and ran full-tilt for the cliff. Even before he reached the edge, just as the hill began to slope downward, he jumped, using his core strength to lift and extend his legs backward. He hooked in, and was gone in flight.

"Went right up like a bird," Ed said.

"That's what we're about to do," Luke said. "Probably with less grace, though."

"We gonna run together?"

Luke nodded. "Yes. How's your chute?"

Ed patted his chest. "It's in there. Doesn't look like much, I can say that."

"It'll hold you," Luke said.

"How do you know?"

Luke stared at him. "Honestly? I don't. I just said that." He shook his head. "That store was like…"

"1973," Ed offered.

"Yeah. And not in a good way."

Ed gestured with his head. "The kid is far ahead."

"I know. It's a bad habit. He's like a dog I used to have. Just a little bit too enthusiastic. I hope I don't have to put him down after this." He looked at Ed again. "You ready?"

"Yes."

"Go!"

They ran, side by side, on either end of the bar. The cliff approached, then came closer and closer. The snow drove down hard. For a second, Luke thought they would reach the cliff before the glider gained lift. Then he felt it pull away from the earth.

"Jump!" he shouted. "Jump!"

Then they were up, out over nothing. The cliff fell away behind them. Luke kicked his legs back and clipped in. Ed held himself up with arm and shoulder strength alone, his thick legs dangling. The glider listed badly to the right, pulling toward Ed's side. There was too much weight on that side. Luke steered hard left, to no avail.

"Ed! Move toward the center."

Ed bounced toward the center, the glider turning and tilting like a dying quail.

"Kick your legs back, man."

Luke had rigged a second hook for Ed's legs. Ed swung back, feeling with his feet, finding the hook.

With the weight more evenly distributed, Luke had better control. He turned a sharp left toward the east, following Ari, who was like a Batman shadow far ahead. Ari was tilted upward, gaining altitude despite the heavy snow. Luke did the same, pushing the glider higher. The city sprawled outward to their right, the high mountains climbing to their left.

"This is a quick trip, so don't get comfortable."

Ed shook his head. "Believe me, I am not comfortable."

The snow spit down, icy, sharp. It was good, Luke decided. Low visibility was good. Who would scan the skies for hang gliders on a night like this? Who could even spot them?

Up ahead, Ari veered left toward the mountains. Suddenly, he dropped away from his glider. He fell straight down like a bomb. A second passed, two, three...

"Oh, man. Don't tell me his chute..."

The chute opened, white against the dark of the sky. It didn't seem to fill. An instant later, it disappeared into the falling snow.

"Did he make it?" Ed said.

Luke shook his head. "His chute opened. It looked like maybe... I don't know. That looked terrible. Whose idea was this?"

The empty glider was still in flight, headed straight into the mountains. Perfect. Certainly, it would crash to the ground a minute or less from now. But if it flew far enough, it might be days before anyone found it.

"You just reach inside your suit and throw that chute out," Luke said. "Just like I showed you. Got it?"

Ed didn't seem sure. "Yeah, man. I don't know. I gotta think about—"

Luke shook his head. "There's no time for thinking. You just gotta trust me and go."

Ed stared at him.

"Go!" Luke shouted.

In one fluid movement, Ed unhooked his legs and swung forward like a gymnast. The glider wrenched crazily. Then Ed was gone.

Luke looked down. It seemed that Ed was just below him for a second, then he wasn't. Had his chute opened? Luke wasn't sure. He couldn't see much in all the snow. He couldn't see the building down there at all.

Should he circle back around? No. The more time he spent up here, the better the chance somebody would see him. He had no idea what awaited him down there. He had no idea what had happened to Ed.

"He who hesitates," he said.

He unhooked his legs, swung forward, and let go.

Instantly, he was dropping very fast. The glider was gone.

One second. Two.

Three.

He reached inside the chest of his flight suit with his right hand, fumbled for the emergency chute. It wouldn't come out! There was no time for this. He used both hands.

Come on! Come on!

He looked between his feet. There was the roof, or the ground. He had no idea. Coming fast.

The chute was stuck. He pulled. It wouldn't…

He was just gonna…

He wrenched it out. It went up.

Open! Please!

The chute opened above him. It was small. The pull was not hard, not like a real parachute. There was a sense of slowing down, decelerating, maybe not enough. He looked down again—the surface was coming…

Super fast.

Fast.

But not that fast.

Please don't rip.

There was no time to look at anything. Here it came. He hit.

It was jarring. Bone-rattling. He bent his legs and fell backward, rolling onto his butt and then his back. The snow was soft. The surface of the building was hard. The chute came down on top of him, not drifting, but falling. It covered his body like a shroud. Fifteen seconds, the drop took. Definitely not twenty. Barely more than ten from the time the chute opened.

That was loud. Did anyone hear that?

He lay in the snow in the dark. For what seemed like a long time, he didn't move. As his heartbeat slowed and the adrenaline coursing through him subsided, he did a mental scan of his body, looking for any pain, any sense of something broken, a puncture wound, anything bad. There was nothing. He wiggled his fingers and toes. They moved easily. No major nerves were severed. He was okay.

He pushed the parachute away and looked up. Ed and Ari stood there, staring down at him. They were not smiling.

"You alive?" Ed said.

Luke nodded. "I think so. Yeah."

"Good, because I'm about to kill your ass. That was the dumbest, most suicidal thing you ever had me do."

"Are we on top of the prison?"

Ari nodded. "Yes."

"See? It worked."

* * *

"I can't see anything," Swann's tinny robot voice said. "Too much cloud cover."

Swann was trying to pull up real-time footage of their location from a spy satellite.

"It's snowing here," Luke said. He was standing at the edge of a low parapet and looking down. Three stories below him, there was a narrow street. Actually, more like a road. It ran between the prison and the mountains—the foothills climbed steeply away from the prison right across that street. There was no one around. If they made it back out of the prison, he would hook the fold-up fire ladder on the wall here and throw it over the side. With a little luck, then they would climb down and be gone.

"Snowing?" Swann said. "That's nice. Christmas is coming."

Luke shook his head. "So how do we do this, Swann?"

"Okay. The building goes lengthwise roughly in an east-west direction. According to earlier imagery I have, there are ten stairwell doors on the roof. The stairwell to Section 209 is the third one from the eastern end of the building. Get that door open, then take the stairs down to the level just below the roof, C-level. Trudy thinks you are looking for cell C31 in Section 209. Bahman, if he's still alive, should be in that cell."

"Any idea about the security situation?" Luke said.

"Guards, I would guess," Swann said. "Armed guards."

"Yeah. Good point."

Luke hung up the phone. Ari and Ed were already standing by the door to the stairwell. The doorway protruded from the roof. Above it was a small fiberglass canopy. It was a steel door, gunmetal gray in color, with a rounded handle and what looked like a heavy duty lock embedded below the handle.

"If we blow the lock," Ed said, "this is gonna be a party very fast."

"If we shoot it, same thing," Ari said.

Luke had a funny feeling about that door, however. Beneath the canopy, very little snow had accumulated. The ends of discarded cigarettes littered the ground here. The guards, other workers, maybe even the prisoners, came up here for smoke breaks. Would they risk locking themselves outside? Especially when there was no way any outsiders could come from this direction?

Who in their right mind would break *into* a prison, anyway?

Luke grabbed the handle and pulled. The door opened easily and without a sound. Inside, an iron slatted stairwell led down to the next level.

"After you guys," Luke said. "No guns, all right?"

Ari pulled a six-inch serrated knife from a sheath on his belt.

Luke nodded. "Nice one."

Ed cracked his knuckles.

Luke reached to his calf and unstrapped the hunting knife he kept there. They were going in quiet. Any shooting of guards would just bring more guards. Now that they were in, the next goal was to get back out.

Ed moved down the stairwell first. His feet made no noise on the iron rung. For a big man, he moved like a cat.

They went fast. At the bottom of the stairs was a landing. They were in a small foyer area, with a door to the cellblock.

Be open, Luke thought.

Ed touched the handle, pulled it the slightest bit. It moved an inch—it was unlocked. The security in this building was atrocious, not like an American prison at all, where every twenty feet you came to another locked door.

There was a man on the other side of the door. They had all seen him. He wore a drab green uniform. Could be more than one guard there.

Ed, Ari, and Luke all looked at each other. They didn't say a word. Luke indicated the door, then tapped his own chest. He pointed at Ed and put his hand over his mouth. He pointed at Ari and indicated the knife. They both nodded.

Luke held up one finger. Two. Three.

He opened the door.

Ed surged through the opening. The guard was there, a big guy. He turned, just in time to get hit by a human tidal wave. Ed grabbed him, spun him around, and covered his mouth with his huge hand. The man's eyes were WIDE.

Ari was there half a second later. He plunged his knife into the man's chest. He did it fast, like a piston, like a prison fighter with a shiv, the knife plunging in, coming out, plunging in, coming out, plunging in, hitting everything, severing everything. Ten times he stabbed the man. Then he did ten more, moving down to his intestines, just in case his heart and lungs weren't dead already. Thorough.

Ed continued to hold him as he died, continued to cover his mouth. He eased him slowly to the floor. The man never made a sound.

Luke moved past them into the hallway. This was the cellblock. The hall was narrow, dim, painted a dingy shade of white. He scanned the walls and ceilings for cameras. He didn't see any. Up ahead, the hall turned a corner. At the top, embedded in the angle of the turn, there was a rounded security mirror—in the fish-eye mirror, a man rushed up the hall toward him, pulling his gun.

They met right at the turn.

Luke flicked his knife out, drawing a quick smile straight across the man's throat, right to left.

The guard stared at Luke. Their eyes locked. The man had a full second to contemplate the horror of what had just happened to him. Then the bleeding started.

"Gluck," the man said. "Guh!"

Luke had nicked the carotid artery and the jugular. Blood sprayed out in dual jets. He stepped back from it as the man sank to the floor, a hand clamped to the side of his neck, to no avail. There was already a lot of blood, and there was going to be a whole lot more. The guy was a one-man abattoir, a slaughterhouse.

"Whew," Luke said quietly. It would have been nice to take the man's uniform, but that was out of the question now. That thing was soaked.

A hand landed on Luke's shoulder and he jumped.

"Impressive," Ari said. "Quite a little dance."

"Yeah. And I barely even know the guy. We really just met."

Ari stepped over the corpse, reached on his tiptoes to the security mirror, and yanked it down. There was nothing behind it. He dropped the mirror onto the body.

"So much for security."

Ed came up behind them, carrying the other guard's key ring.

"C31," he said. "Right? Let's do this, man. This place gives me the willies. I feel like I'm on a submarine."

They moved through the corridor in single file, passing heavy steel doors on either side, each painted white. The building was old—the doors were on big rollers, like barn doors from an earlier time. Each cell's number was in both Persian and English. Why was that? Luke glanced at a small engraved plaque visible on one of the doors—the edges were gooped in white paint, but the center had never been painted over.

Cuyahoga Steel Door, Incorporated—Cleveland Ohio, 1901.

Nice. American made, and built to last. Still working fine, more than a century later. There were no windows in the doors, and there was no sound coming from any of the cells. It smelled in here, like an open sewer.

"Is this place even open for business?" Ed whispered.

They came to the door. C31.

He jangled through his keys, looking for the one that matched the Persian script above the doorway. He kept glancing at the keys, then back up at the door.

"Man, this alphabet is gibberish."

After a moment, Ari's hand snaked out and a grabbed a key.

"This one."

Ed shrugged. He slipped it into the lock and opened it. Then he slid back the door.

A man lay on the cement floor. He was thin, bordering on emaciated, shivering and curled into a ball. His striped prison uniform was ragged and threadbare, and it was cold in here. His feet were bare and the color of eggplant. His hair was long and matted, and his beard was thick and unruly. The cell was narrow, with no furniture. In one corner was a green bucket, nearly full with human excrement. The man barely looked up as Luke stepped inside.

"Ed, watch those hallways. Anybody comes, they die. Quietly if possible."

"Naturally. Quiet as a church mouse."

Luke kneeled to one side of the man. Ari stood over them.

"Hamid Bahman?" Luke said.

The man stared at him, his deep-set eyes nearly blank. His head was like a skull, the skin cracked like old paper. His mouth opened.

Most of his teeth were gone. There were small round scars everywhere on his exposed skin, like little craters. Luke had seen it before. Burn scars, and lots of them. People had been burning this man with cigarettes, on a regular basis, and for a long time. Luke suspected that was probably the least of it.

This was the guy, the prominent nuclear physicist who was going to lead them to the missile sites?

The man spoke, his trembling voice barely above a whisper. Luke knew enough Farsi to understand what he said.

"Who wants to know?"

Luke glanced up at Ari. Ari said something in rapid-fire Farsi. The man nodded.

"It's him," Ari said.

"What happened to him?"

Ari spoke again, and the man responded. The man spoke slowly and simply, as though he were a child. It was easy enough for Luke to follow.

"I am a traitor," he said. "I must be punished."

"What did you do?" Luke said.

The man shook his head and closed his eyes.

Luke repeated the question. "What did you do?"

Tears began to spill out from behind the man's closed eyelids. "I don't know," he whispered. "They won't tell me."

He body shook with silent sobs. The guy had been broken, then broken again. He had been broken so badly, and so many times, there was barely anything left of him. The Iranians were doing a Joseph Stalin experiment in human rights violations. Luke knew that before coming here, intellectually, but it was still a bit of a shock to see it up close.

He thought of all those silent cells they had passed, all filled with broken men just like this one. Then he thought of this whole sprawling building, blocks and blocks long, three stories high, thousands of cells. No wonder internal security was lax. None of these prisoners were a threat to anyone. They couldn't even get up off the floor.

Luke stood. "Ask him if he knows anything."

Ari squatted and began speaking to the man. The man responded with simple answers. They spoke for several moments. Luke poked his head out into the hall.

"How we looking?"

Ed was down the corridor several feet, at a corner where it made another turn. His head turned back and forth, watching the next hallway, and also watching back the way they came.

"Okay for now. But I'd say let's get this thing moving. We ain't got all night."

Luke looked back into the cell. As he watched, Ari opened a plastic wrapper and gave Bahman a small blue and white pill. Bahman brought the pill to his mouth, his bony hand shaking uncontrollably. With what looked like a lot of effort, he swallowed the pill, his head wrenching back, his throat working. It went down.

Ari patted the man on the shoulder and murmured something. The man nodded. Ari stood and turned.

"Let's go."

"What was that pill?"

Ari stared ahead. His eyes were hard. "That was my cyanide tablet. It's very fast acting, no coating, releases right into the bloodstream. He doesn't want to live anymore, and I don't blame him. You wouldn't want to know the things they've been doing to this man. And I don't care to repeat them."

Luke nodded. They weren't going to be able to drag this shivering wretch along with them. Not out into the cold, not really anywhere. They weren't going to be able to find him medical care. They would never get him out of the country alive.

"Okay," he said. "Did he give you anything?"

"He has no idea where the missiles are, or if they even exist. He doesn't remember if the nuclear weapons program was real or a hoax. Everything is just a fantasy to him now, a bad dream. All he could give me is a name. A university professor he used to work with on uranium enrichment. Maybe. He wasn't sure if he actually knew the guy, or read his name in a magazine. But he thinks the man is an enemy of the regime."

Luke rolled his eyes. "Terrific. Is he even going to be alive?"

Ari shook his head. "I have no idea."

This was more than frustrating. They had risked their lives getting here, and it was nothing but a series of dead ends. Meanwhile, there was a war on, which might go nuclear at any time. They had to get this thing—

Suddenly, Ari slapped himself on the forehead. "Dammit! I can't believe I just did that." He looked back at Hamid Bahman. The skinny man's abused body was already convulsing, the seizures barely visible.

"What?"

"I gave that guy my only cyanide pill. I'm never going to get out of this shitty country, and now I have no way to kill myself."

He looked at Luke. "Do you have an extra?"

"An extra what?"

"Cyanide. Don't you listen?"

Luke shook his head. "Buddy, are you crazy? We don't carry cyanide pills."

"What will you do if you get captured?"

Luke glanced out the doorway at Ed again. Big Ed Newsam, muscles stacked on top of muscles, fists like concrete, bristling with weapons. Hard eyes scanning the hallways for more people to kill. The man was a human wrecking ball. He was hell on wheels. He didn't have an ounce of surrender in his body.

"We don't get captured."

CHAPTER THIRTY

8:15 p.m. Iran Time (12:15 p.m. Eastern Standard Time)
Persian Gulf (West of the Strait of Hormuz)

"Sir, we've got trouble."

Commander Brian Berwick stood on the bridge of the USS *Winston S. Churchill*, an Arleigh Burke class destroyer that had just passed through the narrows of the Strait of Hormuz. He had been interrupted during his evening meal only five minutes before by the Officer of the Watch, a young guy named Perry. Perry was a tall drink of water, maybe a little high-strung for life at sea.

Berwick peered into the darkness of night through the windows, though there was nothing out there to see. In his mind, he watched as his ship's situation deteriorated.

"Tell me again."

He already knew the story, and if it was true, he knew what he had to do. The USS *Cole* disaster had changed the rules of engagement, and had taught men like him what *not* to do. But he wanted to hear it again, let it seep into his pores before he did anything. He had to get this right the first time.

Perry was shaking. Trembling, just a bit. "We've got fast-moving vessels, dropping in and off radar, sir. We think it may be a swarm of Iranian Seraj speedboats, and they may be running cover for a couple of Thondar class missile boats behind them."

Berwick shook his head. The Seraj were fast—they were an Iranian rip-off of the British Bladerunner 51. They could do between fifty and seventy knots, were a stable firing platform, and were armed to the teeth with rockets.

If possible, the Thondar were even worse. They were slower than the Seraj, but armed with C-101 supersonic anti-ship missiles.

The Iranians had based their navy around fast attack boats, because they thought it was the only way to counter the might of the giant American warships. And they were right—these boats were low to the water, had a limited radar cross section, and were very, very fast. If a Thondar was out there, and it fired one of those C-101s...

Berwick didn't want to think about that.

The bridge was tense—Berwick could feel it. Nobody up here wanted to be the one that let the Iranians punch a big ugly hole in the hull.

Berwick took a deep breath. The men sat at their stations, their backs to him, silent, waiting, the control arrays spread out in front of them. The scene took on an almost surreal tone. These men were hanging on his next words.

"Where are they?"

"Port side, sir. They were port, just off our stern until a few moments ago. Now they're straight off port. Red 90. They're like a flock of birds out there."

"Distance?"

"Three miles, holding steady."

"Uh, sir?" the radar man said.

"Yes."

"Not holding steady, sir. We've got incoming."

"Incoming ship or missile?"

"Ship, sir. Or ships. I can't tell. I've two radar signatures now. A ship or ships incoming, forty-five degrees."

"A feint or an attack?"

"I don't know. Your call, sir."

Berwick felt his hands ball into fists. The Iranian Revolutionary Guards manned those speedboats. They were crazy. They were trained for asymmetric warfare. They were as liable to load their boats with bombs and use them as torpedoes as they were to fire the torpedoes themselves. This sort of kamikaze harassment from them was a constant on these waters.

Zoom in, run away. Zoom in, run away.

But there was a war in Israel now. The Iranians had made threats. This was not idle chatter. And this boat was not a sitting duck. The vertical launch torpedoes were no use here. But the fifty-caliber guns? Well…

"Distance?"

"Still incoming. Two miles, sir. Collision course."

Berwick took a deep breath. This was going to happen fast.

"Give me those fifties."

"Port side fifty-caliber guns ready."

"Acquire surface targets."

There was a pause, a hesitation. Those things were moving fast out there. They were hard to see.

"Targets, sir?"

"Targets, son. *Targets*. If we're going to do this, we're going to teach them a lesson. This is the United States Navy. They're not going to punch us, they're not going to sink us, and they're not going to harass us. End of lecture. Take the whole fucking swarm."

Another moment passed.

"Distance?" he said.

"Primary target, one mile and closing. Secondary, two miles and closing. Closing, sir. They're coming in behind the primary. They are coming in. Both groups closing. Repeat, both groups closing. Coming fast."

"Steady," Berwick said.

"We've war-gamed this," the radar man said. "Oh my God. It's an attack, sir! I know it is."

"Acquire targets," Berwick said again.

He was fed up. That's what it was. He hated these people—*hated* them. It was an endless game of cat-and-mouse out here. Was he supposed to wait until they hit him, wait until his own crew got killed? There were 281 men and women aboard this ship.

No, thank you. No. Not tonight. Not ever.

"Targets acquired and locked on, sir."

"Distance?"

"Half mile, sir. Half mile and closing."

"Kill 'em, son. Kill 'em all. Fire when ready."

Berwick watched through the port side windows as the guns lit up the dark night sky.

CHAPTER THIRTY ONE

7:31 p.m. Israel Time (8:31 p.m. Iran time, 12:31 p.m. Eastern Standard Time)
Samson's Lair – Deep Underground
Jerusalem, Israel

"Now what?" Yonatan Stern said.

"There's been a provocation."

He looked at the young aide who had come into the war room with the news.

"A provocation? When, in the past two days, hasn't there been a provocation? Please. Don't be shy. Tell us everything."

Yonatan hated the tone of his voice when he spoke like this. He hated that the aides feared him and avoided him. But he had a temper, and he had contempt for hesitancy. It was so deep inside of him, he didn't know how he ever might remove it. Probably not in this lifetime, whatever amount remained of it.

"In the Persian Gulf," the young man said. "The Strait of Hormuz. Just over ten minutes ago, an American warship fired on and destroyed a group of Iranian speedboats. There are very few details available. We do not know which side attacked first. We do not know how many are dead, on either side."

"What do we know?" Yonatan said.

"We know that the Iranians are going to a war footing throughout their military. Captured transmissions suggest that fighter and bomber planes are scrambling, and at least a hundred speedboats have been released into the Gulf east of the Strait—they may be attempting a blockade. The Revolutionary Guards' missile command is on alert, with orders to bring all silos to the highest state of readiness within the hour."

Yonatan let the words seep into his mind. He looked at the other men in the room. He saw their wheels spinning, searching for the meaning of this. Efraim Shavitz was here. Shavitz closed his eyes and rubbed his temples. Perhaps he was thinking he should have gone out dancing after all. It might have been his last chance.

"The Americans," David Cohn said. "They tell us to refrain from bombing the Iranians, then they bomb the Iranians themselves."

"Thank you," Yonatan said to the aide. "Bring us an update every five minutes. Sooner, if necessary."

"Yes sir," the aide said. He went through the automatic sliding door to the elevator foyer. Yonatan pictured the high-speed elevator that would bring this boy to the surface twenty seconds from now. Zooom! Yonatan was rapidly losing his faith in the blessings brought by technology.

"Thoughts?" he said to the gathering of minds.

"Prepare our own silos," said Sheldon Eisner. "Launch the final attack. It's time. You know it has been coming to this. You know they will do the same."

Sheldon was old, older than his years, with white hair and a craggy face. He was one of the few who still chain smoked. He was theoretically the Minister of Culture. He had spent forty years in the IDF before finding this love of culture. Yonatan reflected that hardly a man in his cabinet hadn't spent decades in the military. Of course the left-wing newspapers had long criticized him for this. But Yonatan trusted military men. And they were not the men of narrow interests the newspapers pretended.

These were Renaissance men.

Efraim Shavitz shook his head. "We cannot launch those missiles. It's too soon."

"Shall we wait until after they destroy us?" Eisner said.

"The missiles are for when all is lost," Shavitz said. "They will pull the temple down on top of our own heads, as well as the heads of our enemies."

"What do you suggest we do?" Yonatan said.

"We wait," Shavitz said. "We monitor the situation. I haven't heard anything that tells me our situation has changed."

"The Americans and the Iranians have started a shooting war," Eisner said.

Shavitz nodded. "Yes. But we didn't. The Iranians claim that they only attack in self-defense. We haven't attacked Iran."

Yonatan shook his head. "Did you not notice the destroyed buildings in Tel Aviv, and the morgues filling up with bodies? Have you missed the severed human limbs at the base of the Western Wall?"

"Hezbollah," Shavitz said. "Hamas. Not Iran."

For a moment, the room broke out in deafening noise. Several men pointed at Shavitz, shouting at him. Yonatan could barely make out the words, but the message was clear. Iran, Hezbollah, and Hamas were all the same.

After half a minute, the sound died down again.

"We sent an intelligence party in Iran," Shavitz said. "We told them they would have forty-eight hours from the time they jumped."

"How long has it been?" Yonatan said.

"About twenty-three hours, by my count."

"Has the mission borne any fruit?"

"From what we know, they have successfully infiltrated the country," Shavitz said. "They have made their way to Tehran. The first informer was dead when they arrived. They are pursuing another informer."

"Tell Yonatan where the second informer is located," Eisner said.

Yonatan looked at Shavitz and shook his head. Shavitz and Eisner, two men who could hardly be more different, were similar in one way: they were both like children, seeking their father's favor.

"Inside Evin Prison," Shavitz said.

"Inside Evin Prison? *The* Evin Prison?"

Was this a joke?

"We can assume the mission has failed or will fail," Yonatan said. "Put all nuclear silos—all silos of any kind—on high alert. Notify the air force. Call all flight crews and support personnel to their stations immediately. Within the hour, I want all fighters and bombers—including bombers with nuclear payloads—ready to scramble at five minutes' notice. I want a twenty-four-hour state of readiness, with shifts changes at eight-hour intervals—fresh crews prepared to go at all times. Alert Civil Defense. Prepare the population to access public bomb shelters and emergency food supplies."

Throughout the room, military men and their aides were picking up old-fashioned telephones and making calls. This far underground, cell phones did not work.

"Yonatan," Efraim Shavitz said. "Do you know what you're saying?"

Yonatan raised his index finger. "We will not start a war," he said. "But if a war comes, we will hammer our enemies with the fist of God."

CHAPTER THIRTY TWO

9:30 p.m. (1:30 p.m. Eastern Standard Time)
The Research Institute of Energy Planning and Management
School of Science and Technology
University of Tehran
Tehran, Iran

The hallways were dark.

They had watched him through a hallway window as he gave a late evening class to a handful of students in a lecture hall that might hold two hundred. His students were not inside the building—they were out in the street, bloodied but unbowed. Twenty had been killed this morning, hundreds arrested.

Luke realized now that was probably the reason for the lax security at the prison—the security forces, the police, the Revolutionary Guards, the prison guards, anyone and everyone with a gun or a truncheon, had been mobilized to put down the student unrest. And still the students were protesting.

Even here, deep in the bowels of the science building, you could hear them out in the streets surrounding the campus, chanting.

The professor came down the hallway carrying a satchel. The satchel was filled with the notes from his lecture. The man was dressed in a tweed sports jacket and corduroy pants—the picture of a college professor in the United States during the 1960s. He wore a striped tie. And he had a long black beard with streaks of white in it.

He reached the door to his office, fished out his keys, found the one he was looking for, and unlocked the door, all automatically and without the need for overhead lights.

He opened the door to his office.

As he did, the three of them emerged from the dark corners. Luke put a gun in the man's back.

Ari said: "Don't scream. Don't try to turn the light on in your office. Just walk in normally and sit down."

They followed him inside, and Ed shut the door behind them. The man's office was a mess—piles of paperwork on every horizontal surface. There were two large windows along one wall—

outside, the snow was still spitting down. The man slid in behind his desk. He looked at Ed for a moment, then looked away.

Luke kept the gun on him the entire time.

"Ashgar Nasiri?" Luke said.

The man nodded in the gloom.

"Of course. Why ask if it is me, when you already know?"

"If you have a gun hidden under that desk, or inside a drawer, better to just hand it over now. If you try anything foolish, I will hurt you very badly."

Nasiri shook his head and made a sound like a laugh. "You and your kind. It would all be very humorous, if it weren't so sad. What do you take me for? I've never held a gun in my life."

"What kind are we?"

"Killers. Government operatives. Patriots. Whatever you prefer to call yourselves. You're all the same, everywhere I go. Do you suppose you are the first such operatives to visit me? Guess again. I have traveled widely. Paris. London. New York City. Even here in Tehran. Someone is always picking my locks or sticking a gun in my ribs. There is nothing remarkable about you."

"We saw your friend Hamid Bahman tonight."

At that name, Nasiri hesitated. "Oh? How is he?"

"He's dead," Ari said.

"But you saw him?"

"We were inside Evin Prison. He begged me to kill him, to end his suffering at the hands of the guards and the interrogators. Your government decided he was a traitor, and they treated him accordingly. How well did you know him?"

Nasiri sighed. "Very well. We worked together for five years."

"He couldn't remember if he knew you or read about you once. That's how bad his torture had been."

Nasiri nodded. He thought about it for a long moment, then spoke.

"Before he disappeared, his ideas had become unsound. He had begun to study radioactive half-lifes, as well as toxic shrouds and the concept of a nuclear winter. He authored papers recommending that Iran step back from developing these weapons, and instead become a world leader promoting nuclear disarmament. Several of us warned him that he was going to a dangerous place, but he was a very headstrong man and would not listen to reason. He was as stubborn as a camel."

"Even a stubborn man can be broken," Ari said.

Nasiri didn't seem to hear him. "By the end, he was becoming increasingly worried, and paranoid."

"With good reason, wouldn't you say? The man we met was more dead than alive. He was skin and bones. He had at least two hundred cigarette burns on his body. And believe me, he had much worse injuries than that."

"Why are you telling me this?"

"I haven't told you the half of it."

"Hamid was crazy. He forgot to keep his toe on the safe side of the line. I cannot help people who forget themselves. I cannot help these students and their uprising. I can only help the ones who want to learn. I can help the ones who don't want to end up in a torture prison. The rioters will be lucky to escape with their lives. I cannot help them."

"We need your help."

"What help can I possibly give you?"

"You worked on your country's nuclear program. You and Bahman."

"Of course. It was my duty. It was the duty of all nuclear scientists in the country to build weapons for our self-defense. Whether we wanted to or not. You think us a backward country, a religious autocracy, and that is true, as far as it goes. But there is much more to the story. Iran is a rich tapestry, full of contradictions. It is one of the grandest, most storied civilizations in human history. Look at this university all around us—one of the great universities, a center of science and culture and the arts, certainly in the Muslim world, but also in the larger world. We are not fools, and we are not religious fanatics—we believe in science. We take the oaths they force upon us because we want to live, and we want our families to live, and we want to make the world a better place. Iran will not always be a religious dictatorship, I can assure you of that. The current student uprising will fail miserably, but one day, the ayatollahs will fall."

"Our two countries are on the verge of a nuclear war," Ari said.

Nasiri nodded. "I know it."

"You will never see the ascendancy of Iran's culture and science if the whole place is destroyed in fire and fury."

"How can I stop it?"

"You can tell us the location of the nuclear missiles."

Nasiri sat still for a long moment. He looked at the snow accumulating on the edges of the window pane.

"What will you do?"

"Destroy them," Luke said. "Call in air strikes. It will prevent a nuclear exchange with Israel. That's a war Iran cannot win."

"While Israel gets to keep their own arsenal?"

"Yes. I'm not going to lie to you. They've had their missiles for forty years, and they've never used them. They won't use them if they're not threatened. It will be a return to status quo. A chance for peace."

Nasiri took a deep breath.

"They will want to kill me. If they find out who told you…"

"We can try to get you out."

The professor slowly shook his head. "Then they will kill my family in my stead. You look like three very capable men. I'm sure that's why they sent you. But you're not a moving company. Can you smuggle out my elderly mother, my uncles, my three brothers and their families, my ex-wife and our two daughters? All quickly and under cover of darkness?"

"No. Just you, in all likelihood."

The air seemed to go out of Nasiri, like a tire deflating. "I only know one location. You must understand. The program was very secretive. We were kept isolated from one another. Different people worked on different aspects of the project in different places. We often didn't even know who the people in the other locations were—we had our suspicions, of course. There are only so many people who know how to enrich uranium and miniaturize warheads."

"What location do you know?" Luke said.

"Parchin," Nasiri said. "Just east of the city. It is a large, heavily fortified military base. I have been there many times. I've seen the missiles with my own eyes. There is a battery of eight missiles there, deep underground, though not as deep as our government might suggest. They drilled a tunnel twenty miles long—it comes from the enrichment facility at Fordo, where I worked for years. It is a highway under the Earth. We were able to develop a secret facility at Fordo that enriched the uranium to greater than ninety percent purity—more than enough for a successful weapon. The weaponized uranium was trucked from Fordo to Parchin. It may still happen for all I know."

"Were there tests to see if the warheads would even work?"

Nasiri. "Yes. But they took place elsewhere. I know nothing about them, except that they were successful."

"Does anyone know every part of this?"

Nasiri shrugged. "Possible. There was one person, the director of my project. He is a brilliant man—a passable hands-on engineer, but a man who can synthesize the input of many fields, and make sense of it all. A man who also recognizes his own limitations. He often took meetings at the highest level of government. He sometimes visited other sites, though he would never talk about what he saw."

"Where is he now?"

"He retired. Became an imam here in the city. He calls himself Ali Mohammed Tehrani and has a popular mosque in south Tehran, near the Grand Bazaar. It's funny. He never seemed to have a religious bone in his body. I suspect he became an imam to protect himself. A wonderful idea, if you are willing to dress in costume and play a role the rest of your life. It's hard to accuse someone of treason when they are so obviously devout."

Abruptly, Nasiri stood. Luke watched him.

He moved to some shelving beneath the window. Everything was a mess. There were stacks of papers along the shelves. He pulled out a pile of folded maps and laid them out on top of the low shelf top. He stood in front of the window.

"I have maps of the Fordo facility, the secret enrichment center there, and how it connects by tunnel to the silos sites at Parchin. It may help you."

"You have the maps here?" Ed said.

Nasiri laughed. "It helps when they call you an absent-minded professor. You can walk out with the secrets of the universe, and they think you are being forgetful."

He reached to his right, to a small table lamp on top of the shelf. It was the kind with a bending, snakelike arm that could direct the light wherever you needed it.

"Don't do that," Luke said.

Nasiri clicked on the light. "I just want to show you how—"

Instantly, a hole punched through the window and Nasiri's head popped apart. Blood and bone sprayed. His body continued to stand for half a second, as if it didn't understand what had just happened, then fell bonelessly to the floor.

Luke, Ed, and Ari dropped as one.

"Dammit!" Ed said. "Sniper."

"Kill the light," Luke said. "Kill the light!"

Ed reached up with a heavy book and knocked the light off the shelf. The glass bulb tinkled as it shattered. More holes appeared in the windows. One of the windows cracked apart and shattered into several pieces.

"Anybody get a look at where those shots came from?"

"These windows are across a plaza from another faculty building," Ari said. "I noticed that coming in. They must have taken up residence in an office across the way. How did they know?"

"Those two dead guards at the prison might have given them a tip," Ed said.

They had dragged the bodies of the guards up to the roof and left them in the snow. But they made no serious effort to get rid of them. What were they going to do with them? Toss them off into the streets?

"How's the professor?" Luke said, already knowing the answer.

"How is he? Did you see his head break open and his brains come splattering out?"

"Yeah, I did."

"Well, then."

No one said another word. They lay on the floor with Nasiri's corpse for several seconds. Luke could feel the clock ticking. Their opponents were already on the move. The bad guys had all the advantages—they were on their home turf, and they knew exactly where this office was located. They knew the layout of the whole area.

Down on the streets, Luke and company were going to be dead men. Even so, they couldn't stay here.

"Ed, grab those maps, man. We better get going."

* * *

They moved silently through the halls, like wraiths.

Even their footfalls were light, making no sound on the marble floors. Luke's senses were on red alert—his hearing, his eyesight, his sense of smell—everything was on, picking up the slightest cues from the environment.

Ed was on point, his MP5 out, magazine in, full auto. He had three more magazines loaded along his belt. If it came to a confrontation, there was going to be no sneaking out of here. Overwhelming force was all that would work, and it was going to be LOUD.

Ari was next, shadowing Ed, moving low along the walls opposite from and behind him. He was ready with his Uzi.

Luke brought up the rear, barely behind Ari, almost touching him, and facing backward. Any attack was likely to come from both sides, a pincer move.

Ed arrived at the door to the stairwell. He crouched at the bottom of it. With the barrel of his gun, he reached across and opened the door an inch.

DUH-DUH-DUH-DUH-DUH.

Someone in the stairwell was overeager, on hair trigger. The short burst of automatic fire shredded chunks from the door, high, near the handle and above. Smoke and dust rose from the impacts. Ed turned and looked back. His eyes met Luke's. His shoulders slumped. He shook his head and pointed downward. Then he pointed upward. There were shooters in the stairwell, both above them and below them.

Ding!

There was an elevator across the hall from the stairs. And someone was inside of it.

"Ed?"

"Fourth floor, right?"

"Yeah."

"Coming this way."

"Don't kill them," Luke said. "Whoever's in there, we need them. Catch them, don't kill them."

"What if there's ten people?"

"Leave two alive."

Luke's mind moved at warp speed, searching for answers. He hit on one. These people didn't know who they were dealing with. Not yet. They had the stairs staked out. They were coming up in the elevator. Maybe they thought the office had been infiltrated by radical students, students they simply imagined they were going to hunt down and kill.

Luke shook his head. He hoped that was it.

He removed his handgun from his shoulder holster. He took a silencer out of a pocket of his cargo pants. He threaded it into the barrel of the gun and screwed it in tight. He was ten feet from the elevator, pressed to the wall, on the same side of the hallway.

"Ed, how's that elevator?"

"One more. Here we go."

"Give me a head count and draw them out. They'll be so focused on you, they won't see me here. I'll take free shots at whatever's available, and you guys finish the leftovers. Copy that?"

"Copy."

Ed and Ari moved to either side of the doorway, guns aimed across the hall and into the elevator. Luke squatted along the wall.

He would only get a shot if someone came out.

"Come on out, boys," he whispered. "Come on out."

Ding!

The doors opened.

Suddenly, there was shouting in Farsi. Ari shouted, the men inside shouted.

"Drop your guns!" the men in the elevator shouted. "Do not move!"

"Three men!" Ed shouted in English. "Three men!"

Two men stepped into the hall, guns trained on Ari and Ed, shouting.

Ari and Ed shouted back, guns trained on the men.

It was a standoff. Dangerous, dangerous. The first trigger pull would cause a bloodbath on both sides.

A third man, taller than the others, stepped into the hallway.

CLACK!

Luke's gun bucked as he took the top half of the man's head off.

The two men turned, looking for the shooter who had just killed their commander. Instantly, Ed and Ari were on top of them, rifle butts cracking skulls. Luke ran forward, gun pointed. He kicked the Iranian's guns away from their outstretched hands.

Luke recognized their distinctive uniforms—dark green coats and pants, black turtleneck shirt with gold logo shaped like a globe at the throat, green baseball caps with the same logo, and white gloves.

These were the fearsome Revolutionary Guards. These were the guys who stomped on the slightest hint of dissent in Iranian society. These two had probably been out killing college kids earlier today.

Luke didn't mind killing men like these.

"Get them up!" he said. "Get them up! Let's go. We're out of here."

The plan had formed instantly, mercilessly. He looked at Ed and Ari. His eyes felt wild. He had been to this place before. Total combat, and these were the men to do it with. There was no fear in their eyes. They were alive, alert, ready to move.

"They're going downstairs, we're going upstairs. To the roof."

He looked at Ari. "Are there buildings close to this one?"

Ari nodded. "Yes. Across alleyways, that sort of thing. A few jumps, we can move away from here. They might be big jumps."

"That's what we'll do. Ready?"

"Ready."

Luke looked at Ed.

"Born ready, white man."

He and Ari lifted the two men off the floor. They were both confused, hands at their sides. Luke went to the door of the stairwell. Ari and Ed were right behind him. He pushed open the door, then ducked back. Ari and Ed shoved their charges into the stairwell and dove in after them.

Automatic fire came from the stairwell below.

DUD-DUD-DUD-DUD-DUD.

The two Revolutionary Guards jittered and moved as the bullets hit them.

Ari sprayed bullets from his Uzi down the stairs.

Ed fired up the stairs.

A body came tumbling down.

They shoved the bullet-riddled Iranians down the stairs. Ari and Ed ran upstairs, Luke three feet behind them. He vaulted the dead body on the stairs. More fire came from behind them, but the bullets hit the wall of the landing.

"Go man, go!"

They sprinted up the stairs, two at a time, guns everywhere at once. This was the dangerous time, trapped in a stairwell. Luke could hear the boots of the Iranians pounding up the stairs behind them. The men shouted, almost screams of horror, of tragedy, as they passed their dead comrades. Well, too bad. The Iranians would have done the same to the students, had there been any.

Up ahead, they were coming to the door to the roof.

Ed was the fastest and reached it first. He stopped short.

"Wait! Wait!" He touched the door. He put his ear to it and listened.

Luke turned around.

"Come on, Ed. Don't wait all night. We got bad guys right behind us."

"Man, a chopper out there and we all get cut to pieces."

Footsteps pounded up the stairs.

Luke worked an angle on the stairwell below him. He checked his gun. AUTO. This was about to become a shit show.

He glanced back. Ed opened the door a crack, peeked outside.

Ah, hell.

Luke pulled an Israeli grenade from his belt, yanked the pin, let the compressor go, and tossed the thing over the railing. He heard it bouncing down the stairs.

He turned and ran. "Fire in the hole!" he screamed.

Ed and Ari saw him coming and heard him scream. Their eyes went wide and they burst through the door as one. He was one second behind them. Then they were out on the roof and running across it in the rain and sleet. There were no helicopters. There was no one up here. The wind whipped across the rooftop.

"Fire in the hole!" Luke screamed again.

He dove to the surface of the roof, sliding in the thin cover of snow and ice. It was a gravel roof and it bit into his hands, his elbows and knees. Ahead of him, Ed and Ari hit the deck and covered their heads. Luke did the same.

He waited. What was taking so long?

He almost rolled over, gun trained on the doorway. But…

BA-BOOOOM.

The roof trembled. The door blew off and flew through the air, breaking into flaming pieces. Red and orange fire burst from the stairwell, a ball of it, the heat washing over Luke's back. The last chunk of burning door floated to the roof. Dirty black smoke poured from the hole where the stairwell used to be.

Ari and Ed were both looking back, their faces red from the reflection of the flames.

"That's a hell of a grenade, man," Luke said.

Ari shrugged. "We make the best."

Ed worked his way to his feet. Suddenly, another man was there. Same outfit, green coat, green baseball cap, white gloves—another Revolutionary Guard. He was a young guy with a thick mustache, and he emerged from the shadows along the parapet. Instantly, Luke knew his deal—he had seen his buddy killed by Ed, and retreated up the stairs ahead of their onslaught.

He had his hand gun out now, drawing a bead on the big man.

Luke scrambled to find his own gun. In all the commotion, he had dropped it, the silenced pistol.

"Ed!"

Ari leapt to his feet and tried to tackle Ed. It didn't work. The two men stumbled along together.

BANG.

The bullet hit… something.

Luke found his gun in the snow. He rolled onto his side, gained his target, and fired. Outside, with the damping effect of the snow, the gun sounded like nothing. A stapler. A typewriter key being punched.

The Iranian kid was pointing his gun at Ed and Ari again. Red mist appeared at the top of his head. His arms flopped up dramatically, and he flopped backward. It didn't look real. Was he faking?

Luke leapt to his feet and slipped and slid over to him. He kicked the kid's gun away, stepped on the wrist of his gun hand, and pointed the pistol at the kid's head. Nothing. The eyes were blank. The mouth hung half open. A chunk of the head was missing at the top left corner. Not a great shot—another inch or two north, and Luke would have missed.

He felt all the air seeping out of him. It had been quite a night, and it was barely getting started.

Behind him, Ari had begun shouting. It sounded more like anger than pain.

"Ow! Dammit! Ow!"

"How is it?" Luke said. Behind him, the stairwell raged and boiled fire. It looked like something had caught down there. This was a science building—not good. They stored things in science buildings. Flammable things. Explosive things.

"He's hit in the shoulder," Ed said. "It's pretty gruesome, but not the worst I've seen. Meanwhile, the Israeli here saved my life."

"I couldn't save your life, you idiot! You wouldn't fall down."

Ed shook his head. "One has nothing to do with the other. You took a bullet for me. You might have really saved my life. Now you've got a bro for life."

"I've never been happier," Ari said.

"How does it feel, Ari?" Luke said.

"It hurts. A lot. It's not a clean wound. I think it took some bone. It's going to get infected, if I don't bleed out first."

Ed laughed. "Nah. Once we're inside somewhere, I'll get that thing cleaned up, at least good enough until we can get to a hospital."

Ari shook his head. "A hospital. Sure, let's go sit in an emergency room for a few hours. You think they accept the Israeli healthcare card?"

Luke unclipped one of his pants pockets, slid the satellite phone out, and dialed Swann.

CHAPTER THIRTY THREE

10:55 p.m. Israel Time (11:55 p.m. Tehran Time, 3:55 p.m. Eastern Standard Time)
Tel Aviv, Israel

The satellite phone rang inside his headphones. He pressed the green button.

"Albert Helu," he said.

"Swann, I don't have time for that right now."

Swann looked at Trudy, who stared at him from across the room.

"He's alive," Swann said.

"Who's alive?" Luke said.

"You're alive."

"Yes, I'm alive. Ed's alive. We're all alive."

"I was just telling Trudy."

"Swann, shut up a second, okay? By the time you stop talking, we're all going to be dead here."

Swann looked at Trudy. "Okay, Luke." He rolled his eyes. Luke was crazy, always had been, always would be. Trudy could certainly second that emotion.

"Can't you put that thing on a speaker?" Trudy said.

Swann put a finger to his lips.

"I need to make a report. This is important. Forward this directly by the most secure means to the Situation Room at the White House. Two sites confirmed. First site. Uranium enrichment facility at Fordo, southeast of Tehran. They are making weapons grade materials there."

"Luke…"

"Are you getting this?"

Swann's fingers flew across the keyboard. "Fordo," he said out loud. "Enrichment site, weapons grade, confirmed."

Instantly, across the room, Trudy had her tablet out and was scrolling through it.

"Second site," Luke said. "Parchin, east of Tehran. Military base. Confirmed, at least eight long-range missiles with nuclear warheads. One hundred eighty meters underground. Reachable target at that depth. Repeat…"

"Parchin, confirmed," Swann said. "Eight warheads. One hundred eighty meters down."

"At least eight," Luke said.

"At least eight," Swann parroted.

"There is a tunnel that runs underground from Fordo to Parchin. Confirmed. It is a four-lane highway, two lanes each direction. Satellites may be able to find evidence of it on the surface. Construction sites, a long restricted corridor, demolished or relocated residential areas, something."

"What else?" Swann said.

"Nothing."

"Nothing else? Luke, there's two other suspected sites. We've got a ticking clock here."

"I'm not on the clock, Swann."

"Luke, there was an incident. A Navy destroyer took out six Iranian speedboats in the Persian Gulf. The captain thought it was a swarm attack. The Iranians say it was practice maneuvers. Everything is on the verge of blowing up."

Swann could hear Luke's heavy sigh bouncing off satellites and traveling all over the world.

"Swann, we've jumped off of hang gliders at over two thousand feet, broken into and out of a prison, killed at least eight men, and watched a fat college professor get blown away by a sniper. I am walking across the roof of a building that is on fire, and it's snowing out. We are going as fast as we can."

He paused, seemingly for breath. There was silence over the line.

"I need you to do something for me."

"Tell me," Swann said.

"Ali Mohammad Tehrani. He's a Shiite imam. He runs a mosque in south Tehran somewhere. It's near the Grand Bazaar. I need to know what the mosque is called, exactly where it is, and how we can get there from here. I need you to find a layout of it, and anything you can find on the personal habits of the imam. We need to see him, preferably without a lot of company."

"Where are you now?" Swann said.

Luke sounded a touch breathless. "We were on the roof of a science building on the main campus of the University of Tehran. We just jumped an alleyway. We're moving away from campus toward the east."

"Okay," Swann said. "I need to call you back. We'll get you everything."

"Good," Luke said. "And Swann?"

"Yes."

"Don't make me call you back this time."

CHAPTER THIRTY FOUR

December 15
2:15 a.m. (6:15 p.m. Eastern Standard Time on December 14)
Amir Abad Neighborhood
Tehran, Iran

"The man's real name is Siavash Zadeh," Trudy's voice said in his ear. "Prominent nuclear physicist turned religious authority. Seventy-four years old."

Luke sat on the floor of a narrow stone balcony, his back against the brickwork. He was invisible here, pressed into a corner in the dark, two stories above a narrow alleyway lined with shabby tenements, the last vestiges of old Tehran.

The night was quiet. The temperature had dropped, and the last of the snow was drifting down in big fat flakes. The balcony was an inch deep in ice.

"Okay," Luke whispered. No one knew he was here. No sense jeopardizing that arrangement.

"His mosque is called Jameh Mosque of the Believers."

He liked to listen to Trudy's voice. It had a calm, musical, very feminine tone that reminded him of home. He made a resolution—if he ever got out of here, he would never try to teach her another thing.

He sighed. He was tired, wrung through. And he was a long way from anything like home. They were hunted men now. Security was tight. It would be hard to leave the country even if they wanted to, even if Luke could tolerate a job half done.

"It's become a popular mosque, often attracting hundreds of people for morning prayers. People attribute that to the popularity of Zadeh himself, and his natural way of making the lessons of the Quran accessible to people from all walks of life. He affects a look like an ancient holy man, or a wizard—he has a long white beard, wears white flowing robes, and carries a white walking staff."

"Yes," Luke said. He was almost falling asleep out here in the snow.

"Do you want me to tell you how to get there?"

He shook his head. "No. You better tell Ari. He knows this town way better than I do, or than Ed. Hold on."

Luke slid through the window, leaving the phone on the sill. He didn't want to lose the call. Satellite phones were temperamental, and bringing them inside often led to dropped calls.

The place was an open space they had ducked into after they were sure no one was following them. It was in a neighborhood of substandard housing, storefronts, and warehouses. This vast room was empty. Luke and Ari sat against a wall, eating condensed protein rations out of aluminum containers. The both looked exhausted. Their faces were sallow and drained. But Ed had cleaned out Ari's wound and bandaged it with black cloth he had found somewhere.

"How's the gunshot?" Luke said.

Ed shrugged. "He's gonna live. I'd say the guy was firing hollow-points, so the round mushroomed on impact and made a mess. The round itself is gone. Luckily, it was a glancing hit, coming from the side, or it would have taken that shoulder apart. As it is, he's got some shredded meat in there. Bones and socket look okay. I sterilized everything and sewed it up. Gave our hero a couple of non-opiate painkillers. It'll tamp down the pain a little, and he won't get sleepy on us. But he's gonna have some soreness and stiffness."

Ari looked at Ed. "Soreness? Is that what you call this?"

"Mild soreness," Ed said. "It's a flesh wound. You should have been there when a high-velocity round cracked my pelvis. Talk about soreness. That was the real thing."

Luke nodded. This sounded okay. Best not to make a thing out of it. There was a lot more to do, and Ari was just going to have to live with the pain. Luke figured that shouldn't be too much of a problem. The man was a soldier, after all.

"Ari," he said, indicating back toward the window with his thumb. "Trudy's going to give you directions. Don't stay on there all night. The battery is dying, and those maniacs are almost certainly looking for us."

Luke sat down as Ari got up.

"What is this place?" Luke said.

Ed shrugged. "I don't know. Some kind of clothing distribution center. Mostly women's clothing, religious stuff. Long black robes. Hijabs. Veils. Flat shoes."

Luke sat back and closed his eyes. He drifted. In his mind, he seemed to be sitting in a park with Gunner. When he opened his eyes again, Ari was closing the window to the balcony. He walked across the open space and handed Luke his phone.

"You get the directions?"

Ari nodded. "Yeah. I just have no idea how we're supposed to get down there."

"How far is it from here?"

"Three miles, maybe three and a half, but that's not the problem. The city is closed down because of the protests, and now they know we're here. There are checkpoints everywhere, which I know how to avoid, but if a single person sees us—a cop, a soldier, someone a little too curious for their own good—that will be the end of this little trip."

Luke cast around for ideas. Start right where you are, that was the old motto. And they were in a clothing warehouse.

"Can we go in disguise?" he said.

"Nah, man," Ed said. "Don't even go there. It's nothing but women's clothes."

Ari stood above them, thinking. After a moment, he smiled. "Iranian women are trying to modernize. Some of the young women really push the envelope of what's allowed. A few years ago, the morality police were arresting thousands of them. But the older women, and the women from the conservative rural tribes—they still dress in the old ways. Many of them even cover their faces entirely. These gowns are called *abaya.* They are hooded. Combined with a hijab and a veil..."

Ed shook his head. "No. Things are looking bleak enough as it is. If we're gonna die here anyway..."

Ari nodded.

"We might as well be dressed as women when it happens."

CHAPTER THIRTY FIVE

7:05 p.m. Eastern Standard Time
The Oval Office
The White House, Washington, DC

"Susan, we have that preliminary report."

She looked up. She was sitting in a high-backed chair in the sitting area, oddly enough, with General Kirby and Haley Lawrence. They were all sipping tea from an antique tea set. All except Susan—she was drinking black coffee. From an outsider's point of view, the little gathering in this beautiful office must look very, very pleasant.

But it wasn't. It was the farthest thing from pleasant. Pleasant would be lounging in an infinity pool overlooking the Indian Ocean with Agent Luke Stone. In a parallel reality, where there were no wars and no nuclear weapons.

This? No. Not pleasant at all.

A Secret Service man had opened the door and Kurt had poked his head in.

Yet another break from the Situation Room had come, which in a little while would be followed by yet another session. Susan had reached her limit—Kurt's thunderous hand claps were starting to make her flinch. She had barely slept last night, and now she was on a twelve-hour day, with no end in sight.

The hours were slipping by now, and things were getting worse. Susan's advisors, and their staffs, didn't seem to have any answers. The situation was slipping out of control.

"What report?" Susan said.

"The report on the Persian Gulf incident."

"Okay, Kurt," Susan said. "Come on in."

Kurt came in with his close aide, Amy. They both glanced at the TV monitor, which had most recently televised Stephen Lief's inauguration as Vice President. That seemed like weeks ago now.

"Amy, can you work this thing?"

"Sure."

Susan had the urge to shout, "*Don't turn that on!*" She was tired of looking at video monitors. If she never looked at another map, or infographic showing troop and missile strengths, or picture of a fighter plane or weapon system, she would be fine with that.

Amy turned on the monitor and fiddled with her tablet computer. In a moment, she had them in synch. Instantly a map of Iran appeared. Kurt turned around, looked at it, and sighed. His broad shoulders seemed to slump.

He directed his laser pointer at the Strait of Hormuz and dove in.

"Just west of the Strait of Hormuz, as you know, is where the live fire incident took place. The commanding officer of the USS *Winston Churchill*, Commander Brian Berwick, felt that the ship was under threat from Iranian fast attack boats. He made a judgment call. Audio transcripts from the bridge have been analyzed at the Pentagon. Commander Berwick followed established protocols. He followed the Navy's rules of engagement, as modified after the terrorist bombing of the USS *Cole*, to the letter."

"Casualties?" Haley Lawrence said.

"Twenty-four Iranian KIAs," Kurt said. "Six missing and presumed dead. No American casualties. The Iranians have appealed to the United Nations general assembly for a resolution condemning us."

"That won't get very far."

Kurt shrugged. "It might, it might not. We see it as our job to keep the Persian Gulf open to shipping. Not everyone agrees."

"What's the chatter?" General Kirby said.

"CIA and NSA listening stations are reporting advanced states of readiness throughout the Iranian military. They are prepared for war and on a hair trigger. We are in a very difficult position. If we wait for an attack, we are going to lose thousands of people in Qatar and in Baghdad. If we launch a preemptive attack…"

"We are going to lose thousands of people in Qatar and Baghdad," Susan said. "I think I've heard this song before. Can anyone tell me why we have thousands of personnel deployed where they can't possibly be defended from attack?"

"Because someone would have to be crazy to attack us," Kirby said. "That's the rationale."

"What else?" Susan said.

Kurt nodded. He was beginning to get the dark black circles around his eyes that Susan had seen a few times before. Those circles appeared when the iron man Kurt Kimball was starting to wear out.

"We got another report from Agent Stone. It just came in."

Susan's heart seemed to skip in her chest. Kurt hadn't told her that Stone had reported in. She understood that, she really did. But she was on the verge of pulling Kurt aside and telling him: *When Stone reports, you have to let me know.*

"His people in Tel Aviv relayed an encrypted message that was decoded moments ago. Amy, give me Parchin and Fordo."

On the screens, the map zoomed in to focus on an area in the north of the country, just to the south and west of Tehran.

"Stone has confirmed the presence of nuclear-armed missiles at the Parchin military base here, outside the capital. He has confirmed that the nuclear enrichment facility at Fordo, here, is capable of weaponizing uranium, and that there is a tunnel beneath the ground that connects the two facilities."

"Has he seen this with his own eyes?" Haley Lawrence said.

Kurt shook his head. "No. I don't think so. I believe this is the result of interviews with two Iranian physicists who worked at these facilities. Both of those men are apparently dead. Also, Stone and his team were engaged in a firefight with Iranian military or police, or both. They are alive, but the Iranians are aware of their presence, and Stone and his team are either in hiding or on the run."

"Is that all they found out?" Kirby said.

"Yes, that was all he had to report, and given the circumstances, I doubt we'll get much more from him."

Susan got a terrible sinking feeling. "Shouldn't we extract them at this point? Just get them out of there? If what they're doing isn't going to work…"

Kurt shook his head. "It's a low priority. We've got bigger fish to fry. They have a rendezvous point in northern Iran agreed upon with the Israeli military."

Kirby looked at Susan. He also shook his head. "You're talking about elite commandos who sound like they're at the end of their run. They'll either get themselves to the rendezvous, or they won't. With Iran on a war footing, the border outposts on red alert, and the entire society in lockdown, anyone we send in there now will likely just get killed. Kurt, are we flying patrols?"

Kurt nodded. "We're flying fighter patrols at the edge of Iranian airspace in the Gulf, over Iraq, over Turkey, and over Afghanistan. The Pakistanis will not let us fly patrols—they want to stay neutral. We are coming into contact with Iranian fighter planes, but nothing has happened. It's tense up there."

Susan was revealing too much, but to hell with it—she was going to do it anyway.

"Any way to get a helicopter in there?"

Kurt barely moved. Clearly, he knew what she was doing and at this point he was resigned to it. "I don't know. Maybe. If we had an Iranian helicopter, painted in their colors, and brought it in over the mountains from the Caspian Sea, as though it were coming in from a patrol. That *might* work. Not sure who would be crazy enough to try it, though. I wouldn't give anyone that order."

Kirby waved his hands. "Never mind all that. Agent Stone volunteered for this mission. He knew what he was getting himself into."

He looked at Susan. "Are you ready, Madam President?"

"Ready for what, General?"

"We have a confirmed nuclear weapons site in Iran. They have abrogated their responsibilities under every existing international treaty."

"We have *one* confirmed missile site, General."

He nodded. "That's right. And as far as I'm concerned, that's all we need. We are well within our rights now to hit them with everything we've got."

"Everything, General?"

"Everything."

He looked around the room, taking Kurt, Amy, and Haley Lawrence in with his suddenly steely gaze. He was a hard man, Susan decided. There was no compassion in his eyes.

After a long moment, those hard eyes found their way back to Susan.

"Let's face it, President Hopkins. It's go time."

"General, I like your enthusiasm. And as much as I appreciate your eagerness to ignite a nuclear apocalypse in the Middle East, which we've all learned will likely cause the mass starvation, sickness, and deaths of millions around the world, I'd ask you to let me be the judge of when go time is."

She looked up at Kurt.

"Kurt, any chance you can contact the Special Response Team? Maybe some people there wouldn't mind volunteering to risk their own lives, go in and save their beloved boss from himself."

CHAPTER THIRTY SIX

December 15
5:05 a.m. (9:05 p.m. Eastern Standard Time on December 14)
Jameh Mosque of the Believers
Tehran, Iran

It was a cold morning, the pale sun just beginning to rise over the city.

The morning call to prayer echoed from loudspeakers throughout the city. Three women draped in conservative Islamic dress, their heads and faces covered, moved slowly through the alleys and narrow streets, the masculine, but high nasal call of the muezzin everywhere at once.

Two of the women were quite tall, unusually so for women. The third was a giant among men or women—tall, strikingly broad, from a lost race of dark Amazons. Chewbacca in a burqa.

From under one of the gowns, Luke glanced up at the small speaker mounted on a wooden pole above his head. The sound of the call to prayer was evocative for him—there was nothing quite like it.

He hadn't slept, and so he had swallowed the pill about twenty minutes ago. It was just starting to hit his bloodstream now.

He could feel the changes happening. His heart rate was up. His vision was sharper. His mind was more alert. Before, he had been asleep on his feet. Now he was awake. He was confident. He was eager for information. These were the same feelings a normal person might get from a strong cup of coffee, only vastly exaggerated.

Dexies. They'd been Luke's friend for a long time.

Around them, more and more people joined their procession. Many of the women, the young ones especially, were dressed in much more modern style—a simple dark hijab covered their heads, and their faces were not covered. They wore heavy jackets because of the weather, slacks, even Western makeup.

The most obvious thing about the Iranian men, no matter how they dressed, was how much smaller they were than the three conservative women. This illusion of being Muslim women was not going to hold up for long.

"Are we close?" Luke whispered.

Ari nodded beneath his covering. "I think so. Another short block, maybe."

"How's your shoulder?"

Ari shrugged. "Ed tells me it's a little sore."

The alley wound its way to the right, and again the gold dome appeared in front of them. People flowed through a set of gates and into the main entrance. Just before the gates, streams of people entered from adjoining alleys on the right and left.

The three of them entered the surge of humanity, everyone moving slowly now, wall-to-wall people, white plumes of breath rising in the air. Effortlessly, the women and men segregated themselves, the men heading to the wide entryway straight ahead, the women veering to a narrower doorway on the left.

Luke, Ed, and Ari followed the women's line, truly dwarfing everyone now. A young woman glanced at them, then looked forward. An older woman, dressed in black, but with her face showing, also looked at them. Then looked away.

It wasn't polite to stare.

They climbed a short flight of stairs, and they were inside the building. Immediately, Ari nudged Luke. To their left, there was a rounded flight of stairs, very narrow, headed down. Luke, in turn, nudged Ed. They all turned, ducked their heads beneath the low ceiling, and went down the stairs.

The stairs led them to a low hallway beneath the mosque. The followed it, looking for somewhere to duck inside. At the end of the hall, they came to a room, all in white. They stepped inside.

A man was here. He was an old man with a white beard, wearing flowing white robes. He almost seemed to shimmer, like an Old Testament figure brought to life. His white walking staff leaned against the wall. He seemed to be going through deep-breathing exercises, perhaps preparing himself to lead the large congregation massing above his head.

He turned, startled, when they entered.

"Who told you to come in here?" he snapped. Luke's Farsi, rusty as it had been when they entered the country, was beginning to improve. He understood the man right away.

"Jesus told us," he said.

The man's eyebrows rose at the masculine voice coming from beneath the *abaya*. His eyes strayed to a red button, almost like a plunger, coming out from the wall several feet from him. An alarm,

Luke supposed. It was too far for him to easily reach. He would have to dive for it. Luke calmly walked over and positioned himself between the man and the button.

"Siavash Zadeh?" Luke said.

"They call me Ali Mohammed Tehrani. I am the religious leader of this mosque."

"But you were known as Zadeh, the nuclear physicist?"

The man shrugged. "Of course. In another life."

"The father of the Iranian nuclear program?" Ari said.

"That's going too far," Zadeh said. "The program is a bastard. It has no one father. No one would ever want to claim such a thing as their own." He gazed at the three men, eyes lingering on the sheer size, and potential brute force, concealed beneath Ed's *abaya*. "And you are… what? Men dressed as women? Assassins come to kill me?"

Suddenly, the red alarm button made a great deal of sense. This man spent his life waiting for the other shoe to drop. He was old, but he didn't want to die. The list of people who might kill him, or kidnap him for his knowledge, was long. The Americans might want him, or the Israelis. The Saudis? Almost certainly. Wouldn't they want a nuclear weapons program of their own? The Pakistani ISI? Sure. The Russians might be curious about him, or any number of terrorist organizations that would want to unlock the secrets inside his brain. The Iranians themselves might decide it was too much trouble to allow him to continue living.

Who would come if that red button were pressed? The guardians of the mosque? The guardians of the imam himself? Luke pictured giant men with broad chests, wearing turbans and a sash across their upper bodies, wielding scimitars.

Wrong movie.

"We're not assassins," Ari said.

Luke glanced at him. That's exactly what Ari was. Luke half-expected him to pull his gun and shoot the white-bearded Zadeh in the head.

"We're here to ask you some questions."

"My flock awaits me upstairs."

"They can wait. This should only take a few moments."

Zadeh eyed that button again. He nodded.

"Remove your veils so I can see who I am dealing with. Then ask."

Luke removed his veil, as did Ed and Ari.

Zadeh's eyes moved back and forth.

"I will guess one large American, one very large American, and an Israelite. Unbelievers all. How did I do?"

Luke brushed that off. "Where are the nuclear missiles?"

Zadeh shook his head. "Why would I tell you that? Why would I tell any man?"

"To save your country," Luke said. "To save millions of people, including eighty million Iranians. If your government launches those missiles, what do you think Israel will do? What do you think the United States will do? No one here will survive. There will be a black burnt cinder on the map where it used to say Iran."

Zadeh shrugged. "The same could be said of Israel."

"Will that matter? When all of your people are dead, will it matter that your enemies are also dead? Are they even your enemies?"

Zadeh said nothing.

A thought came to Luke, an argument, a way forward. "What did Abu Bakr command?" he said, referencing the successor to the Prophet Muhammad. "He said, 'Neither kill a child, nor a woman, nor an aged man. Bring no harm to the trees, nor burn them with fire. Slay not your enemy's flock, except for food.' Nuclear weapons do all of these things. They're against Islamic law. You know this is true."

The old man stared at him.

So did Ed.

"Where do get this stuff, man?"

Luke looked at Ed. "I read."

"I didn't even know you *could* read."

"And yet Christian law and Jewish law have no such prohibitions?" Zadeh said. "How convenient for all of you."

Luke turned back to the old man. Something else occurred to him then. There was more going on here than met the eye. The college professor, Ashgar Nasiri, had been wrong about his former boss. Zadeh hadn't become an imam, and dove headfirst into religion, to keep the government from killing him. The government of Iran didn't care who they killed, and they made no apologies for killing people.

If they wanted to kill an imam, they would find a reason why he was an apostate. If he was too popular to arrest and execute, or if he followed Islamic law to the letter and couldn't be accused of heresy, they would kill him in some other way. Poison his food. Have him murdered in a robbery gone wrong. Inject amphetamine between his toes and have eyewitnesses watch him die of a heart attack. Being religious was no protection from the government in this country.

"Why did you become an imam?" Luke said. "After a long career in nuclear science, technology, weaponry…" Luke indicated the man's robes, the spare room, the mosque above their heads.

"Why all this?"

Zadeh stared at him for a long moment.

"You are wise, my friend. You see things that others do not see."

"Tell me," Luke said.

"You already know. I did it to seek Allah's forgiveness. To lead people into the light. To find some way to peace. My God is merciful. I am quite certain that the Perfect One does not agree with nuclear weapons. I am sure that He weeps to think of his beloved children creating such things. They are not a gift. They are a curse."

He looked at Ari. "Only the accursed should wield them."

Ari shrugged. "You will get no argument from me."

"What will you do?" Zadeh said to Luke. "If I tell you the locations?"

Luke didn't hesitate. "Destroy them."

"Can you be sure?"

"We can't be sure of anything. All we can do is try."

Zadeh nodded. "I've waited years for someone to come to me and tell me they were going to destroy the weapons. I've prayed for it in the night so many times that I've lost count. But don't tell me you will try. I didn't pray for someone to try."

"We'll destroy them," Ed said. "I've never tried to do anything in my life."

"You tried to knock me out with one punch," Ari said.

"No, I didn't. I tried to get your attention, and it worked. If I tried to knock you out, you'd still be sleeping."

The old man sighed. A long silence followed as his eyes glazed over, and something inside him seemed to shift.

Finally, he looked right at Luke.

"Remember these names. Parchin. There are at least eight functional missiles there, deep underground. Possibly ten missiles now. You must destroy the entire military base, because some of the missiles are not real. Many people think the missiles are in the southwest corner of the facility. Many have seen those ones, all in one place. They are replicas. The missiles are spread in silos throughout the complex. To get them all, you must destroy the entire complex. It is very large, and many people are there. I'm afraid there will be grave loss of life."

"What else?" Luke said.

"Fordo," Zadeh said. "The enrichment facility there. It is our foremost enrichment facility. It must go. If it remains, they will simply begin the work again."

Luke nodded. Now they had confirmation, from a second source, of what Nasiri had told them. He was very confident that both of these men were not lying. Their stories were even subtly different. Nasiri thought the grouped together missiles were the real ones.

"Are those all?"

Zadeh shook his head. "There is Isfahan, well to the south of here. It is an enrichment facility. There is one centrifuge there that can enrich weapons grade uranium. It is not as advanced as the facility at Fordo. It takes longer to enrich the material, and the results are not as pure. The warheads therefore are smaller, and less powerful. Those missiles, six that I know of, are deployed in deep silos very near to Isfahan. The warheads were moved on conveyer belts through small tunnels to their deployments. The silos make a rough semicircle to the south and west of the facility, each just a few miles away from the others. There is no secondary facility there—just the enrichment facility, and the silos. If you look closely with the most advanced satellite technology, you may notice minor disturbances in the dirt. Beneath those disturbances are iron bunker hatchways leading to the silos.

"You will have to hit those silos at the exact moment you attack Parchin. At each silo, teams of six men live in underground compartments, each taking eight-hour shifts. They are prepared to fire at any time, and independently of one another. It is a very deep secret. Only the designers of the project, and soldiers of the Revolutionary Guards, can be trusted with this information."

Luke looked at Ari.

Ari nodded. "Yes. This was a suspected site." He looked at Zadeh. "And what of Bushehr, on the Persian Gulf? Our intelligence estimates suggest that this—"

Zadeh shook his head. "It's a decoy. We built many things there, all fake. It is a… do you know this phrase? Potemkin village? The enrichment facilities near there could not be made to produce the necessary material. It was obsolete technology. But we carried on building silos anyway, to frighten the Saudis. For a ballistic missile, it is a three-minute flight to Saudi territory from there. It is eight minutes to Riyadh."

"There are no nuclear warheads at Bushehr?" Luke said.

"No. Not one. It's not possible to build them there, and we cannot truck nuclear warheads overland. Too many eyes are watching."

"Anywhere else?"

Zadeh hesitated.

"We have to know," Luke said. "There's no sense telling us all that, but not telling us everything."

"Bandar Abbas," Zadeh said. "The navy base there has at least four nuclear missiles. They were purchased from North Korea and brought in by ship, perhaps because the centrifuges at Bushehr could not make weapons grade uranium."

"Bandar Abbas?"

Zadeh nodded. "It is a two-minute missile flight to the American air base in Qatar from there. Ten thousand American soldiers, plus their families, all dead two minutes after the start of any war. It is the choke point of the Strait of Hormuz. Also, the Safaniya underwater oil fields of Saudi Arabia are very easy to hit. In fact, we calculated that launching just those four warheads could close the Persian Gulf to shipping for a hundred years. Thirty-five percent of the world's oil passes through there, and ten percent of its natural gas."

Luke stared at him.

"You Americans," he said, "always wonder how long we could hold the Persian Gulf against you. In the event of an American attack, we don't need to hold the Gulf. All we need to do is make it impossible for you to use it."

"You would detonate nuclear weapons that close to your own territory? You would poison your own people, and destroy your own access to the Gulf?"

"It was for a worst-case scenario, when all else was lost."

"How deep are the weapons buried?"

He shook his head. "Not deep at all. They are deployed on the eastern end of the base, just below the surface, not far from the football pitches. They are two miles from the town of Bandar Abbas proper."

"That's dangerous," Luke said. "An attack on that base could destroy those nukes. You could have a civilian disaster there."

"What you don't seem to realize is that an attack there will trigger the launch of those weapons, as well as the ones at Parchin and Isfahan. An attack on the other missile sites will trigger the launch of the ones at Bandar Abbas. Like Parchin, it is a military base, not an isolated silo deep underground. They are constantly monitoring the military situation. They have access to instantaneous information. It will take a great deal of luck to destroy all of the missiles in this country, and not expect them to be launched. Any attack on Iran will cause a civilian disaster, not just at Bandar Abbas, but in Jerusalem, in Tel Aviv, in Baghdad, and in Riyadh. In many places."

"Do you have any way for us to confirm what you're telling us?" Luke said.

Zadeh shook his head. "Just my own word. I no longer work in government. I never kept any materials or paperwork. Possessing such things is dangerous."

"What if you're lying?"

"Why would I do that?"

Luke shrugged. "To make us look bad. To make us use overwhelming force against Bandar Abbas, causing civilian casualties."

"Do you really think," Zadeh said, "that in the eyes of the Muslim world, the United States and Israel could look any worse than they already do?"

Luke shook his head. "I don't know. Anything else?"

That had to be it, right? Three nuclear sites. That's all Israeli intelligence had been expecting, and they'd been keeping a pretty sharp eye on this place.

Zadeh stared at him for a long moment.

"Look, I don't have all day, and neither do you," Luke said.

"There is one more," Zadeh said.

From the corner of his eyes, Luke noticed both Ari's and Ed's shoulders sag. Too many. Too many nukes to hit.

"It is a rumor only. I've never seen the facility—it was from before my time in government."

Luke found himself calculating backward. Before this man's time? The 1980s, the 1970s…

"The Shah?" he said.

Zadeh nodded. "Yes. From before the Revolution. Mohammad Reza Pahlavi, the one you call the Shah of Iran. It is said that this despot and traitor deployed several very large Cold War–era nuclear missiles just west of the city, in Khojir National Park, high in the mountains and very near to the ski resort at Tochal. They were meant to threaten the Soviets. That all seems rather quaint now."

"We were allies with the Shah," Ed said.

"The Americans? Yes. Who else would want to threaten the Soviets?"

"And we gave nuclear missiles to Iran? You know this for a fact?"

Zadeh shook his head. "I don't know anything for a fact. It is, as I indicated, a rumor. The weapon transfer, if it took place, happened in the early 1960s, before satellite surveillance had become so… thorough, shall we say? I have never confirmed it. No one from my department ever visited the facility, if it even exists."

Luke needed to call Swann and Trudy. There was a lot to check out.

It was possible, he knew. There were cover-ups and secret histories. Certain operations remained carefully undocumented. Evidence was destroyed. Deniability was maintained. The right hand didn't know what the left hand was doing. Then the people on the left hand grew older, moved on, forgot everything, died.

As he watched, three shapely young women in flowing but form-fitting white robes and white hijabs entered the room from the hallway Luke and his team had come down.

"Teacher," the first one said. "The congregation is awaiting your arrival."

She looked at Luke and Ari. For a moment, she didn't seem to understand what she was seeing. Then she looked at Ed. His hood was off. His veil was down. His beard was not as carefully trimmed as it normally was. His eyes were bloodshot from exhaustion. He was very tall. And thick.

She looked down at the bottom of his black gown. It barely reached his calves. He was wearing combat boots. His feet were big.

The young woman screamed. It reminded Luke of a scream from an old Hollywood horror movie.

People were the same wherever you went. She saw a monster, so she screamed.

Her two companions turned instantly and went running back up the hallway, screaming as they ran. The young woman walked to the red button.

"Don't do that," Luke said.

She pressed it, pushing it all the way in.

Suddenly, a clanging erupted, very loud, in this room, and everywhere. It seemed to echo throughout the building, and maybe even in the streets outside.

"Run!" Zadeh shouted at the woman. "Save yourself!"

She did as instructed, darting out of the room as Ed and Ari watched her go.

"You operating some kind of harem here," Luke said. "Teacher?"

Zadeh shrugged. The ghost of a smile appeared on his lips. "Life is short. May as well enjoy it."

He indicated another doorway, smaller than the one they had come in. "You better go that way. Follow it out to the alley. It will be your only chance. But hurry, or they will beat you there."

There was shouting in the hall that came from the mosque. It was narrow, and the men had to push past the young women. Now heavy footsteps pounded on the stone floor.

"Here they come," Ed said. He pulled a gun from under his gown, but Zadeh darted to him and put a hand on his arm.

"Don't shoot," he said. "Don't shoot my people."

Ed slammed the door and slid the bolt across the door. A second later, pounding came from the other side. Ed and Ari stepped back.

BANG. BANG. BANG.

Bullet holes began to appear as the wood splintered.

"We better go," Luke said.

* * *

They ran through a narrow tunnel, up a short flight of stairs, and they burst out into the cold morning light of the city. It was a curving alley between the mosque and nearby buildings.

A crowd of men ran at them from the left side.

The first man in line, the fastest, young, bearded, brandished a knife. He lunged at Ed, perhaps hoping to bring down the biggest one.

Ed sidestepped and punched the man in the jaw as he flew past. The young man crashed to the pavement. Luke waded in—he ducked a punch, chopped a right hand across a man's throat, followed with a hard left to another man's face. The man staggered backward and fell down. The next two stumbled and fell over him.

Ed threw a man against the mosque wall like a bag of laundry. The man's head bounced off the white wall and he slowly slid to the ground.

"Hey!" someone shouted. "Hey!"

Luke and Ed turned. Ari stood behind them.

"This way. You can't fight them all."

Luke looked. Dozens of men were racing down the alley. A man came running up the stairs to the door Luke and his team had just come out of. Ed planted his boot in the middle of the man's chest, and pushed him and everyone behind him right back down the stairs. It was a domino effect—a logjam of people.

"Let's go," Luke said.

They ran, *abayas* flowing, the alarm bells pealing, a crowd of raging men just seconds behind them. *Assassins!* Luke heard. *Assassins tried to kill the teacher!*

The alley emptied onto a larger thoroughfare. Light car traffic passed in either direction. Across the street, five young men had gathered on Vespa scooters, parked in a semicircle, chatting and smoking. They wore heavy jackets and gloves. Smoke and white plumes of breath rose from their mouths.

Ari darted across the street. Ed and Luke followed, the mosque congregation on their heels.

Ari punched the closest Vespa rider, knocked him to the ground, and hopped on his scooter. He turned the key in the ignition and took off down the street. Luke and Ed, one second behind, did the same. A young man tried to fight Luke for the Vespa. He kicked him away. Ed knocked his Vespa owner unconscious.

Already the crowd of mosque-goers was here, swarming across the street. Why didn't they give up?

A man stopped in the middle of the street and pulled a gun from under a dark robe. He trained it on Ed's massive bulk.

Luke pulled his own gun and fired from the hip. The gun bucked in his hand.

In the street, the gun flew out of the bearded man's hand. He looked down at the hand, shaking off the sting.

"Go!" Luke screamed at Ed. "Go!"

They roared off, pulling away from the congregation. They barreled down the thoroughfare, but now they had a new problem. The two remaining Vespa riders were right behind them.

Up ahead, traffic had stopped for a light.

Ari slowed, then cut right, over a sidewalk and down a narrow alley. Ed did the same. Luke followed. So did the two Vespa riders.

The alley was barely wider than the bikes, the doors to people's homes lining either side. Snow from the night before had accumulated in the alley, and the bikes skidded and slid. An old woman in black stooped over to feed a cat, saw them coming, then dove back inside. The cat leapt in the air. The plate of food went flying, crunchy kibbles landing in the shallow snow.

Luke could see a pursuing Vespa from the corner of his eye. The front tire was *right there* next to him. He waved a hand at the man.

"Get away!" he shouted in Farsi. "Get away!"

Ari hung a sharp left at the end of the alley, his wheels sliding across the wet ground. Ed did the same. Luke followed. So did the men behind him. Five Vespas barreled along the next street. To their right was a long building. Along the side of it, people were unloading boxes from carts and small trucks, shouting or shaking fists as the bikes zoomed by.

Somewhere nearby, sirens began to wail.

A police car was coming up the street from the opposite direction, lights flashing. It straddled the middle line.

Ari turned right and passed through a narrow green iron gate. Men with dollies piled high with boxes jumped out of the way, boxes spilling to the ground. To their left was a green wrought iron fence, ornate spikes at the top. To their left was a series of fountains, closed for the winter.

They passed through a tall minaret-shaped doorway, and instantly Luke knew where they were—the Grand Bazaar, the *bazaaris* getting their wares ready for the coming day. Six days a week for centuries, the Bazaar had been open for business on this same spot, and it wasn't about to stop now. Political unrest, police crackdowns, the threat of nuclear war—that wasn't about to keep the underwear, carpet, and hundreds of other kinds of merchants at home.

Luke was impressed.

They zoomed down a high, narrow stone passageway, festooned with silk tapestries on either side.

The man behind him had crept up next to him again. Was he insane? Luke glanced at him. The man had his helmet on, and his gloved hand was reaching for Luke. The two, very close, sped through a stone archway and entered a wide, vast room filled with colorful rugs laid out on slabs.

Luke pulled his gun again. He brought it across his body and shot the man's front tire. The fat tired exploded and the bike stopped suddenly, the man going head over handlebars. Luke roared ahead.

He glanced back and the man had landed on a pile of rugs.

But the last Vespa was still back there, trailing at a distance.

Ari and Ed were still up ahead. They crossed the rug showroom, entered another narrow passageway, and blasted along, people scattering.

They came out into a tall circular atrium, where several passageways entered at once. The walls were mosaic tiles. Men carried heavy boxes on their shoulders, bent under the weight. Men pushed yellow metal dollies loaded with boxes.

A woman and her little boy stood in the middle of the crowded circle; she was pointing at the ceiling showing something to the child.

Ari came screaming into the atrium, swung sharply to miss the woman and her child, and crashed into a table of books in front of a store. The metal gate of the store was still down. The books went flying. Ari flew through the air and hit the metal gate. He fell to the ground, staggered to his feet, and shook his head to clear it.

Luke and Ed stopped in the middle of the atrium.

Whistles shrieked. Uniformed police came running down the passageways.

"Ari?" Luke said.

Ari seemed confused. He glanced at Luke and suddenly his eyes came alive, as if he had just remembered where he was.

"Go!" he shouted.

Luke looked back. The last Vespa was here. The young man on it stared at Luke and Ed like a dog that had finally caught the car he'd been chasing. Now what? Behind him, two police motorcycles were coming across the rug showroom, sirens blaring.

Luke's head was on a swivel. Cops in this passageway. Cops in that passageway. Where to go? What to do?

Ari hopped on his bike. He rode over to them.

"That way," he said, pointing off to his right. "That way is clear."

Luke looked. To the right was a ramp that went straight up to a catwalk of some kind. The set up brought Luke a wisp of memory from his childhood—the ramps that the daredevil Evel Knievel used to ride on to approach his stunts.

There seemed to be a second level up there, at the far end of the catwalk, possibly with stores or food stalls. Above the narrow concrete catwalk was a giant crystal chandelier, the largest thing of its kind that Luke had ever seen.

What the...

"Come on, let's go!" Ari said.

Luke and Ed didn't have to be asked twice. Any second, this foyer would be swarming with cops.

Ed took off, Luke half a second behind him. They raced up the ramp and across the catwalk, beneath the shadow of the sparkling chandelier. The sheer size of it was like a great whale above their heads.

Luke crossed the catwalk, skidded to a halt, and looked back.

Ari wasn't with them. He had climbed off his bike again. He had his Uzi out now. What the hell as he doing?

He looked at Luke. "What are you doing?" he shouted. "Go!"

Now Ed was back again. "What's going on?"

Suddenly, Ari opened fire at the chandelier. He ripped into it, hosing it with bullets near its base. Crystal bulbs shattered, shards of glass flew. Then the entire massive fixture fell from the ceiling, dropped twenty feet, and crashed into the catwalk. An instant later, the concrete of the catwalk cracked, fell apart, and the entire bridge went tumbling down, crashing to the floor of the empty level below it.

Luke and Ed found themselves across a chasm from Ari and the police, who were now closing in. There was no way to get over there. Ari might as well have been on the other side of the Grand Canyon from them.

Ari dropped the gun.

The first policeman arrived. Ari punched him to the ground. Another came. And another. He fought them. More came. He waded in.

He fell back, his arms nearly pinned by police. He pulled his arms free. Ari's bike crashed to the ground, three cops tumbling on top it. Ari swung. More cops came.

He disappeared beneath them.

Luke and Ed exchanged a disbelieving look.

Ari had just sacrificed himself for them.

And there was no way to go back and save him.

CHAPTER THIRTY SEVEN

5:30 a.m. Israel Time (6:30 a.m. Tehran Time, 10:30 p.m. Eastern Standard Time on December 14)
Tel Aviv, Israel

The phone was ringing.

Swann opened his eyes. The heavy blinds were drawn, and it was still dark in the hotel room. He was curled into a ball on the couch. If he tried to stretch out, his feet and his head extended past the arms. It was a small couch. He rolled over and sat upright with his feet on the floor.

The satellite phone rang through his computer speakers—pleasant tones, rising and falling almost like chimes. He looked around the hotel room. The place was a mess. Clothes strewn about, computer equipment all over a fold-out table, wires snaking everywhere, empty food boxes and trays, dirty plastic utensils, cans of soda and beer.

"Swann!" Trudy said. "Are you going to answer that?"

He looked at her through a pair of half open French doors. She was on his big, king-sized bed, also curled into a ball. Why was a tiny little person like Trudy curled into a ball on his huge bed? It would make a lot more sense for Trudy to be curled up on the couch, where she would easily fit, and Swann to be sprawled out as much as he wanted, limbs extended like a giant bird, on the bed.

Certainly he would have slept better under that arrangement.

"Why are you even in here?" Swann said. "Don't you have a room?"

"Swann! It's probably Luke."

Luke. Shit.

A rush of adrenaline kicked in. Swann checked his watch and snapped out of it. 5:30. He had stayed awake all night waiting for his call. He remembered being up and seeing 4:52 on the clock. He must have fallen asleep shortly thereafter.

Swann stumbled across the carpeted floor to the computer. He slid into his chair, put his headphones on, and answered the phone.

"Helu," he said.

"Swann. Two things. I need to make a report, and then I need you to help me."

His voice was frantic, as always.

"Is everything all right?" Swann asked, sensing the worst.

"No. We lost Ari."

Swann's heart dropped.

"Is he…"

"He was captured. We need to get him back. That's what I need your help with. In the meantime, pass on this information."

Luke started talking. He had confirmed another nuke site, debunked one the Israelis thought was a nuke site, and uncovered one they hadn't known about. He had also heard of a rumored site, where there might be leftover Cold War–era nukes.

What he had achieved was mind-boggling. As Swann typed it all down, Swann dimly realized that the information he was about to convey could change the course of human history.

Swann got it all. He glanced at his watch. Getting on toward 11 p.m. in Washington, DC. He'd better relay this before they broke for the night.

"What's the story with Ari?" he said.

"There was a chase and he sacrificed himself to save us. And we're not going to leave him behind."

Swann shook his head. He knew this was going to be bad.

"What can I do?" Swann said.

"Find him. We're in Tehran. He's a foreigner, and they're going to assume he's a spy. They must have somewhere in town that they take prisoners like that. They must have to transfer them from place to place. Look, if they find out he's an Israeli, they're just going to torture and kill him. We need to break him out before that happens."

The pit in Swann's stomach deepened.

"Break him out? Luke—"

"Swann! I don't want a lecture, okay? When you were captured in Syria, we came and got you, and everybody was trying to give us a lecture. This is a good kid. He's on the team. We're going to get him out."

There was a long pause over the line. Swann pictured himself relaying this information to the White House. With missile systems everywhere on red alert, Luke Stone was going to go rescue someone.

"Here's what I need from you guys," Luke said. "Any chatter at all about a new foreign prisoner. Could be Iranian government networks, could be Shiite terror networks, anything. He was captured early this morning at the Grand Bazaar, before it opened. Maybe Trudy can find out where they normally take captured spies."

"Got it," Swann said.

"Now the hard part," Luke said, and Swann rolled his eyes. "I need to know exactly where he is. The location, the exact building, the room number on the door. If he's being transported, I need the vehicle description, the route, the license plate number, the name of the driver and his home address."

"Luke, I don't even speak Farsi."

"I'm not asking you to do it, Swann. I'm asking you to get it done. Use our resources back home. Borrow people from the CIA. Commandeer a spy satellite. Put a hundred analysts on it. Just find me the kid, okay? I'll do the rest."

"Okay, Luke," Swann said. "Okay."

CHAPTER THIRTY EIGHT

11:05 p.m. Eastern Standard Time
The Situation Room
The White House, Washington, DC

"Military base Parchin is a confirmed nuclear missile site," said the disembodied voice coming through the black speakerphone console in the center of the conference table. The voice was that of Mark Swann, the data analyst on Stone's team. He was calling them from a hotel room in Israel.

Susan was beyond tired now.

She couldn't remember ever seeing the Situation Room this crowded. There were at least fifty people packed inside. The walls were lined with chairs, each chair with a person on it, and an aide or two aides standing nearby. The young aides were typing into their tablets, or scribbling furiously into notepads.

The conference table was littered with coffee cups and empty plastic takeout containers. It looked like a war zone. Every seat at the table was taken. Susan was at the head of the table, Kat Lopez crouched next to her. There was a steady hubbub of noise, the low background hum of whispered conversations. There was also a smell in the room—the smell of people who had been on the job for sixteen hours without a shower.

Stone had resurfaced again, with a lot more intelligence to offer this time. It had set off a frenzy, as staff from the White House, the Pentagon, and the spy agencies scrambled to make sense of it.

The fact that Stone had resurfaced made Susan want to vomit with relief.

Kurt Kimball stood in front of a screen at the other end of the table. He was in his shirt sleeves. The dress shirt was too small for his big chest and arms.

"Reconfirmed," Kurt said. "You already confirmed Parchin before."

Over the speakerphone, a woman's voice said something in the background. Swann hesitated. Was that the voice of the infamous

Trudy Wellington? Susan imagined it was—she knew Trudy was going on this trip with them. Thankfully, Stone hadn't tried to hide it.

Trudy probably didn't want to call any attention to herself, being a former enemy of the state and fugitive from justice.

"Reconfirmed, but changed," Swann said. "The previous data was that the missiles were clustered in one section of the base. We believe that was a ruse. You need to hit the enter base. Repeat, the missiles are salted throughout the base—to get them all, you have to take out the enter base."

That set off a burst of chatter.

Kurt raised his big hands, looking for quiet.

"That's a large base," General Kirby said. "It'll be tough to take out the whole thing."

Susan looked at him. "Aren't you the same General Kirby who was calling for massive strikes earlier tonight?"

Kirby shook his head. "Susan, there is a very big difference between precision strikes and massive, preemptive ones. You're calling for precision strikes, but at the same time you want to take out one of the largest military bases in Iran. If you want to do that, you have to go in with overwhelming force."

Susan shook her head. At some point, she was going to get through an entire day without a man lecturing her. She didn't know when it would be, but on that day she was going to bake herself a cake.

"If we need to take out an entire base, General, we will do that. Without resorting to sending in our entire air force."

"Can I continue?" Swann said over the speaker. "I've got other things to do. You might want to let me get through everything, and then argue about it."

"Please," Kurt said. "Continue."

"Isfahan enrichment facility, due south of the capital. Confirmed."

Another burst of chatter went around the room.

Kurt clapped his hands. CLAP. CLAP. "People! Agent Swann has a hot date. So let him get to it. Take your notes. If you have questions, raise them formally to the group. Don't waste time talking to each other."

"At least six warheads at Isfahan, silos arranged in a rough semicircle a few miles south and west of the main facility. One hundred and eight meters deep. I believe I have found surface evidence of at least three of these silos from satellite data. I'm uploading that to you now—the silos are marked in red in the second image. I think your analysts can probably extrapolate the other locations from these."

"Good. Amy?"

Kurt's assistant, Amy, sat near him at the far end of the table. "It's coming in. One more minute."

"Isfahan is deep in-country," a woman in military dress greens said.

"Yes," Kirby said. "But six silos right near each other are perfect for a precision strike. One sortie can take the whole thing, especially at that depth. A second can go in for insurance."

"If they make it that far," the woman said.

"Next," Kurt said. "Next!"

"Bushehr," Swann said. "Debunked."

Another swell of chatter. To Susan, Kurt looked like he wanted to bite someone's head off.

"It's a decoy," Swann said. "They were never able to build nukes there. The source claims that the nukes are instead at Bandar Abbas military base, well to the east of there, also on the Persian Gulf. This is a new suspected location—it was not part of Israeli intelligence. These missiles are in shallow silos at the east and west sides of the base. I believe these are easy to see from satellite data. Your own analysts should be able to scroll back through years of data and…"

"Yes," Kurt said. "See the progression of the silos, before they were built and after."

"Right," Swann said.

"Anything else?"

"Suspected, not confirmed," Swann said. "Khojir National Park, just east of Tehran. In the mountains, possibly near the Tochal ski resort."

There was quiet in the room, finally.

"Amy?" Kurt said.

On the screen behind Kurt, and on screens throughout the room, a large green mass appeared, east of the capital city of Tehran. It was at least as large as the city. Amy zoomed in on an area in the southeast section of the park. Tochal.

"That's it?" Kurt said.

Swann was noncommittal. "That's what the man said, apparently. I've looked at satellite data, but I don't personally see anything on the surface worth reporting. It's a big area."

"Who is the man?" General Kirby said.

"His name is Siavash Zadeh," Swann said. "He's considered the father of the Iranian nuclear weapons program."

"Did he give more detail about the location?" Kurt said.

"He doesn't know anymore. He said it happened before his time."

"I know about Zadeh," Kurt said. "The man is in his seventies. Before his time was fifty years ago."

"Yes."

"Are you saying there are fifty-year-old nuclear weapons buried somewhere in an Iranian national park?"

"I'm saying that's the rumor."

"Who put them there?" Kurt said.

"We did," Swann said. "The CIA. To target the Soviets, if you believe rumors."

The burst of chatter now was more of a wave, rising, rising, reaching a crescendo, before breaking and then rising again. The idea of American ballistic missiles, nuclear weapons, sitting quietly underground for half a century, while Iran transformed from a secular ally to a theocratic enemy dominated by mullahs… well, that got people talking.

"Where is Stone now?" Kurt shouted.

Susan leaned in to hear the answer. It sounded garbled, drowned out by the talking in the room.

"Shut up!" she shouted before she realized what she was doing. "Everybody! Please shut up!"

The room instantly went silent. The President of the United States had just shouted for everyone to shut up. The stricken faces around the room suggested that nothing like that had ever happened before.

"I'm trying to listen to the intelligence report," she said.

"Agent Stone is in hiding inside Tehran. They lost one member of the team—the Israeli member. He was captured by the Iranians. Agent Stone and Agent Newsam intend to go back for him."

"Uh, negative," Kurt said. "If Agent Stone is still operational, we're going to need him to go to Khojir National Park and confirm the existence of those weapons. That is a civilian facility. We need to know, before any strike, if the weapons are really there. We also need to know where."

"Can't you find that out by having people with high-level clearances go back through old top secret documents from the CIA?" Swann said.

"We may be able to, we may not. That could take days. Also, we might be able to determine a location or locations, but if the CIA was really involved, there may be decoy sites. There probably will. We are still going to need eyes on the ground to confirm."

Over the phone, the entire room could hear Swann's sigh.

"I'll tell him."

"Swann?" Kurt said. "Tell him it's a direct order from the President of the United States."

"I'll do that," Swann said. "And I'm sure it will work. I've never known Agent Stone to disobey a direct order before."

CHAPTER THIRTY NINE

7:20 a.m. Tehran Time (11:20 p.m. Eastern Standard Time)
Near the Grand Bazaar
Tehran, Iran

Hide in plain sight.

They hadn't gotten very far. Not far at all. But staying close was better than running in the open, especially when everyone was looking for them, especially when they had no idea where they were going.

They were in an old warehouse diagonally across an old plaza from the Grand Bazaar. There were tapestries and rugs piled in here, but it looked like no one had used this place in years. The tapestries were worn and eaten through. The rugs were in huge piles. Everything was covered in dust.

Ed leaned against the wall near a window smeared with soot. He watched the streets outside, the *bazaaris* still bringing their wares, early customers starting to arrive. The police were out there, too. Dozens of them. Military vehicles went shrieking by from time to time.

Ed's pistol was drawn. The M79 was slung over his back.

"You know, the Bazaar looks like it's seen better days," he said.

"Everybody shops uptown now," Luke said. "You go to the north end of the city, it's all malls, expensive restaurants, beauty salons. Tehran is going high end, high-tech, cosmopolitan. It was already going that way the last time I was here. Old Tehran is slowly being forgotten."

"They still torture people, though," Ed said.

"Some things never go out of style."

Luke sat on a dirty bench, waiting for the phone to ring. Trudy and Swann were going to find them the kid. He knew that was true. Then they were going to call here with the information. This phone wasn't going to be cooked just yet, and the cops weren't going to come tumbling in here the instant Swann called.

Ed shook his head. "He shouldn't have done that, man."

"He did it to save us," Luke said.

"Misguided. We all could have made it."

"No we couldn't," Luke said, looking at him. "You know that."

Ed frowned in acknowledgment. As much as he clearly hated to admit it, Ed would be dead right now if it weren't for that kid. Not only that, but the kid had saved Ed twice. Of all people, it had been the kid. That arrogant, annoying, loud-mouthed Israeli kid whom Ed had hated at first.

And as much as Ed hated to admit it even more, he had taken a liking to that kid. Ed didn't do that easily. That kid had sacrificed himself for him. And in Ed's eyes, that had made him a brother for life.

Now a brother of his had been taken. And Ed never left a brother behind.

Ed clenched his jaw and bunched and unbunched his fists.

Once they got free from the Bazaar, they never considered for a moment leaving the kid behind. There was no way they were leaving without him. He was on the team.

"If those guys find out he's an Israeli…" Ed said.

Luke nodded. "I know it."

"How long you think it will take to break him?" Ed asked.

"I don't know. Depends on what they do. He seems pretty tough, but you know the deal. When they really get to work, it doesn't take long."

Ed nodded. "I know." He paused. He looked back at Luke.

"Is Swann going to call, or am I gonna have to go back to Tel Aviv and press his fingers to the keypad?"

Just like that, the phone started to beep.

"Speak of the devil," Luke said. "Watch for any activity. If this phone is burnt, we need to know that."

Ed nodded and looked back out the window. "Got it."

Luke pressed the green button.

"Yes."

Swann launched in without preamble. He spoke without revealing anything specific. He must have been worried about the phone as well. If Swann was worried, that was a bad sign.

"Here's the deal. I called them. Got right to the top. They were very interested in what you had to say. They told me negative on the retrieval. Negative. Do not do it. They need you to stand by. There's going to be more coming from them in a little while. They want you to take a walk in the park and find something they lost a long time ago. They can't remove it unless you find it."

Luke didn't say anything. He let all that sink in. They wanted Luke and Ed to go find the nukes near the ski resort. How were they supposed to do that?

"That comes straight from the person in charge," Swann said.

"The man or the woman?"

"The woman."

He pictured Susan sauntering to her closet the morning he left, while he sprawled out on the bed. She must be pulling her hair out by now worrying about him. That, and she needed to handle all these other little details, like when to call in massive air strikes and spark a nuclear war.

"Did you get me what I asked for?" he said.

There was long pause over the line.

"Swann?"

"Yes. We did."

"Tell me."

"We're going to burn this thing, if it isn't cooked already."

"I don't care," Luke said. "I need it, so give it to me."

"Okay," Swann said. "I'll go as fast as I can. Trudy pulled up some intelligence on an old police precinct house on the far southeastern edge of the city. "Police Precinct Thirteen. It hasn't been a precinct house in twenty years or more. It's a notorious torture spot. They bring detainees there who they don't plan on logging into the system."

Luke listened, said nothing. They were going to bleed Ari for whatever they could get out of him, then they were going to toss him away like a used rag. He might hold up for a while, he might not. The Iranians probably wouldn't even care. God help him.

An image came to mind. The Iranian scientist in Evin Prison—ragged, emaciated, shivering, broken, and asking to die.

"What else?" Luke said.

"I got some satellite data over the past several hours. Nothing consistent, but there has been activity—a van pulled in there soon after you called, then left again five minutes later. I'm looking at the building now, real time, probably a one-minute delay with all the bouncing around I'm doing with these signals. The skies have cleared and I have a nice shot of it. The place is pretty run down, like no one has been in there in years, but there are four cars parked in a lot behind the building. There's a security fence, with a guy who opens it and closes it manually. A black Mercedes limousine pulled in there a little while ago, and a man went into the building surrounded by bodyguards. Looked like somebody important. I can't guarantee anything, but I'm going to guess that's where he is. Trudy says she would swear by it."

"Put her on."

A moment passed, then her deep, feminine voice was there.

"Luke?"

"Give me the scenario, your entire reasoning, in thirty seconds or less. If we guess wrong here, the whole thing goes up in flames."

"They took him there," Trudy said simply. "The timing is perfect. It's close by. There's activity onsite. What Swann didn't tell you is satellite data suggests no one has even gone inside that building in the past three weeks. Suddenly people are there? Data from CIA, Mossad, ISI, MI6, and NSA-captured transmissions all indicate the place is used for torture and elimination of special prisoners. It's a disappearance center. That's the only reason it's ever used. They have a special prisoner, a foreign spy, right when they're on the verge of a nuclear war. Where are they going to take him? To a real jail? I don't think so."

Luke took a deep breath. "Okay."

"Luke?"

"Yes."

"It's very, very dangerous. It's a black site. They're not going to let you just waltz in there."

"We're not going to waltz."

Something occurred to him then.

"It's on the far southeastern end of town?" he said.

"Yes."

"Would you say it's on the way to the national park?"

"It is, yes."

"So theoretically, we could just swing by there, pick up our friend, and then head out to the park?"

"Luke, you're insane. But yes. In theory, you could do that."

"Good. Now, I'll need exact directions."

Trudy put Swann back on the phone. Luke listened as Swann described to him where the precinct house was. It was only four miles east and south of their current location. If they could pick up a ride, they could be there in ten minutes.

"Let's keep in touch, shall we?" Luke said. "I have a hunch I'll be needing you again."

He hung up.

Ed stared at him. "Details?"

Luke explained the details to him. For a few moments, Ed became lost in thought. He eyes were looking at something far away from the dim and dusty insides of this warehouse. After a little while, he seemed to return to the present. His eyes focused on Luke again.

"We find a back way out of here. A quiet street. We carjack something, preferably a military vehicle." He shrugged. "We go over there to Precinct Thirteen, and we ram the gate. They're not expecting us."

He pulled the M79 around to his front. He patted it.

"We knock a couple holes in the wall with this. Go in, get Ari, pop a cap in a few Iranians, then we leave. Go check out these nukes or whatever. Call it in, then we go home. How does that sound?"

Luke made a face. It was a face where he gritted his teeth and his mouth dropped away from his jaw. It was a face he made in childhood a lot when his mother said something he wasn't happy about. It was a face he rarely made in adulthood. Somehow, the muscle memory was still there.

"It sounds hot."

Ed shrugged. "We hit hard, we move fast, we get a couple of lucky breaks…"

His voice trailed off. Suddenly, Ed looked tired.

"How does it sound to you?" Luke said. "Honestly."

Ed shook his head. "It sounds like the hottest thing ever."

Every second they waited was another second they would be torturing Ari. They both knew that.

And so, with a small nod, they each jumped and bolted from the room at the same moment.

CHAPTER FORTY

8:05 a.m. Tehran Time (12:05 a.m. Eastern Standard Time)
Precinct House 13
Tehran, Iran

"I'll ask you this again. What is your name?"

Mohammed Younessi stood over the young man chained to the metal chair. The chair had narrow arms, which the young man's arms rested upon. His wrists were manacled to the ends of the chair arms. The young man was stripped to a white T-shirt and shorts. His T-shirt was stained with dark blood.

They were in an old, long disused meeting room, in a long disused police station. The room was mostly empty. The carpeting had been pulled up. The walls were bare. The large windows were covered by wooden boards. The only light came from a single bulb depending from the ceiling. A guard stood by the door, and two others stood along the wall by the boarded windows. All three carried rifles.

As barren as the room was, there was still electricity. In case they needed it, there was electricity to spare. They might get to that later. Right now, they were only working on preliminaries.

Younessi ran a hand over his perfectly bald head and took a drag on a Turkish cigarette as he stared at the helpless man. The man's face was bloodied, but not broken. The police had beaten him before bringing him here, but it seemed to have little effect on him. Although his head drooped down from time to time, his eyes did not show fear.

That alone proved he was not Iranian. All Iranians, when they met Mohammed Younessi, were already terrified.

"My name is Alireza Saadat," the young man said in Farsi. Yet it was Farsi with very little regional accent or flavor. It could be Farsi learned from a book, or from many months in a classroom. "I told this to the police. I come from Rasht. Everything is a mistake. I have done nothing wrong."

Younessi smiled. “But you lied to the police. You were with two men, and you sacrificed yourself to help them escape.”

The young man shook his head. “Not true. I have no idea what they are talking about.”

“Tell me,” Younessi said. “Where is your accent from? It sounds rather… generic.”

“Rasht, of course. It is an international city, and a melting pot of many cultures. Many of our countrymen come from all of Iran. You fall into an accent that is from everywhere and nowhere at once.”

Younessi took another drag on his cigarette. He decided to change directions a little bit. “They call me the Director of Accountability, did you know that? It’s my title. They also call me the Director of Compliance. I would like you to comply with my questions.”

The young man nodded. “I am trying to do that.”

“Why did you visit the mosque of Siavash Zadeh, the one they call Tehrani?”

The young man shrugged. “I had been told his Quranic talks were excellent. The best in the capital city. I wanted to hear for myself.”

“He told us you are an Israeli assassin, and that you came to his room with two Americans. If an assistant did not ring the alarm, you would have killed him.”

“No such thing happened. I heard that men tried to attack Imam Tehrani. But I was not there. I was worried for him.”

“Well, you needn’t worry any longer. All the excitement was too much for him, I’m afraid. You and your friends did not kill him, but the work was done anyway.”

Younessi shook his head. What he did not say was that Zadeh had died while being interviewed. The moment the hard questioning began, a few slaps, a couple of heavy punches, and poor old Zadeh’s heart had given out. Rather inconvenient, that. They had just been getting started.

“I am very sorry to hear that,” the young man, the supposed Israeli, said.

Younessi almost laughed. “No you aren’t.”

He was already growing tired of this person. It was time to accelerate past the preliminaries. A few simple actions would take them straight to the heart of the matter. He stepped very close to the young man, the Israeli who claimed his name was Saadat, and squatted next to him. Younessi put his face near the young man's cheek.

He still had the lit cigarette in his outstretched hand. He held the glowing red ember very close to the young man's forearm.

"I want you to do something for me," Younessi said, his voice hardly above a whisper. "I want you to show me how very strong you are. I want you to demonstrate your manhood. Don't scream. Deny me the pleasure of hearing it."

He pressed the ember to the brown skin of the young man's arm, right into the muscle there. The cigarette sizzled as it punched into the flesh.

A tiny stream of smoke rose.

The young man's eyes were pinched. His mouth was clamped shut.

Younessi held the burning cigarette there. Smoke continued to rise. "That's right, take it like a man," he whispered. "Show me your manhood. Show me your toughness." The Israeli's entire body shook, like he was strapped to the electrical rail of a commuter train system.

After a long moment, Younessi pulled the cigarette away and took another drag from it. He remained crouched next to his prisoner.

"When I discover for a fact that you are a Jew," he said conversationally, "I am going to put the cigarette in your eyes."

"Put the cigarette in my skin again," the young man said, his eyes hard. "And I promise I will kill you."

Younessi smiled and looked back at the guards. They were all smiling as well. Younessi almost laughed. "What an enjoyable young man you are. Now we know you're not really from Rasht. Rasht is such a cosmopolitan place! What a desirable destination. Delicious foods and coffee. Art and fashion. It is so forward thinking, with so many comforts, the men there have nearly become women. I don't think I've seen a man from Rasht take a lit cigarette without screaming in pain. And then to issue threats afterwards? I've never heard of such a thing."

Younessi extended his cigarette toward the young man's forearm again. He held it less than an inch from the skin, very near to the bright red welt of the previous burn. He paused, the cigarette dangling so close.

"Do it," the young man said. "I dare you."

Younessi pressed the cigarette into the flesh again. He drove it in hard and deep, burying it. It was amazing the way the cigarette just punched in there. Younessi never tired of seeing that. He would like to conduct an experiment that explained the mechanisms involved.

The young man's body bucked. He closed his eyes, his breathing coming in harsh rasps, but he didn't say a word.

After a moment, Younessi pulled the cigarette away again. This time it was out. He had put it out in the man's flesh.

He stood. "Of course you are a foreign agent. You've been trained to withstand torture. That's fine with me. Wonderful. When the sessions are longer, I enjoy them more." He looked down at the young man, whose eyes were still closed, and who was still breathing heavily.

"You and I are going to become great intimates," Younessi said. "Do you think cigarette burns are the extent of my skills? I hope not."

Suddenly, an alarm sounded. It was very nearby. Indeed, it was here on the grounds of this old police station. In his years of coming here, no one had ever sounded an alarm. Younessi, surprised, found himself looking skyward. All he could see above him were the rotting boards of the ceiling.

Had the war started already?

He looked at the guard near the door. "Find out what that is," he snapped. "If bombers or missiles are incoming, we need to find shelter."

Another sound came then, the sound of a very large engine accelerating. It was coming from outside the room, on the other side of the boarded windows. He looked in that direction. The two guards stationed along the windows turned around to look. The sound was right behind them.

CRASH!

The boards blew inward, shards of wood and shattered glass flying everywhere. The two guards were thrown back, instantly eviscerated. Their bodies fell to the floor in two heaps. The grille of a large truck appeared where the boards had just been, headlights on, steam rising from the hood. It looked like a malevolent face.

Younessi reached for his firearm.

Already, the guard at the door was firing at the truck, obliterating the windshield. There didn't seem to be anyone in there.

To Director Younessi's left, the wall of the building suddenly blew apart and caved in. He sprawled on the ground like a snake.

He knew there had been an explosion, but it was so loud, he hadn't heard it. His gun was gone. Burning debris floated everywhere. There was a loud ringing in his ears. He had been in combat against Iraq when he was a young man. In just a few seconds, he pieced together what had happened—someone had fired a mortar or small rocket at the side of the building.

Who would do this? A bombing attack was one thing, but a ground-based mortar attack? Younessi found that he could not stand. He looked and a long shard of wood protruded from his right leg. He began to crawl toward the door.

Where was the other guard? Fled, probably.

As Younessi watched, a large black man stepped through the whole where the wall had just been.

And for the first time in his life, he understood what those whom he tortured felt.

True terror.

* * *

Luke lay on the floor of the truck beneath the steering wheel. He pushed the heavy mat of broken safety glass from the windshield off his body.

Ed had just blown out the wall, and that seemed to have put an end to the shooting for now.

Luke kicked open the driver's side door and slid out. He looked around. There was big Ed Newsam, kneeling by the kid, cutting his manacles off. The kid's face was a mess. His shirt was covered in blood. That was okay. He looked all right. At least he was alive.

Closer to Luke was a tall, bald man in the green uniform of the Revolutionary Guards, injured and crawling on the floor. He was moving a little faster than a snail's pace, and he seemed to be headed toward the door. Probably Ari's interrogator. Luke would deal with him in a minute.

"Did I tell you?" Luke said to Ed. "Right on the money."

Swann and Trudy had found an old diagram of this small, squat building. They had guessed, correctly, exactly which room was used for prisoner interrogations.

"That's why they get the big bucks," Ed said.

Once he was free, the kid walked toward the bald man, a maniacal look in his eye. Luke had seen that look: it was the look of vengeance. It was a look that said nothing would stand in its way.

After a moment, the kid stepped up behind the man crawling on the floor.

"Hey!" Ari shouted. "Turn over."

The bald man rolled over to look at him. There was sheer terror in his face.

Luke heard a noise and looked down to see the man had wet himself.

"I wasn't going to hurt you," the bald man said, pathetically.

Ari snorted at that.

He bent down, grabbed the piece of wood buried in the man's thigh, and twisted it. Hard.

The man shrieked like a girl.

"Hey, Ari," Luke said. "We don't have all day."

There was a Mercedes limousine parked behind this building, probably armored, and their next step was to fight their way to it before reinforcements arrived.

Ari extracted the wood slowly from the man's thigh, then raised it high and plunged down the jagged end between the man's legs.

The man's shrieks, if possible, rose another decibel, as blood pooled out between his legs.

"Please!" the man whimpered.

Ari was not finished, though.

"Remember you said my eyes were next if you found out I was Israeli?" Ari asked.

"I didn't mean it!" the man pleaded. "It was just an empty threat."

But Ari's scowl deepened.

"Well, you were right. I *am* an Israeli," Ari said. "And this is for you."

Ari raised the jagged wood and high and brought it down into the man's eye. The man shrieked as Ari plunged it deeper and deeper.

Finally, the man was quiet. Still.

Dead.

Ari stood and looked at Luke, his eyes glazed, as if coming out of a daze. He seemed almost sheepish.

"I promised him I would do that. And I always keep my promises."

Luke shrugged. "We're not taking prisoners today. If you didn't do it, I would have."

Ari slowly smiled as Ed stepped forward and clasped his small hand in his huge one with a genuine affection Luke had never seen him display before.

"Welcome back to the team, brother."

CHAPTER FORTY ONE

12:30 a.m. Eastern Standard Time
The Family Residence
The White House, Washington, DC

It was late. She had been awake for eighteen hours.

She sat alone in the kitchen of the Residence. She was ensconced in the breakfast nook, eating a giant bowl of raisin bran topped with almond milk. She was trying to give up dairy products. It was a tough road.

A Secret Service man was posted just outside her door.

She had come up here to take a little break, and get away from the madness of the Situation Room. Kurt had broken up the meeting and sent most people home a little while ago. Still, a skeleton crew was going to stay the night, in case any more crises developed. Kurt was part of that crew. So was Kat Lopez. So was Haley Lawrence.

It seemed like they were expecting another crisis any minute.

The cell phone at her elbow rang. This was a secure phone, encrypted, and ran on a government network. Long gone were the days when Susan had a private cell phone.

She picked it up without even looking at it. This time of night? It was probably Pierre. It was just after nine on the west coast.

"Hello?"

"Susan?"

She could barely believe it. It was Stone.

"It is so nice to hear your voice," she said.

His voice sounded like it was coming from inside a sewer grate. There was a delay of several seconds between them, which made talking awkward. Still, it was him.

"Funny thing," he said. "It only just occurred to me to give you a try. All this time, I've been communicating in the most roundabout fashion possible. I could have just gone straight to the horse's mouth."

"Should you do this?" she said.

"No. I shouldn't. But I'm doing it anyway."

"Where are you?" she said. Somewhere in her mind, she hoped he would say, *"At the American embassy in Baghdad,"* or *"On a flight back to Israel,"* or best of all, *"I just landed at Reagan National."* Of course, none of these answers were possible.

"I'm driving a black limousine with smoked windows. We are headed to a famous national park to check out the sights."

"How is your friend?" she said.

"He's fine. A little bleary, a little wear and tear on him, but all in all, better than I expected."

"You know," she said, "you don't have to do this. Anyone would say you've done enough. You could just come home now."

"You know that won't work," he said. "You know that as well as I do."

"I don't care," she almost said. *"I just want to see you alive again."*

But she didn't say that. Instead she said:

"I love you."

There was a long pause over the line. The delay accounted for part of it, yes, but it was longer than the delay. Much longer.

"I love you, too," he said at last.

"I know," she said, and a tear appeared at the corner of her eye. It broke free and slid down her cheek.

"Don't die, okay?"

"I haven't died yet, have I?"

Before she could answer, his voice changed. "Listen, I've got to run. I'll talk to you soon." Then he was gone.

"Don't go," she said into the blank telephone.

The Secret Service man poked his head in the door. He was holding his earpiece to his ear. "Madam President?"

"Yes?"

"I'm just getting word. They need you in the Situation Room. There's a problem."

* * *

"Hello, Yonatan," Susan said.

She looked around the Situation Room at the tired, shocked faces that surrounded her. Kurt was here. Kat. Several others. Everyone looked like they had already been hit by a bomb. Everyone in the room was holding a phone to their ear, to listen to this call.

"Susan, this is a courtesy call," Yonatan Stern said. "We have made our preparations for war. We can no longer wait. As of five minutes ago, we have begun a full mobilization of Israeli civil society. Everyone is being sent to the bomb shelters. Our nuclear silos are reporting readiness as we speak. Within thirty minutes, we will begin our attack."

"Yonatan, we sent a team of covert operators to you. They've risked their lives. You said you would give this plan forty-eight hours. That was the time frame your own people came up with. The plan is working. They have one more site to confirm. You can't just—"

"Susan, we can and we will. We are already doing so. Are your listening stations not tuned in to the chatter on Iranian military networks?"

"I'm sure they are," Susan said.

"They are aware that there are infiltrators inside their country, attempting to discover the location of their nuclear sites. As a result, they have moved to a state of full readiness. They are not going to wait for the United States to come in and destroy their weaponry. More than eighty percent of their missile silos are now prepared to launch, with more coming on line all the time. They are just waiting for the order. That's what we're hearing."

"They're *waiting* for the order, Yonatan. They have not launched."

"I'm sure you'll understand that we cannot wait until after they launch. We must strike first."

Susan shook her head. "What good will that do you? You launch first, they launch three minutes later. You both get destroyed. I hate to see your society destroyed, Yonatan, don't get me wrong. However, that's your decision, and your affair. But by doing this, you're also putting tens of thousands of Americans in Qatar and Iraq at risk. And you're putting millions of people around the world at risk. Many people who don't live in Israel, and who don't live in Iran, will die from radioactive fallout. I really don't like you doing that."

"There is a chance..." Yonatan said. "If we launch first, and we hit them with everything we have, there is a chance that—"

"There's no chance, Yonatan. Give up on that idea. There's no chance. Almost all of your people will be killed. Your country will be turned first to flames, and then to dust. A toxic shroud will envelope the Earth, leading to sickness and starvation for millions throughout the Middle East and Asia. Eventually the effects will reach everyone in the world. Is that what you want?"

"I won't be here to see it," Yonatan said. "I cannot just sit here and allow my country to be destroyed. They started this war. Not us. They attacked us first. We are going to launch a full-scale conventional attack on their military bases. We are not launching nuclear weapons. If they should respond with nuclear weaponry, as they have claimed, then we shall retaliate. Good day, Susan. Good evening for you. You are very far from danger. I am afraid your relative safety has clouded your thinking."

"Yonatan, you're the one whose thinking—"

The phone went dead. For the second time in the past half hour, a man had hung up the phone on her in a wholly unsatisfactory manner.

Kurt didn't even bother to make his customary throat-slicing gesture. He simply put his phone down in its cradle. Susan did the same.

She looked at Kurt. "What are we supposed to do?"

"Bomb Iran," Haley Lawrence said. "We have B-2 bomber sorties outfitted with thirty-thousand-pound GBU-57 Massive Ordnance Penetrator bombs, along with fighter escorts, flying at the limits of Iranian airspace right now. They are prepared to make their runs at a moment's notice. We have three sites confirmed. We bomb those with precision strikes. And we bomb that national park back to the Stone Age. We hit the whole thing. Carpet bomb it."

A military man in dress greens shook his head. General Kirby had long ago gone home, or wherever it was that generals went.

"It would take at least a hundred sorties to bomb that entire park," the man said. "It's larger than the capital city. We don't have that many airplanes in place. We don't have that many GBU-57s."

"Hit them with MOABs," Haley Lawrence said.

The man, a colonel, shook his head. "Secretary, you're showing the limits of your expertise a little bit. The MOABs won't go deep enough. If you wanted to wipe out villages, they'd be fine, but they're not bunker busters—they're not going to take out nukes buried deep underground. And villages bring me to my next point.

"There are more than a dozen villages inside the confines of that park. The decision to carpet bomb would mean killing thousands of civilians. It wouldn't work anyway, because we just can't do that many bombing runs inside Iran—it would take hours. And after the first few strikes the Iranians would know what to expect, and they have robust anti-aircraft defenses. We could lose a lot of men, and a lot of equipment in there. Also, if we didn't hit the nukes on the first try, what's to stop the Iranians from launching? We either know where those missiles are, and we hit them with a handful of deep bunker busters, quick precision strikes, or we can't go in."

Susan looked at him. "Colonel…"

"Colonel Criden, Ma'am. Buck Criden."

"Well, Buck, that's the most sense I've heard a man make all day."

She looked at Kurt.

Kurt shook his head. "It leaves us without a plan."

Susan sighed. "Here's the plan. I want our people out of there. I want any nonessential, non-military people still loitering in Qatar and Baghdad evacuated, starting now. If Israel won't wait, I want Stone and his team extracted from Iran. But we do everything in our power to buy Luke more time."

She looked around the room.

"That's my plan. Do you have a better one?"

"No."

Susan clapped her hands. The claps were not nearly the thunderclaps that Kurt was famous for, but they got people's attention. All around the room, tired faces snapped awake.

God help you, Luke, she thought. *Come through for us.*

CHAPTER FORTY TWO

8:01 a.m. Israel Time (1:01 a.m. Eastern Standard Time)
Samson's Lair – Deep Underground
Jerusalem, Israel

The command center was dead quiet.

Yonatan Stern sat at the head of the conference table without moving. Every set of eyes in the room, thirty pairs, were looking directly at him. They were waiting for him to give the final order—the order that would bring an end to their enemy Iran, of course, but also to themselves. It was an order that would dash the dreams of countless generations over two thousand years.

It seemed that insanity had won. It seemed that terror had won.

All along, for many years, his hope had been to reach a place where Israel achieved complete peace through unassailable strength. Eventually, Israel would become too powerful to attack, and their enemies would simply leave them alone. Or even better, become their friends. It hadn't happened. Nothing of the sort had happened.

Suddenly, Efraim Shavitz spoke. The Model's suit jacket was off and his shirt was rumpled. There were sweat stains under the arms. He had a day's growth of beard, and his hair hung limp and dirty and mussed. He was the Model no more.

"Who are you, Yonatan? Who are you to make this decision?"

Yonatan shrugged. "I was elected. The people chose me to make this decision. I've been preparing for this moment my entire life."

"For what moment? The moment you gave the order to kill tens of millions of people? You've been preparing for that? It seems an odd thing to prepare for. And I'm sure no one elected you to do it. I'm sure your ancestors would cry to see you now. This isn't what they wanted for Israel. They wanted to live in peace, and in prosperity, in God's Holy Land."

"What would you have me do?" Yonatan said.

"Wait. Wait until we hear from the infiltration team again. Give them the chance to do their jobs."

"And if our enemies attack in the meantime?"

Shavitz shrugged. "Let our friends avenge us. And let them remember us by knowing that all we wanted—all we ever wanted—was to live here in peace."

No one spoke. Unlike earlier, no one shouted Shavitz down.

A clock on the wall ticked.

Tick-tock. Tick-tock.

Yonatan watched the second hand. It seemed to move with impossible slowness.

Tick.

Finally, he sighed.

"We will give them one more hour," he said. "Pass that information to them, if they are still reachable. One hour. We cannot wait any longer than that."

He looked everyone somberly in the eye.

"God help us if that's too long."

CHAPTER FORTY THREE

9:25 a.m. Tehran Time (8:25 a.m. Israel Time, 1:25 a.m. Eastern Standard Time)
Khojir National Park
Iran

"This should be interesting."

Luke sat behind the wheel, piloting the black Mercedes limousine up into the mountains along a back country road. The Mercedes was a luxurious car. Deep leather seats. A dashboard like the control panels on a corporate jet. A thick glass panel between the front seat and the rear, which Luke had already lowered.

They were all wearing green Revolutionary Guards uniforms, right down to the baseball cap with the gold logo on it, that they had looted from the dead bodies back at the police station. Luke's uniform was a pretty tight fit. Ed looked like he had borrowed some dress clothes from a ten-year-old boy. The hat fit okay, but the rest?

Ari had managed to wipe most of the blood off his face, so that was good. But he was pretty lumped up. Ed had started calling him Lumpy. Ari was wearing the uniform of a major. His Farsi was the best of the bunch.

The plan, such as it was, involved Ari pulling rank and shouting. It was a cockamamie plan, one that Luke had no faith in at all. It was all the worse because Luke was the one who had thought of it. It was all he could come up with.

Hey, at least the road had been cleared of snow.

Swann was watching them on a real-time satellite feed, at a fifteen- or twenty-second delay. Analysts had found a spot they thought might be the missile site. No one was sure. If it was wrong, Luke had no idea what they were going to do next. Each step that they took further down this path, the more it seemed like there was no way back out. Eventually, they were going to come to a dead end. The bottom of a missile silo seemed like about as dead an end as you could find.

"When you get to the top here in a minute, you're going to come to a gate," Swann said in his ear. "It's got a couple of guards.

You're either going to have to convince them you're legit, or you're going to have to kill them. I don't see a lot of other options."

"Then what?"

"Then proceed further up the road half a mile to an outbuilding. It's got a couple of guards, as well. Four, to be precise. We're guessing that's the elevator."

"Pretty lightly defended, wouldn't you say?" Luke said.

"I don't like it," Ed said behind him.

"Right?" Swann said. "For a nuclear installation, it's crazy. But they've been pretending for decades this place isn't even here. That's the only thing I can figure—they hide it by making it look like it's nothing worth looking at. Either that, or we've got the wrong place."

Through the snow-covered trees, Luke could already see the fence to his left. The guard gate was going to be right up ahead.

"Okay, I have to run," he said.

"Hey, Luke," Swann said. "Just a friendly reminder. You've got about thirty minutes until our friends unleash the Apocalypse. No rush. No pressure."

"I'll keep that in mind. Shouldn't you guys evacuate?"

"We're waiting for you, buddy. And Ed."

The road came around a corner, and there was the gate. The guards wore winter coats and heavy fur hats. It looked chilly up here. The views to the right were of undulating, snow-covered hills, with larger mountains in the distance. To the left, on the far horizon, was the city.

"Okay, Lumpy," Luke said. "This is for all the marbles."

"That's fun," Ari said. "This new nickname is fun. I hope I live long enough for it to catch on."

"I think it will," Ed said. "Since nobody knows your real name."

Luke powered his window down as a young guard came up to the car.

"Orders," the kid said in Farsi, his hand out. It seemed he was expecting Luke to give him a piece of paper. Luke shrugged and indicated the back of the car with a tilt of his head. Just the driver, nothing more.

"Orders," the kid said again.

"There are no orders," Ari said from the back seat.

The kid looked at him. "Sorry, sir. No orders, no entry."

Suddenly Ari shouted. A blur of angry Farsi flew past Luke's head. He tried to slow it down, pick out the actual words. He caught "Director of Accountability," and "you better open this gate."

Director of Accountability?

That sounded ominous. In the context of Iran, being held accountable did not seem like a good thing. The next words were easier to catch.

"You see my face? He did this! I'm a ranking officer! What do you think he'll do to you? Open this gate. NOW."

The kid hesitated, backing away.

"Now, I said!"

The kid unlocked the padlock and pulled the gate back on its rollers. Luke glanced at it. Twenty-foot-high chain-link fence, topped with looping razor wire. A fence like that kept honest people honest. Bad guys would beat it in a minute.

There had to be more ahead. Either that, or the fear of crossing the government kept even the bad guys honest.

Luke pulled through the open gate. The kid bent over and looked inside. "Do you know where to go?"

Ari snapped at him. "Of course we know where to go, you idiot." He waved his hand violently. "Get away! Get away from my car!"

Luke pulled away slowly, suppressing a laugh. He powered the window back up. He glanced into the rearview mirror. Ari's face really was a mess.

"That was pretty good, Lump. Looks like you fooled them."

Ari shook his head. "I fooled them for the next five minutes, maybe less. In a moment, he's going to go in that little guardhouse, phone his superiors, and find out that the Director of Accountability is dead."

It was a short trip to the next stop. The concrete outbuilding was one story high, with a corrugated iron door. Four men with machine guns stood outside. They wore the same heavy coats and hats as the men at the gate.

Luke pulled the car up about thirty yards from the men, reached under the steering wheel, and untied the ignition wires. Ed had hotwired the car—Luke didn't want the guards to notice there was no key.

They stepped out and crossed the small lot. An icy breeze blew, easily penetrating Luke's uniform. Rolling snowy mountains surrounded them, though this was the highest point nearby. Maybe fifty yards to their left was a black tarmac—light wisps of snow and ice blowing across it. A helipad.

Ed had rolled up the sleeves of his shirt to make the arms look as if they weren't too short. There was nothing he could do about the pant legs. There was nothing he could do about the tightness across his chest, the buttons straining, holding on for dear life.

"You look like a stripper about to bust out of that thing," Luke said.

As they approached, one of the guards punched a green button on the side of the building. The metal door slid upward, taking its time. Inside was a concrete foyer, and the door to an elevator. The guard went to the elevator, turned a key in the locking mechanism, and the door slid open.

"Bingo," Luke wanted to say, but didn't.

The guard seemed as if he would join them inside. Ari held up a hand as if to say STOP.

"Watch my car," he said in Farsi. "Don't touch it."

The guard nodded and the door slid shut. Immediately the elevator began to drop. It moved slowly, inexorably, toward the center of the Earth.

"You're getting pretty good at throwing orders around, Lump," Luke said. "You might have a future as an officer in the Iranian army."

"Or on the Special Response Team," Ed said.

Ari put a finger to his lips.

The elevator had no windows. It moved smoothly along, barely making a sound, and going very slow. Minutes passed. There was nothing to look at. These missiles were deep underground. Luke began to wonder if conventional weapons could reach this far down. Nukes could do it, but they weren't firing nukes. Had a bunker buster ever taken out something like this?

More time passed. How the hell were they going to get back out?

At last they stopped. The elevator bounced just a touch, and the door opened.

They stepped out onto a catwalk.

Below them was a vast cavernous space. Banks of ancient computer consoles were in the near foreground. The consoles had small video screens, clock faces, dials, and buttons. Every ten feet or so was a command keyboard.

About two dozen men and a handful of women in military uniforms moved about or sat at the consoles. Above their heads were more four modern video screens, like the jumbotrons at a football game. Each screen appeared to show a different ballistic missile, mounted in a silo. The screens scrolled through various angles—upright from a distance, worm's-eye view looking straight up the length of the missile, a view from above the nose cone. There was Persian writing on the fuselages of the missiles. There were also American flags, which had never been painted over. The missiles themselves were silver, and were at least five stories tall.

"Ed?" Luke said.

"It's real, man. Those are American-made Titan I missiles, deployed in the early 1960s, then scrapped almost right away—like three or four years later. That thimble-looking thing there at the top is a W38 nuclear warhead. Three and a half megatons, if I'm not mistaken. More destructive power than all the bombs dropped during World War Two combined, including the bombs dropped on Hiroshima and Nagasaki."

"And they've got four of them here," Ari said.

"Yeah."

"What's that computer system?" Luke said.

"UNIVAC Athena," Ed said. "Vintage, circa late 1950s. It was designed to launch missiles and nothing else, and that system is probably married to the onboard computers of those specific missiles. Real primitive, but the kind of thing that used to launch men into space. I'd say this one predates the earliest versions of the Internet by at least ten years, which means it was probably never networked to the regular world. These days, I doubt anything is left that can communicate with it."

"Meaning the system is isolated," Luke said. "Launch and control can only come from here?"

"In all likelihood, yes."

Luke's hands started to roam his own body. He had two Israeli grenades left. He glanced at Ed. Ed had at least a couple of Israeli grenades. His M79 was gone. It wouldn't have looked right walking into an Iranian missile silo with a big American grenade launcher strapped to his back.

"Why were the missiles scrapped?" Luke said.

No one seemed to notice them up here on the catwalk yet, or if they had, they didn't show the slightest interest in them. They had a minute, maybe no more than that, to talk. If he could get a sense of the capabilities of these things, and their vulnerabilities, maybe he could figure out what to do about them.

Ed shrugged. "Technology was moving too fast. These things were obsolete almost before they were deployed. They operate on liquid fuel. An oxidizer has to be added at the very last moment to get the fuel to ignite. If you look closely, you'll see they're sitting on hydraulic platforms. They have to be lifted to the surface before they're launched. The whole mess can take fifteen minutes or more, if people know exactly what they're doing. Longer if the people are clueless. Who's got that kind of time?"

"Can they hit Israel?"

Ed nodded. "Oh yeah. And with pretty good accuracy. They're fast, and they're big. If they can still get airborne after all these years, just one of these things would turn Tel Aviv into a Rorschach test."

Luke looked at Ari. "Can Israeli missile defense knock these out of the sky?"

Ari shrugged. "I'd hate to have to find out."

"If we blow that command system…" Luke said.

Ed was noncommittal. "The UNIVAC? Maybe."

"It might be worth a shot," Luke said.

"Yeah," Ed said. "The only problem would be if they switched the missiles over to a different operating system years ago, and the UNIVAC, and all these people, are just for show. I wouldn't put it past them."

Luke pondered that. Right until the alarm bells went off.

It started with a loud buzzer that went for several seconds, then stopped as abruptly as it had started. An instant later, the clarion started. CLANG, CLANG, CLANG, CLANG, CLANG.

Then another sound joined in.

WHOOOP. WHOOOP. WHOOOP.

The two shrieking sounds overlapped and engulfed each other.

"What is that, the war?" Ed said. "They started the bombing?"

"I don't think so," Ari said. "Look!"

The catwalk started to shake. Luke looked down toward the other end. A door had slid open and a squad of men ran toward them.

"I think they figured out my ruse," Ari said.

"Oh man," Luke said. He drew his gun, the last one he had left—a pistol he had taken from a dead Iranian officer at the police station.

Without thinking, he ran straight at the approaching men, gun pointed. He fired.

BANG!—the sound deafening, echoing through the cavern of the command center. Ahead of him, a man dropped. The other men were bringing their weapons around.

He fired again.

BANG!

Another man dropped. Below him, people were screaming.

He threw the gun and barreled into the crowd of soldiers. Now his fists were flying, beating men down. Suddenly Ed was next to him, doing the same. Fists, knees, elbows, they battered the Iranian soldiers, and were battered by them. Ed flipped a man over the side. A rifle fell to the steel surface of the catwalk.

Ed picked it up. He shot a man on the ground. Luke barely heard it. His ears were ringing. The others were running back the way they came.

Luke looked down at the floor of the command center. Ari was down there. He stood amidst chaos, as people scrambled to get away. He was shouting something.

Between the alarms and the ringing in his ears, Luke could barely hear him.

"What?"

"Your grenades! Throw me the grenades!"

Oh. Luke unclipped his grenades and tossed them over the side, one after the other. Ari caught them both. He pulled the pin on one and placed it on one of the large UNIVAC consoles. Then he ran.

"Don't look now, man," Ed said. He pointed to the other side of the command center. Another squad of troops had emerged from a door over there. They weren't coming up here. Instead, they were assuming firing positions.

BOOOM!

The grenade went off.

The explosion was insane. The catwalk shook, knocking both Luke and Ed to the deck, but it did not fall. For an instant, the cavern was filled with red and orange light. The overhead lights flicked and went out, making this part of the command center dim, but not dark. Not black of night. Somewhere nearby, emergency lights were still operating.

Luke blinked. In his mind's eye, he rewound a few seconds. He saw the computer system blow apart, and then black smoke begin to pour out. No way that smoke was good for you. The smoke began to rise up all around him.

Machine gun fire strafed the catwalk, bullets ricocheting.

"Ow!" Ed shouted. "Ow! Ow! Ow!"

"Ed?"

"It's okay, it's okay. I'm hit. I'm hit in the bicep."

Luke couldn't see him. Ed was obscured by smoke.

"You all right?"

"I'm hit, man. Every time I come out with you, I get hit. Do you ever get hit?"

"Yeah, I do. I got hit a few weeks ago. Remember? It's not like I never get hit."

BOOOM!

Another grenade went off. Somewhere, on the other side of this smoke, sparks and flames flew. It was impossible to see down there now. Gunfire erupted everywhere.

The catwalk began to shake again. A man came running out of the smoke. At first, he was nothing more than a silhouette. A moment later, he turned into Ari.

"You guys ready?" he said. "I blew the computers. I think we better get out of here."

The elevator ride to the surface was interminable. At every moment Luke expected it to stop. The three of them stood there, silent, sweating, the place filled with acrid smoke, the distant rumble of ongoing minor explosions.

And yet, somehow, none of the Iranians, in all the smoke and chaos below, thought to do the simplest thing—to stop their elevator.

They reached the top and the three of them burst out.

Luke was expecting a blazing gun battle when they came out of the elevator building. Instead, the four guards were gone. So was the Mercedes. Iranians knew how to hotwire things, too.

Luke pulled out his phone and pulled up Swann's number. For several seconds, the phone beeped, then his voice came on.

"Helu," Swann said.

"Khojir National Park," Luke said. "Confirmed. Four Titan I 1960s-era ICBMs. Very deep underground. Massive bunker busting ordnance required. You have the coordinates."

"Roger that," Swann said.

"Good bye, Swann."

"Good luck," Swann said. "Be safe."

Luke hung up the phone. He wasn't sure what was going to happen, but it certainly seemed like he had just called an air strike in right on top of their heads. They stood in the empty lot for a moment, white plumes of breath rising from their mouths. In the far distance, south and west of the city, giant explosions erupted. A few seconds later, three supersonic fighter planes streaked overhead, one by one, very low, their engines screaming, splitting open the sky.

Ed was covering his ears with his hands. Blood ran from his right arm. His shirt was shredded there. He had the Iranian rifle slung over his back.

"Those were American fighters," he said. "It looks like the war *has* started. This is probably not a good place to stand for very long."

"With no car, I don't know where you'd like us to go," Ari said.

Close by, Luke spotted a chopper in flight. Had it always been there? It seemed to appear out of nowhere. It was a Bell helicopter, a variant of the common UH-1 Huey troop transport that Americans flew. A lot of militaries used that chopper. This one had the distinctive yellow and black markings of the Iranian Air Force. It was coming down to the helipad.

"Maybe we can borrow that chopper," he said.

He started to walk toward the pad. Ed unslung his rifle.

"Watch those forward guns, man. M60s, they'll slice us to ribbons in two seconds flat. Don't irritate those pilots."

Luke saw the two forward machine guns, loaded with big 300-round ammunition belts. Slice them to ribbons? Those guns would liquefy the three of them, and barely leave anything for the crows.

The chopper touched down lightly. Luke put his hands in the air and walked slowly, moving straight toward the cockpit. Suddenly, a woman's head popped out of the right hand side of the cockpit.

He couldn't believe it.

It was an American.

It was Rachel.

"Luke!" she shrieked. "What are you doing? Run! We don't have all day."

* * *

The chopper lifted off, banked hard left, and turned toward the north. In a moment, they were flying fast over snow-capped mountains, the sprawl of Tehran to their left, and then behind them. Straight ahead, maybe twenty miles away, was wide open water.

More fighter jets zoomed overhead, moving faster than sound. Compared to them, this helicopter crawled at a snail's pace.

Luke poked his head into the cockpit. There was a woman and a man in here. The woman was putting her helmet back on over her auburn hair.

He knew these two—of course he did. Rachel and Jacob. They were old friends of his, and they had followed him to the Special Response Team. Both of them were former U.S. Army 160th Special Operations Aviation Regiment—code names Nightstalkers. The Nightstalkers were the Delta Force of helicopter pilots.

Rachel was as tough as they came. She had a muscular body, like the old Rosie the Riveter posters from World War Two. She had recently given up her long-held career as an amateur cage fighter. Meanwhile, Jacob was as steady as a rock. He was very thin, all angles and jutting Adam's apples. He looked nothing like your typical elite soldier. But his calm under fire was legendary. He was one of the best helicopter pilots on Earth.

Luke liked Rachel. He liked her fire. Always had. He liked them both, and that was putting it mildly. Right at this moment, he liked them more than ever before.

"What are you guys doing here?" he shouted.

"Your girlfriend sent us," Rachel said.

"My girlfriend?"

Jacob shook his head and smiled. "She's teasing you. The President asked for volunteers to come in here and extract you people. We had nothing better to do, so we raised our hands."

Behind them, an explosion rent the sky. An instant later, a shockwave hit them and the helicopter shuddered. Luke nearly fell forward into their laps.

Jacob raised a hand. "We're okay."

Luke went back to the side bay door and looked back. A massive bomb had just hit the Khojir facility, right where they had been a few moments ago. A cloud of smoke and dust reached high into the sky from the explosion. An instant later, another bomb hit, and another gigantic explosion went up.

Luke held on tight as the next shockwave hit. He looked at the sky. The bombers were so high, he couldn't even see them.

South of the city, anti-aircraft guns opened up, looking for something to hit. Luke turned and looked forward. The chopper was dropping in altitude. Already they were almost out over the water. They were flying fast—better than 130, Luke would say.

He passed through the hold again. Ed and Ari were strapped into their seats. They'd both taken some lumps this morning. They were sitting back with their eyes closed. They looked ready to call it a day and let the pilots do their jobs. Luke poked his head into the cockpit again.

"What's the plan here?" he said. "I know we're not flying this thing back to DC."

"We're running for daylight," Rachel said. "We get over the Caspian Sea, then out past Iranian territorial waters, we should be—"

Just then, the radio squawked. A voice shouted in Farsi. Luke heard it and knew instantly what it meant.

"Helicopter, identify yourself."

"Oh boy."

Below them, the land ended and they passed over the water. For an instant, Luke caught a glimpse of waves breaking white against the shore.

"What do they want?" Jacob said.

"They want us to identify ourselves. Got anything for that? A mission name, call numbers, anything bogus that might hold up for a few minutes?"

"No. I really don't. We launched this thing off a ship out at sea. It's just an old captured Iranian Huey. It's a little outdated, but it rides pretty much the same as one of ours. Swann sent us the coordinates through channels, and we flew in there without talking to anybody. I don't know why they need to talk to us now."

"Identify yourself now," the voice said over the radio. "Or we will shoot you down."

"Sounds like they don't trust us," Rachel said.

Luke looked out through the windshield. The dark sea buzzed by below them, maybe fifty feet down, almost close enough to touch.

"I don't even see anybody out here. I'd just ignore that guy and keep moving. What do you think?"

Neither pilot had time to answer. The second Luke spoke, a jet flew by overhead, the shriek of its engines impossibly loud.

"Fighter plane," Rachel said. "Same colors as this, yellow and black."

"Did you get a make on it?" Jacob said.

"Looked like a MIG-21, Russian made."

"Terrific. Luke, if I were you, I'd go strap myself—"

Another jet screamed by. A dark shadow went by, to the left and behind the plane. Then another.

"We've got trouble."

"Can't we do anything?" Luke said.

"Against those guys?" Rachel said. "Supersonic fighter jets?"

"Just asking," Luke said.

Jacob glanced to his left and skyward. Suddenly he shouted. It was an act so out of character Luke didn't know what to make of it.

"Incoming!"

"Right stick!" Rachel screamed.

Luke dashed backward, moving toward a seat to strap in. Suddenly, the chopper lurched hard right. Luke fell to the floor of the hold. The chopper banked, flying nearly sideways. Luke clung to the floor. Through the right side bay door, the water was right in front of him.

Then gunfire erupted all around them. Bullets ricocheted inside the cabin. Metal shredded and sparks flew.

Luke caught an image of Gunner. Not tall, thirteen-year-old Gunner. But tiny, eight-year-old Gunner, already into zombies at that age, wearing Dawn of the Dead footsie pajamas.

"Circling," Jacob said, his voice calm again. "Coming back around. Jesus."

"Circling?" Luke shouted.

"The jets are circling," Rachel said.

Luke pulled himself upright. He had to get strapped in. He fell into a seat, pulled the leather straps around himself.

"Fighter number one," Jacob said. "Making a run. Here… he… comes."

Another burst of gunfire came. THUNK, THUNK, THUNK, it shredded the metal skin of the chopper.

Rachel made a squeak, almost like a mouse.

Something was severed up front and steam began to shoot out in a violent cloud.

Ed opened his eyes. He shook his head. "This day just gets better and better."

"How's your arm?" Luke said.

Ed nodded. "It hurts, man." The shirt was soaked through with blood.

"Sorry," Luke said. "I should have patched it up when I had the time."

"When was that?"

Luke shook his head. "I don't know."

"Fighter number two," Jacob said matter-of-factly. "Incoming."

Luke closed his eyes.

THUNK, THUNK, THUNK, THUNK, THUNK.

It sounded like hard rain falling on a tin roof. Metal peeled and shredded all around them. Somewhere glass shattered.

An alarm in the cockpit began to sound.

BEEP, BEEP, BEEP…

Jacob's disembodied voice said: "Mayday, mayday. Tail rotor is hit. We're going to lose it. Assume crash positions."

The world zoomed by with dizzying speed. Luke glanced out the bay door. They were maybe thirty feet above the water.

Suddenly the chopper went into a spin.

"Tail rotor gone!"

The chopper zoomed along, spinning like a pinwheel. Luke was pressed against his seat. The chopper lost altitude, dropping with a sickening lurch. He looked out again—they were just above the water.

"Prepare for impact."

The chopper smacked the water hard, skidded along the surface for a second, then flipped. Luke felt it go, nothing gradual about it, upright one second, upside down the next. The chopper rolled, tumbling in darkness. Luke's head whipsawed and:

Everything went black.

CHAPTER FORTY FOUR

10:12 a.m. Tehran Time (9:12 a.m. Israel Time, 2:12 a.m. Eastern Standard Time)
Deep Underground
Islamic Revolutionary Guard Corps
Al Ghadir Missile Command
Iran

General Lotfi Farhadi walked quickly through the hallways of the missile command center, on his way to what he often thought of as "the war room." Several aides flanked him, trailing him by a few meters. The group's footsteps echoed along the otherwise empty corridor.

The general had a sinking feeling in the pit of his stomach.

Just ahead, a wide automatic door slid open. He passed through the doorway and into the swirling chaos of the command center's main room. The chatter of voices hit Lotfi like a wall as he entered.

The ceiling was three stories high, causing an echo effect. At least two hundred people filled the room. There were fifty computer consoles, many with two or three people huddled around them. Twenty feet above the heads of the personnel were a series of video display monitors.

Screens showed digital maps of Iran, Iraq, the Persian Gulf, and Saudi Arabia, as well as the wider Middle East. There was a map of Israel, the Palestinian Territories, Lebanon, and Syria. Satellite imagery showed smoke rising from explosions inside Iranian territory. Digital reports scrolled across a screen in Persian script—hundreds of conventional missile silos across the Iranian heartland were reporting combat readiness.

It was now or never, as people sometimes said.

Farhadi clapped his hand on the shoulder of a young man, a first sergeant monitoring a computer screen.

"What has happened?" he said.

"Simultaneous precision attacks at Parchin, Isfahan, and Bandar Abbas, sir. Moments later, a deep penetration attack at Khojir National Park. The first three are our nuclear missile facilities, are they not?" the sergeant said. "That makes sense. But why would they bomb a national park? There's nothing there."

General Farhadi ignored the question and asked his own instead.

"Air defense response?"

"Ineffective, sir. High-altitude American bombers with stealth technology, escorted by advanced supersonic attack fighters."

"Okay," Farhadi said.

It was interesting to him how resigned he was—not just to the destruction of nuclear capabilities so many years in the making, but also to his own fate.

Just then, a wide-eyed colonel rushed up to him. "Brigadier General Javan requests an immediate response to these unprovoked attacks."

"What are the reports from the nuclear silos?" Farhadi said.

"None. Complete destruction. All systems down. Preparedness at zero."

"Khojir?"

"A firestorm, as far as we can tell."

"Then what response can there be? We are left only with conventional missiles, and we will receive nuclear apocalypse in return." He paused. "Have they attacked anywhere else?"

"No, sir. Only the nuclear facilities. They made precision strikes, then fled as fast as they arrived."

"The Americans?"

"Yes. We believe so. Almost certainly."

Then that was it. The Americans, or Israelis, had succeeded to wipe out all of their nuclear weaponry. Somehow, they had found it all.

Now it was too late. Just moments ago, he had been prepared to launch all of Iran's nuclear missiles.

But with them all destroyed, there was nothing he could do.

"Then, as I indicated, there is no response."

Suddenly, the colonel stood ramrod straight and tall. "Sir! The Brigadier General insists on a response in kind."

Farhadi shook his head. "I cannot help him with that. It is suicide. I will kill myself before I kill the entire Iranian people."

It occurred to General Farhadi then that he would like to take retirement, if such a thing were possible. Of course, it was far too late for that. He turned to leave the war room. There was no sense staying here. If there was time, he would at least like to see his wife again.

"Sir! Need I tell you what the reaction of the Supreme Council will be to this abject failure to act?"

The automatic door slid open, ejecting Farhadi into the long corridor. It felt like a release from bondage. He didn't even bother to answer. For every epic failure, there must be a scapegoat.

"You were right, General. You are killing yourself."

Farhadi nodded. "I know."

CHAPTER FORTY FIVE

Time Unknown
Whereabouts Unknown

Someone slapped him across the face.

"Wake up, mister! Wake up."

There was going to be hell to pay.

For what seemed like hours, Luke had faded in and out of consciousness, resisting his body's urge to wake up. He knew very little. They had made a run for it over the Caspian Sea. They had been shot down. They hit the water.

And he was alive.

He was on a cot somewhere, and in pain. The cot was narrow and uncomfortable, with a hard backing—like a prison cot. His eyes were covered by some kind of bandage, so he couldn't see. It was impossible to toss or turn, even if he wanted to—his body seemed to be fastened to the cot somehow.

He realized he was not in his right mind. He assumed he was in Iran, likely to be tortured and executed just as soon as they got around to figuring out who he was. But the people around him seemed to speak a language he could not understand—if it was Farsi, they were speaking too fast for him to catch even a single word.

All until a moment ago. Now, the man slapping him was speaking English.

"Wake up, please!"

Suddenly, the man's hands removed the blinders that had covered Luke's eyes. Light flooded in, and Luke blinked and squinted in response. A smallish man with café au lait skin stood over him. His brown eyes were bright and merry. He slapped Luke across the face again, not hard, not soft, but firm. It was a firm slap. There was no menace in it.

"Don't slap me," Luke said. "Okay?"

"I'm just waking you up."

"Thanks."

Luke glanced around. He was in a room, very rustic, with wood paneling, a wooden table, and a chair. It was chilly in here. There was a large window. Through it, Luke could see the water in the distance. This building appeared to be on a hillside.

He looked at the cot he was on. He wasn't fastened to it. He was under wool blankets, including his arms, and the bed was made so tightly, and tucked so well, that Luke could barely move. It was less a preparation for torture than the handiwork of an overzealous maid.

"Where am I?" he said.

"You are in Turkmenistan," the man said with evident pride. "Your helicopter crashed into our territorial waters, and our navy rescued you. We thought you were Iranians, but now it seems you are Americans. I am fluent in English, so I am your assigned guide and translator. My name is Gurbanguly Gorski. You can call me Gurbanguly, if you like."

"Thanks, uh…" Luke said.

"Gurbanguly," the man said again.

"Yes. Are any of my friends alive?"

"All of them, of course. We rescued everyone. A pilot, a large black man, another man, and a woman who was sitting next to the pilot."

"She's also a pilot," Luke said.

The translator seemed momentarily troubled by that idea. "Oh? Yes, of course. All of them alive and well, in any case. With minor injuries only."

"What now?" Luke said.

"Well, you've been identified as the leader of this group."

"Yes."

"The President of our country is eager to meet with you. He loves Americans."

"Ah," Luke said. "What is his name, please?"

Gurbanguly looked at Luke closely, again momentarily troubled. "Saparmurat Berdimuhamedeow," he said with a shrug, as if such a thing should be obvious. It was a household name in Turkmenistan. Would it not be in America?

"And when would he like to meet with me?"

"Now."

"Now?"

"Yes, right now. He is outside the door, waiting for me to awaken you. That's why I was slapping you. It seemed the speediest way. I will inform him you are awake."

As the translator went to the door, Luke worked to wrench his arms free of the blankets. A moment later, another small man appeared in a blue suit, a custom fit. He seemed slim, with somewhat beefy jowls and very black hair. It was impossible to guess his age. A procession of people followed behind him. Luke tried to determine who they were. A few functionaries, several big bodyguards carrying Uzis, and finally a photographer snapping pictures.

The President walked to Luke's bedside, accompanied by the translator and the photographer. He took Luke's right hand and first gave it a Western-style handshake, then held it between both of his own. He said something.

"President Berdimuhamedeow welcomes you to Turkmenistan," Gurbanguly said.

The President continued to talk, the words tumbling from him like a waterfall. To Luke, it sounded like beautiful nonsense. "He invites you to dine with him at Oguzkhan Presidential Palace this very evening."

"I'd be delighted," Luke said.

"President Berdimuhamedeow is great friends with your President Susan Hopkins, and he would like to present you this photograph as a welcoming gift."

One of the functionaries behind the President handed him an eight-by-ten color glossy photo. The President took it, held it for a moment, then passed it on to Luke. It was a shot of the man standing between Susan and her husband, Pierre, in the Rose Garden on a sunny day. They were all smiling—positively beaming, in fact. Susan in heels was three inches taller than President Berdimuhamedeow. Pierre was close to a foot taller. Susan wore a red mini-dress, the hem just above her knee. She looked beautiful, ethereal. She made it very hard to notice the other two.

"As you know, Turkmenistan and the United States confer most favored nation trading status upon each other."

Luke nodded. "Oh yes."

"It is President Berdimuhamedeow's great hope for you that one day you too will meet the American President Hopkins."

"Thank you," Luke said. "That is my great hope as well."

CHAPTER FORTY SIX

December 18
1:00 p.m. Israel Time
Mount Herzl Cemetery
Jerusalem, Israel

It was a sea of people.

The mourners, thousands of them, walked quietly through Mount Herzl, the military cemetery. The body of Daria Shalit had been returned to Israel as part of the ceasefire agreement with Hezbollah. Hezbollah claimed she had been killed in the Israeli bombing of southern Lebanon. The Israelis claimed she had been shot at close range, execution style, by her captors, probably moments after her abduction.

So it went.

The people who knew her stood in the center of the massive crowd, near her freshly dug grave. Luke, Ed, Trudy, and Swann stood high on a green hill, overlooking the scene. Luke and Ed wore United States Army uniforms, flown in especially for the occasion. Trudy wore a black dress, a headscarf, and a veil. Swann wore a bizarre white suit with what appeared to be polka dots. Luke didn't know for sure because he couldn't bear to look at it.

Many people near them were openly weeping.

Below them, a military honor guard, men in olive drab dress uniforms, wearing brown berets, moved through the crowd with a coffin on their shoulders. The coffin was draped in the blue and white flag of Israel, the Star of David across the top. Carefully, they placed the coffin on the ground near the open grave.

A young pregnant woman stood over the grave. Soon, she started to speak. A man next to her held a microphone near her mouth. The woman rubbed her own belly. Her voice hitched in her throat. "Daria," she said, her amplified voice echoing across the hillside. "I can't say goodbye to you. I want my son to know you. I want you here with your big smile. I want to thank you for all the years you were my dearest little sister. How can we live on without you? You left us orphaned."

She stopped speaking, tried to start again, stopped. She shook her head, indicating that she couldn't continue. A man wrapped his arms around her, and they moved away from the grave.

Everywhere, the women were crying. Now the soldiers were crying, too. Men and women in the maroon berets of the paratroopers and the special forces, the gray berets of the air force, the many colors of the many different corps, all weeping for Daria, and maybe for themselves.

A rabbi stood over the grave now. "Glorified and sanctified be God's great name throughout the world," he said, his voice strong and booming. "May He establish His kingdom in your lifetime and during your days, and within the life of the entire House of Israel. Say Amen."

"Amen," said the entire crowd, thousands speaking as one.

"May His great name be blessed for ever and to all eternity."

Luke felt a tug on his uniform. Ari was there, wearing a black suit with a dark blue tie. He wore a black yarmulke on his head. The welts on his face were beginning to heal. He indicated with his head to come with him. Luke nudged Ed. They both followed Ari up the hill. The ranks of mourners were thinning up here. Below them were rows upon rows of gravesites covered in green grass, embedded in concrete plazas, thousands of individual graves.

"Hey, Lumpy," Luke said. "Looking sharp."

"I wish you wouldn't call me that," he said.

"We'd call you something else," Ed said, "if we knew what it was."

Ari shrugged. "I guess Lumpy will have to do."

"What are we doing up here?" Luke said.

"Saying goodbye."

"Really?" Ed said. "Just like that? I thought we were at least going to have drinks. The man took a bullet for me, I'm going to buy him a beer."

Ari shook his head. "I don't drink alcohol."

"Against your religion?" Ed said.

"No. Against my fitness regimen."

They stared at each other in a silence of mutual respect.

"I could use you on the Special Response Team," Luke said.

Ari's eyes widened just a bit, clearly surprised by the offer. Luke could sense that he was touched and honored.

"I come up from underground. Then I go back under. That is who I am," he said.

Luke nodded; he understood. And yet he wondered if one day their paths might cross again. He had a feeling that they would. And his feelings were never wrong.

"But look," Ari said. "There is another reason why we are up here. One other person wanted to give his regards before we go. He said he'd like us all to be together."

He gestured to his right, down the hillside, but away from the crowds. A short, thick-bodied man walked up the hill, surrounded by half a dozen larger men, all in dark suits. The bigger men carried Uzi submachine guns close to their bodies.

As they came a little closer, Luke recognized the ears and the silver comb-over on the smaller man. This time, the hair was covered with a dark blue yarmulke with the Star of David in gold across the top.

Yonatan Stern labored just a bit to make it up the last of the steep hill.

"Gentlemen," he said, shaking each man's hand in turn. "I will be speaking in a few moments, so I'm afraid I must make this brief. You have my thanks, and the thanks of every person in this nation, from the youngest to the oldest. Your abilities are matched only by your courage. You have our greatest respect."

As the pleasantries were being exchanged, Luke felt something that he had rarely felt before. It took him a moment to identify it. It was homesickness. Yes, he wanted to see Gunner desperately, and he wanted to see Susan.

But watching all these people, and their ties to this land, made him realize that he had a land as well. He wasn't as much of a vagabond as he may have imagined himself. He wanted to go home.

"You know," Yonatan Stern said. "You would all be candidates for the Medal of Valor, our highest military honor, if it were not for one thing."

"What is that one thing?" big Ed said.

The Prime Minister sighed, and then smiled. "We must all agree that this recent mission never happened."

CHAPTER FORTY SEVEN

December 20
6:35 p.m. Eastern Standard Time
The Family Residence
The White House, Washington, DC

It was starting to feel a lot like Christmas.

Susan sat in the White House family dining room, at the small round table. The overhead lights were dimmed, but that was because the whole room was strung with Christmas lights. Also, there was a nice fire crackling in the fireplace, and having the lights down was a nice way to enjoy it.

The doors to the dining room were closed, one Secret Service man right outside, listening in on an earpiece. Susan had a feeling she was safe right now, Secret Service or no Secret Service.

She took a sip of red wine and glanced across at her guests.

Luke Stone and his son, Gunner. Luke's hair was cut short and his face was clean shaven. The look brought forward the rugged handsomeness of his features. This was the engaged Stone, the one who was going to stay awhile. When his hair and his beard started to grow, and he started to take on that wild-man look, you had to keep your eye on him because he was liable to disappear.

Gunner's hair was longer than his father's. He wore a black T-shirt with a ticking clock logo on the front. White letters spelled the words ZERO HOUR.

Susan didn't even bother asking Gunner what that was. She knew all too well that it was a rock band popular with the kids nowadays. They had played a short acoustic set at a party her twin girls had held this past summer at the Malibu house.

She wasn't going to tell Gunner *that*, now was she? Not to worry, however. The girls probably would.

"How's your macaroni, Gunner?" Susan said instead.

The chef had made them all a turkey dinner, with homemade cranberry sauce, stuffing, six kinds of vegetables, and macaroni and cheese. He had paired it with two different kinds of wine. God only knew what the dessert was going to be like. As far as Susan was concerned, the White House chef was the best cook on Earth. And Susan had eaten in a lot of restaurants in a lot of places. You might even call her a foodie.

The only thing Gunner had touched so far was the mac and cheese.

"It's really good," he said. "I'm a big macaroni eater, and I have to say it's good."

Susan nodded. She almost laughed. Gunner, once he got to know you a little better, started to come out of his shell quite a lot. He was going to be a lady killer, if his dad wasn't careful.

"The chef likes to focus on mac," Susan said. "That's a big part of why I hired him. We eat it every day here, pretty much."

"I do too," Gunner said. "The best is the one from Velveeta, the one you put in the microwave. The cheese comes in a packet, and you squeeze it out like toothpaste. It's already mixed. This is good, but that one's the best."

"I bet it is," Susan said. "I'll have to try it."

"I'll bring you some," Gunner said. Then he glanced back and forth between his father and Susan. "The next time we come."

Susan looked at Luke. He hadn't said much so far tonight. He sipped his wine and stared back at her, half a smile on his face. He seemed relaxed, maybe even well rested. He and Gunner had gone Christmas shopping today, Susan knew. Then they played video games at an arcade. Bland, domesticated activities suddenly seemed to agree with the elusive, daring, high-flying Luke Stone.

At least for now.

"Talking about next time, I wonder what you guys are doing for Christmas dinner. My daughters, Michaela and Lauren, are flying in tomorrow. They're about your age, Gunner, maybe just a little older. I think you'll like them. Your dad saved Michaela's life once upon a time, did you know that?"

Gunner shook his head. "No. Dad doesn't really tell me anything."

"Well, he'll have to do better."

Now Luke did smile. He took another sip of his wine. He looked like a cat who had just swallowed a small yellow bird.

"What's up with you, Smiley?" Susan said.

Luke shook his head. "It's nice to be home."

HOUSE DIVIDED
(A Luke Stone Thriller—Book 7)

"One of the best thrillers I have read this year. The plot is intelligent and will keep you hooked from the beginning. The author did a superb job creating a set of characters who are fully developed and very much enjoyable. I can hardly wait for the sequel."
--Books and Movie Reviews (re *Any Means Necessary*)

HOUSE DIVIDED is book #7 in the USA Today bestselling Luke Stone thriller series, which begins with ANY MEANS NECESSARY (Book #1), a free download with over 500 five star reviews!

A passenger jet is attacked in northern Africa by terrorists wielding RPGs, resulting in an enormous loss of life. Yet U.S. intelligence reports this is merely a distraction, a prelude to a worse terror incident.

A cargo ship is pirated off the African coast, and terrorists are puzzled to find in its vast hold just one mysterious crate. It contains a weapon they do not understand—one of vital interest to Al Qaeda. It is a weapon, we learn, that will inflict catastrophic damage on the United States if not stopped in time.

The weapon disappears deep into the heart of Africa, and as all hope seems lost to retrieve it, Luke Stone is summoned. Forced to cross deserts, to enter jungles, Luke and his team embark on a mad race across Africa, on a suicidal mission: to destroy the weapon before it is too late.

A political thriller with non-stop action, dramatic international settings and heart-pounding suspense, HOUSE DIVIDED is book #7 in the bestselling and critically-acclaimed Luke Stone series, an explosive new series that will leave you turning pages late into the night.

"Thriller writing at its best. Thriller enthusiasts who relish the precise execution of an international thriller, but who seek the psychological depth and believability of a protagonist who

simultaneously fields professional and personal life challenges, will find this a gripping story that's hard to put down."
—Midwest Book Review (re *Any Means Necessary*)

Book #8 in the Luke Stone series will be available soon.

BOOKS BY JACK MARS

LUKE STONE THRILLER SERIES

ANY MEANS NECESSARY (Book #1)
OATH OF OFFICE (Book #2)
SITUATION ROOM (Book #3)
OPPOSE ANY FOE (Book #4)
PRESIDENT ELECT (Book #5)
OUR SACRED HONOR (Book #6)
HOUSE DIVIDED (Book #7)

Jack Mars

Jack Mars is the USA Today bestselling author of the LUKE STONE thriller series, which include the suspense thrillers ANY MEANS NECESSARY (book #1), OATH OF OFFICE (book #2), SITUATION ROOM (book #3), OPPOSE ANY FOE (book #4), PRESIDENT ELECT (book #5), OUR SACRED HONOR (book #6), and HOUSE DIVIDED (book #7).

Jack loves to hear from you, so please feel free to visit www.Jackmarsauthor.com to join the email list, receive a free book, receive free giveaways, connect on Facebook and Twitter, and stay in touch!